ISBN: 978-1-63950-031-4   [Paperback Edition]
      978-1-63950-032-1   [eBook Edition]

Printed and bound in The United States of America.

Writers Apex

Gateway Towards Success

+13176596889
www.writersapex.com
8063 MADISON AVE #1252
Indianapolis, IN 46227

476 Hamilton Park Circle
Saint Cloud, 34769
407-593-8138
Email: rsteck5@yahoo.com

Take A Chance,

True Love Waits

RACHEL F. STECK

Chapter One

Millie Green stands in front of her refrigerator, surveying its contents. Since her diet was quite unique, she was looking to see if she had anything her son, Jake, would eat. He arrived late in the night from college to surprise his mom. He was enrolled in legal school at Stetson University; The ringing phone jolted Millie and she tried to gray it quickly so it would not wake up Jake.

"Hello" she said quickly.

"Hi, Millie," her neighbor Roberta said. "my husband is bringing his boss home for dinner tonight and I need to go to the store. When I tried to start my old car, nothing happened. The starter has been acting funny lately. By any chance are you going to the store this morning?"

"Well, I hadn't planned to, Roberta, but i could get some lunch meat and chips for Jake. He came home last night to surprise me.

"Oh, Millie, you are a God-send." she said appreciatively.

Are you ready to go?" Millie asked. "If so, I'll be right over so we can get back quickly."

"Yes, I'll have to clean after I get the pot roast on…" she said.

"No, problem." Millie replied. "See you in about five minutes."

When Millie and Roberta got to the supermarket, it was crowded.

"Since I only need a few things, let's split up and shop separately. "Take your time and I'll be sitting somewhere near the store."

Roberta replied, "It will take me a few minutes but I will hurry. Like I said, I still have to clean my house before they get there. I can't clean until I get the pot roast in the oven." Roberta explained, as she hurriedly pushed her shopping cart towards the produce section.

Millie pushed a shopping cart to the lunchmeat section of the large superstore. Two very attractive men were standing in front of the packaged meats, surveying the selections. She stood patiently, not saying anything. The taller of the two men glanced at her and smiled.

"Are we in your way?" he asked.

"That's okay; I'm not in a hurry. They make it hard, don't they? Give us so many choices…" she said, smiling at him, just to be friendly.

He shook his head affirmatively, as the other man picked up several packages of sliced lunchmeat and walked away. Without giving the incident another thought, Millie made her selections, and then pushed the shopping cart to the bakery section to get some fresh rolls.

She was surprised to find the two men in the bakery, picking up some loaves of bread. They notice Millie, smile and walk away.

The taller of the two men looked back at Millie and smiled again. She could not help but notice how handsome he was; and, when he smiled, his eyes sparkled.

Millie grabbed a package of sandwich buns, and proceeded to the dairy section to get some sliced cheese.

Finally, after picking up a bag of potato chips in the snack section, and a bottle of Jake's favorite soft drink, she pushed the cart to the express lane and paid for her selections. Then, she carried the bag of groceries to her car and put it in the trunk.

After she walked back into the store, she looked around to see if she could see Roberta. Unable to find her, Millie sat down on a bench by the front door and became somewhat preoccupied with the valentine balloons that were tied to the end of the bench. The balloons reminded her that it was almost Valentine's Day. For a moment, she toyed with the idea of picking up something for Jake; but decided that since she had already sent him a valentine with a twenty dollar bill inside, she wouldn't do anything else. After all, Jake didn't eat candy; and, she did not want it around the house.

Millie pulled the strings on the balloons and made them sway, oblivious to her surroundings. She felt an unexplainable loneliness that morning. She sighed, wishing she had a valentine. After all, it had been a long time since she had felt a man's arms around her.

Millie noticed the two men she had spoken to earlier. They were walking towards the checkout lane next to where she was sitting. The men split up, and one went into the checkout lane to pay for the groceries. However, the other one, the taller, more handsome man was now walking towards her, with a broad, confident smile.

Millie noticed the man's muscular physique as he walked towards her. He was wearing a black-watch plaid shirt and dark blue jeans. He was also wearing expensive-looking embossed leather boots, and a denim jacket.

Even before he sat down at the other end of the bench, he began to talk. "Do you like to fly?"

"Sure," she replied, "I love to fly. Why do you ask?"

"My partner and I," he said, pointing to the other man, "came from Southern Pines, North Carolina, for the race. Do you like racing?"

"Sure, I like racing. When I lived in Ohio, I'd go to the Indy 500 whenever I could. I loved to hear the announcer say, 'Gentlemen, start your engines." There's something about the roar of those powerful motors. To me, it's the most exciting part of the race." she said, with excitement, surprised by her own gabbiness to this stranger.

"My partner and I are drivers...here for the Daytona 500. Our operation is based in Southern Pines; but we travel all over the country...

Phoenix, Atlanta, and Pontiac, Michigan. The crew moves the cars for us in semis; but, we prefer to fly to different locations."

"Really! Are you serious? The NASCAR race in Daytona? Winston Cup?"

"Yeah, so, answer my question, do you like to fly?" he again asked.

Millie was somewhat leery of the attractive gentleman; yet, at the same time, she knew he could be planning to invite her to the race. The handsome stranger was looking deeply into her eyes, as if he could see into her soul. She trembled as his sparkling blue eyes mesmerized her. Frightened by her own fear at talking to a stranger, she broke eye contact and looked at the floor, saying nothing. He asked the question again.

"Yes, I like to fly." she said. "Wait, you say you drive a race car. What's your name?"

"Oh, you don't know who I am? I just assumed you knew who we were... I mean, you smiled as if you knew us."

He paused, then, taking a deep breath, he continued, "Yes, sometimes I drive. We travel the Winston Cup Circuit all over the country."

He was noticeably shaken by the fact that she didn't actually know who he was. He had become accustomed to being recognized in public, and was shocked that she did not know him.

Millie further observed him. He had coarse black, collar-length hair, intermingled with streaks of gray; piercing blue eyes; and measured over six feet tall, rugged-looking, deeply tanned, and muscular. Millie summarized by his physique that he was a body-builder. Although his boyish embarrassment was attractive, she was still skeptical.

"Wait a minute, Daytona's on the other side of the state. What are you doing in our little town of Brandon?"

"We came over to pick up some friends, and do a couple promos for one of our sponsors. We've already done one promo, and are scheduled to fly back to Daytona in a couple hours. We need to do some practice laps today. They call it 'Happy Hour'."

"What's your name?"

"Dave Masden."

"Oh, sure, I've heard of you. Are you driving the race car tomorrow? Did you ever race at Indianapolis?"

"No, Indy's a different circuit; but, NASCAR's trying to work something out so the Winston Cup cars can race there once a year. My partner, Ben Colson," he said, pointing to his friend, "does most of the driving. Sometimes, we flip a coin to see who'll fly the plane, and who'll get qualified to drive the car. On this trip, I'm flying, and Ben's driving. We have several cars; so, sometimes; we both get qualified, and compete against each other in the race. That's a lot of fun! Once in a while, we enter the Busch Grand National; but, most of the time, we both get qualified and take our practice laps, in case one of us has a last-minute physical problem, you know, springs an ankle, gets the flu or something."

"What an interesting life you must have..." she said wistfully.

"So, what do you say? Would you like to go to the race tomorrow?"

"Oh, gosh, I'd love to; but, I don't think I can. My son came home for a surprise visit. He's a pre-law student at Stetson, studying really hard for the bar exam."

"How old is he?"

"Twenty-four."

"Really? You look so young! Are you sure you're old enough to have a twenty-four year old son?" Dave asked, as he surveyed her left hand for a wedding band. He noticeably smiled when he didn't see a ring on her finger. Millie had already noticed his left hand was devoid of rings, except for a gold nugget ring on his little finger.

Dave looked at Millie flirtatiously, waiting for a response to his question. She was flattered. It had been a long time since anyone had flirted with her.

"I'm a widow; and, yes, I'm afraid I am old enough to have a son that old!"

"Well, then, how about it?" he asked. "Want-to go to Daytona for the race? I'll bring you back on Monday. Monday's a holiday, right? President's day?"

"Yes," Millie said, "Monday's a holiday. Oh, I don't know, Dave. I'm a cautious person; not exactly the type who'd go away, at a moment's notice, with a perfect stranger."

"Well, I don't know if I'm perfect; but, you'll be safe with me." He said kiddingly. "The bottom line is, I like your smile; and, I'd like to get to know you better."

Millie noticed Ben had finished checking out, and was walking towards them, carrying two bags of groceries. Her mind was racing. She was tempted by the offer; but she knew she didn't know this handsome stranger well enough to go away with him.

Ben handed Dave one of the bags of groceries and said, "Hey, Man, let's go! We've got a lot to do."

"Okay, give me a minute..." he said, putting up his hand in protest. Then, turning back to Millie, he said: "Well, listen, I've got-ta go. Last chance, do you want to go? I'll take care of you; fly you home on Monday. How about it? Are you willing to take a chance?"

She felt an unexplainable, overwhelming physical attraction to him, and was not ready for him to walk out of her life forever.

"Where are you going right now?" she asked. "If I give you my phone number, will you call me in a half hour so we can discuss this? I'd love to go; but, since I don't know you, I'm a little skeptical."

"Sure, I'll call you. What's your name and number?" Dave asked as he grabbed a pen from his shirt pocket.

"Millie Greene, with an 'e'. My number's unlisted, 555-7072. I'm waiting for my neighbor 'cause her car wouldn't start this morning. I see her in the checkout line now, so I should be home by then. Its ten o'clock now..." she said, glancing at her watch. Then she stood up, and watched as he wrote her name and phone number on his hand. He was so tall; Millie felt tiny standing beside him.

"Okay, I'll call you in a few minutes, Millie." he said, putting his pen back in his pocket. Then, giving her another approving look, he continued, "I hope you'll come with me. It'll be fun ....no strings attached, honest!"

"I'm certainly thinking about it! Call me, Dave, okay?"

He shook his head affirmatively and gave her a thumbs-up signal. Millie sat down on the bench, and watched them leave the store, flattered that the attractive stranger had singled her out.

Although it would be a risky move, she wanted to go to the race with him, to take a chance on a potential romance. What a nice Valentine's Day gift she could give to herself. Regaining her composure, she took a deep breath, stood up and practically floated across the store to Roberta's check out line.

"Roberta, you'll never believe what happened to me! I'm trying to decide if it was a dream. Pinch me and see if I'm dreaming...." she said, holding out her arm.

"Why? What happened?" Roberta said, as she gently pinched Millie's arm. "You look like you've seen a ghost."

Millie quickly told Roberta about the chance meeting, and her conversation with Dave Masden. Her skin tingled with goose bumps at the thought that someone as handsome as Dave could be remotely interested in her. She was so excited, she was trembling.

"You know, Millie, I meant to tell you earlier. You look great with your hair combed like that. You should wear it down more often. Well, you know, it's time you had a date. How long has it been? Why, it was over seven years since Jacob was killed. Are you brave enough to go with him?"

"Oh, I'd love to go; but, you know I'm not much for taking risks. It's been so long, though, since I actually wanted to do anything. Nah, forget it; I can't go! Remember Jake's home for the weekend. I should stay with him."

"Horse feathers!" Roberta said, "There you go again with those 'shoulds!' Do you think Jake's gonna sit around with his Mom after he passes the bar exam? No, of course not. He'll be practicing law in some exciting big city; and, what about you? Well, you'll be sitting at home, rocking in your rocking chair, waiting to die. You need a life for yourself, Millie. You're not getting any younger!"

"I know... I know!" she said, waving her arms in protest. "Would you go?"

"Probably not, I'm a big chicken. But, that's not fair. I really can't answer that question because I'm married. There's a big difference."

"Well, I have to make a decision 'cause he's going to call at ten-thirty for an answer. I want to talk to Jake about it before he calls.... if he calls. Maybe he won't call, and then I won't have anything to decide, will I?"

"Oh, I bet he'll call. You'll see."

Roberta paid for her groceries and they drove home. Millie helped Roberta carry in her bags.

"Thanks, Millie, for taking me to the store. Good luck with whatever you decide about going to the race. I'm pullin' for you."

"Thanks, if it's meant to be, it will be. I'm praying to know what I should do." she said, as she put her car in gear to drive away.

When she got home, she quickly went into the house, carrying her groceries. "Jake....Jake! Are you awake?"

"Yeah, Mom, you woke me up when you left." he said, taking the groceries.

"Oh, I'm sorry; but, you'll never guess what happened, Jake. I met Dave Masden.... You know, the race car driver? He invited me to go to the race in Daytona Beach. Who knows, I just might go! What do you think about that?"

"What? Mom, are you crazy? You don't know him. I can't believe you're even thinking about going."

"I know that I don't know him; but, he said he'd fly me back to Brandon on Monday. They're flying back to Daytona this afternoon."

"They?"

"Ben Colson, his partner. They're in Brandon for...what did he call it.... a 'promo.' I can't explain it, but I just want to go!"

"Come on, Mom, think about it. He's a stranger. What would Dad say? Even if he brings you back on Monday, what about tonight? And tomorrow night? Where will you be sleeping?"

"Well, I'll get a motel room, I guess."

"Oh, sure. Where? I'm sure Daytona's locked up because of that race. There's probably not an available motel room in the whole city."

"I know, but I've got to think fast. He's going to call me at ten-thirty."

"Well, its ten thirty-five now. If he doesn't call, we don't have to worry about it, Mom. I hope he doesn't call!"

The telephone rang at ten thirty-seven. Jake ran to the phone; but Millie was able to grab the receiver before he could reach it.

"Hello." she said into the telephone receiver.

"Hi, Millie?"

"Yes, this is Millie. Dave?"

"Yes, I've only got a minute. So, how about it? Do we have a date? Would you like to go to the race tomorrow? I'd love to have your company...." he pleaded confidently.

"Well, as I explained, my son surprised me by coming home from Stetson this weekend. I haven't seen him since Christmas."

As Millie talked to Dave, Jake was shaking his head, and waving his arms in protest, warning her not to go. Then, finally, he waved his arms again in disgust, and proceeded to the kitchen to fix himself a sandwich.

"Well, maybe he'd like to come along." Dave suggested. "He'd have fun. Kyle Petty's having a private party for the drivers and their friends tonight. If you want, I'll take you both to the party. Usually, there's some country singers or actors at these parties. Why don't you ask him if he'd like to come along? Then, you won't be afraid to come...."

Millie asked Dave to wait while she discussed his suggestion with Jake. Jake shook his head, and folded his arms in disgust.

"I guess I don't have a choice 'cause it looks like you're hell-bent on going. Since my car's at school, I'll may be able to get a ride back to

Stetson from Daytona...some of my classmates are going to the race. But, Mom, I'm warning you; I'll be watchin' this guy!"

Going back to the phone, Millie said, "Dave, he said he'd love to go; said he'd get a ride back to Stetson from there. By the way, where will we be staying? There probably won't be any motel rooms because of the race."

"We have a place. They'll be room for you and your boy. Don't worry. It'll be okay, Millie, you'll see."

"Okay, so.... How are we gonna do this?"

"Do you know where Albert Whitted Airport is.... in Brandon? Dave asked her.

"Sure."

"Meet me there at two o'clock? We have to go see some people and do another promo; but we're scheduled to leave at two-thirty this afternoon. The flight back to Daytona only takes a few minutes. Well, listen, I've gotta run. I'll catch you later, at the airport, okay?"

"Okay, we'll be there by two o'clock."

"It's a date, then. See ya' later, Millie. I'm glad you're going to come. Bye."

"Bye, Dave. See you at two..."

The phone line went dead. Millie cradled the phone in her hand. She couldn't believe she had accepted a date with a handsome stranger. Normally, people who were recognizable in public did not impress her in any way. Over the years, she has had some very glamorous customers. Why was Dave Masden an exception? she wondered. Why do I get weak trembles just hearing his name?

Chapter Two

Dave hung up the phone and shouted, "Yeah, Man, she's gonna go! I've gotta date for the weekend!"

"Man, you're crazy! If you wanted a date, you could've had your pick of those pretty girls who hang around the track. Why do you want to bring a stranger into our group? Why her?" Ben smirked.

"Oh, come on, Ben, you know those groupies could get me into some serious trouble with the local law enforcement agencies. What do you think their average age is? Fifteen? Millie's the first woman who's caught my eye since the divorce; and, God knows, I didn't want the divorce..."

"Right! You sure screwed up our gang. We've always been a foursome, 'ole fuddy-duddies.' Now, Lynne wouldn't come because you and Patricia split up. You screwed up everything!"

"Hey, Man, I didn't screw up. She wanted the divorce. I did everything I could to change her mind, you know that. She said I was 'married' to the race car. Now, I hear she's getting married again."

"I heard that, too. I wondered if you knew. You do know who she's going with?"

"Yeah, Butch Smith, our worst enemy! Right?" Dave asked.

"Yeah. Life's a bitch, ain't it? Well, for God's sake, Dave, why this woman? She's fat! Sure, she's attractive as hell, and she knows how to dress. I'll give her that; but, why her?"

"There's just somethin' about her, Ben. I don't know what it is myself. Maybe because she was friendly...had a nice smile. She kinda turns me on. Besides, I like a woman to have a little extra meat on her bones. I've had it with skinny, self-centered women. I read an article that said if you want a woman who'll be good to you, choose a heavy-set woman. The article said they're usually lonely and will be true-blue. The article made a lot of sense to me. It's worth a shot. Most men chase after the hot, skinny women. Before long, those women are sneaking around, messin' with other men. This magazine article said that if he treats her right, a heavy-set woman would be true to her man. It said she would make him feel like a king. Something tells me Millie's a good woman." Dave replied.

"Oh, you and your books! I give up on you, Romeo! What time's she gonna be here?" Ben asked, somewhat exasperated.

"At two o'clock...and, oh, her son's comin' with her."

"What! That's all we need. A kid! Have you lost your mind?"

"He's twenty-four years old, Ben. He goes to Stetson...a law student."

"Really? Hum.... she must've had him pretty young. Well, okay, Romeo, there's no stoppin' you; but, I warn you, don't let her distract you during the race tomorrow. I need you to concentrate. You can't be flirting' around 'stead of keeping your mind on what's happenin' on the track. We need a win...or at least finish in the top ten. Our sponsors are gettin' nervous. I can't blame them 'cause we didn't do so hot last year."

"Everything'll be fine. You know I'm always one hundred percent when we're racing. I'm sorry Lynne wouldn't come with you; but, hell, don't blame me for that. Hey, listen, I've got a great idea. I'm gonna take Millie to Kyle's party tonight. Why don't you come along?"

"No, thanks, Man, I'll pass. I don't like parties. Hell, enough about that. Let's get movin' so we can get everything done before we have to leave. I need those practice laps today."

Millie took a shower and packed an overnight bag while her long hair was drying. She decided to wear her most slenderizing outfit— black parachute pants and black embellished sweater. She packed the new nightgown and the robe she had received from her sister at

Christmas, and her red and black jogging suit to wear to the race. The weather forecast was predicting colder weather; and, even though it was Florida, Millie knew it would be chilly at the track. As an afterthought, she packed a black skirt, and high-heeled boots, in case they decided to go to the party Dave had mentioned.

In the back of her mind, Millie wrestled with the morality of what she was doing. It had been twenty-five years since she had participated in the dating scene. She and Jacob's marriage had been terrific, and they had an incredible sex life. When he died, that part of her life died, too. Since his death, she felt empty, disinterested in the phony head games of modern dating. She had built a solid brick wall around her emotions. Men had asked her out since Jacob's death; but, she always refused, realizing that she wasn't ready to date—that is, until today, when Dave Masden came crashing through her solid brick wall.

Although she had not figured out what it was, she knew Dave Masden had something unusual. Her attraction had nothing to do with the fact he was a NASCAR superstar, or his physique. She noticed a desperate loneliness when she looked into his deep blue eyes, eyes that would not be denied. They mirrored the desperation she knew all too well herself.

So, Millie decided she would allow herself to have this "gift"— the gift of exploring this potential adventure. She was, however, still somewhat apprehensive. After all, maybe he wasn't who he said he was. He could be a serial rapist! Self-doubts quickly flooded her mind. Could she still hold a man's interest, she wondered. After all, this date would last three days! "I can do this," she said to her mirror image.... "I NEED to do this!"

When Jake came out of his bedroom, he was wearing jeans, a blue oxford-cloth shirt and his black leather jacket. Millie kidded him, "You look great, Son, so much like your Father. You watch out, there'll be a lot of pretty girls hanging around the track."

"Mom, right now, all I can think about is passing the bar exam. I want to score high so I'll qualify for the top firms ...maybe in Chicago or LA. I don't have time to be bothered by a girl right now. Well, let's just say, for more than one night!" he said, as he knowingly smiled at his Mother.

"Jacob Greene, you're a brat! I can't believe you said that to me."

"Well, I can't believe you're going on this date! Have you thought about what Dad would say?"

"Hey, Jake, I'm not damaging your father's memory. He wouldn't want me to sit around forever. He died seven years ago, Jake. seven years ago! You're grown. What kind of life do I have?" she demanded, justifying her actions. "My life consists of going to Church and coming home; going to work and coming home."

"Do you think Dad would approve of your going away with a stranger? Someone who 'picked you up' at the grocery store? For God's sake, Mom, Dad was a cop!"

"But you're gonna be my chaperon." she reasoned.

"Don't bet on it, Mom. Listen, I give up. Your mind's already made up. Go ahead! Go, have fun. You need it! You've been a grouch long enough," he said, softening his attitude by messing her hair affectionately with his hand. "I just don't want anything to happen to you. I'll be watching' this guy!"

"I'm not really a grouch, am I?"

Jake laughed at her remark. "No, but you probably need to go out and have some fun. Just be careful! Do you know about the diseases, and using condoms, and all that stuff?"

"Come on, Jake, give me a break! I read the newspapers and watch television.

I know what's happening in the world. Surely, I won't have to think about that this weekend. After all, we just met."

"Mom, things happen a lot faster today than they did when you and Dad were dating back in the 'Stone Age.' You need to know what COULD happen."

"If you're not careful, Jacob Greene III, I'll turn you over my knee. I didn't punish you enough when you were a child!" she kidded. "You are such a cynic."

"Who knows, Mom, maybe everything will work out. I figure we might as well make the best of a bad situation; and, who knows, maybe we'll have a good time."

"Jake, forgive me for acting like a mother; but, you haven't actually been as promiscuous as you sound, have you?"

"No, Mom, but, I do know what diseases are out there."

Millie couldn't determine if Jake was telling her the truth, or if he was, in fact, still a virgin. Their Catholic faith was deeply embedded in his demeanor. He had always been very active in their church, and continued to attend church while in college. She couldn't think about that right now. Time was short and it was time to leave. She decided to think about that later.

Jake drove his mother's Cougar to the small airport and parked the car. Millie swallowed hard, suddenly losing her nerve. "Jake, have I lost my mind? I can't do this..."

"My point exactly, Mom. Come on, let's go home." he pleaded.

Before Millie could consider that option, Dave opened her car door and was holding out his hand to help her get out. He continued to hold her hand until she introduced him to Jake.

Dave shook Jake's hand firmly, and helped him get their overnight bags. Then, he ushered them towards a small group of people who were clustered near a medium-sized silver plane. The airplane had a lightening bolt emblem painted on its side, along with the numbers 'N7744M' painted on its fuselage.

Millie noticed everyone in the group was wearing jackets with matching lightening-bolt emblems.

"Hey, Man, is that your plane?" Jake asked.

"Yeah, we've had it about five years. She's a real beaut. We bought this little Beechcraft Baron from the man who used to own this airstrip.

What was his name? … Oh, I remember now, C. W. Pratt. It's a little twin-engine prop…. seats eight."

"How long have you been a pilot, Dave?" Millie asked.

"Six years. Oh, I love to fly. This plane's an easy solution to our necessity to get around to so many places in such a short time. Our schedule's pretty tight. It just made good business sense to buy it."

Dave introduced them to the group of people, which included the Mayor of Brandon, her husband, and country entertainer, Lee Henderson, a Lee Greenwood want-to-be. Since Millie already knew the Mayor, she spoke to her and her husband, Paul, first, then she shook hands with Lee Henderson.

"Hi, Lee," Millie said, "Lee Greenwood is one of my favorite country singers. I enjoy his music. You can really sound just like him,"

"Do you have a favorite Lee Greenwood song?"

"I have all his albums. My favorites are too numerous to mention. But, tell me, I'm surprised to see you in our little town of Brandon, Florida. If you don't mind me asking, why are you here? Did you perform here?"

"No, I had some business to take care of so I flew over with Ben and Dave. Since we've been friends for years, I try to catch most of their races. Believe it or not, it's a form of relaxation from my hectic life."

"Well, welcome to Brandon."

"Thanks, Millie, and thanks for enjoying and buying my music."

"I'm not just saying it because you're here, I really love his songs. They reach deep inside me…say exactly what I'm feeling. If I could write songs, I'd write exactly like that."

"Don't you have a favorite?"

"*God Bless the USA*' is my all-time favorite, I guess. It caused me to 'fall in love' with Lee Greenwood, so to speak. He performed the song for the Ellis Island celebration a few years ago. The song, and the fireworks, were so beautiful I had a puddle of tears in my eyes. My next favorite is, '*You've Got a Good Love Comin'*." she replied.

"That's a good one, too." Lee agreed.

"Hey, Henderson," Dave kidded his long-time friend, "Quit trying to make time with my girl!" Then, looking at Millie, he said, "You guys need a jacket so you'll be recognized as part of our group. Come with me."

Jake and Millie followed Dave into the airplane, and to a small compartment near the cockpit. Dave pulled out several jackets and held them up. Surveying Millie and Jake for size, he handed them each a jacket. "Here, try these."

"Cool!" Jake said as he placed their overnight bags in the overhead cargo hold. He pulled off his leather jacket, draping it across one of the seats. "This is fine, thanks!"

Millie said a silent prayer as she slipped hers on, hoping it would fit. She'd be embarrassed if she had to ask for a larger size. To her amazement, the jacket fit perfectly. It was cherry red; and, along with the lightening-bolt emblem, it carried a Coca-Cola endorsement logo.

Jake went back outside to talk to the group of distinguished people, leaving them alone. Millie started to follow him at first; but Dave put his hands on her shoulders, and looked at her intently, as she looked at her jacket.

When he had her attention, he said, "You look great in my jacket, Millie. Glad you came? You'll see, it'll be fun."

"I hope so..."

"Don't look so concerned. I'm not some kind of monster or serial killer. There are no strings attached. You don't have to do anything you don't want to do. I'll bring you back to Brandon on Monday night, regardless of what happens, or doesn't happen, between us..." he assured her.

"I know, Dave. I'm a little nervous. I shouldn't tell you this; but, it's been a while since I had a date."

"Well, relax. You're doing great! I'm a lucky man to have a pretty lady like you for company. These trips can be rough... a man gets lonely."

Millie tried to think of something clever to say. To her relief, she didn't have to say anything, because Ben stepped onto the plane, following by the group of dignitaries.

Looking directly at Millie, he said, "Why don't you take my seat in the cockpit? I'll sit back here and play host to this group."

"I don't know how to fly," she stammered. "Will I have to do anything?"

"Not a thing, Darlin', just talk to the pilot." Dave answered her, pointing to himself, and giving her a smile that only she could see.

Ben opened his mouth to speak, and then changed his mind. He turned around and opened a small portable bar and began to mix drinks. As he stood there, Millie noticed he was shaking his head, occasionally waving his hands in the air, mumbling under his breath.

Jake chose to take the seat directly behind the cockpit.

He had changed his mind about this trip, deciding it was, in fact, a great idea. It had been a long time since he had seen his mother smile the way she was smiling at Dave. He also realized that this trip could be good for his career. The mayor, a country singer, race car drivers, and the promise of more influential people to meet—he could end up with a legal career in NASCAR.

Ben handed Dave and Millie a can of Coca-Cola; then turned around and asked everyone to fasten their seat belts and prepare for take-off. "Gee, I feel like a stewardess!" he kidded as he made feminine gestures.

Everyone laughed at his antics, then, he continued by saying, in a more serious tone, "They say we're in for some turbulence over Orlando, so keep your seat belts fastened." Then, joking again, he said, "and, no smoking please. Coffee, tea or little ole' me!"

"Come on, Jake, sit back here with me and Ben." Lee said. "We may need some legal advice!" Jake got up obediently and moved to the back of the plane, where the group of passengers immediately accepted him.

Millie looked around the cockpit. Gauges and switches surrounded her. Dave methodically checked the airplane before radioing for take-off clearance.

The take-off was smooth. uneventful and Millie relaxed. It was obvious that Dave was very skilled as a pilot. The sky was clear and deep blue in color, and the little town of Brandon, Florida was beautiful from the air. Once they'd reached their cruising altitude, Millie broke the silence.

"Well, Dave, if you're as skilled at racing as you are at flying, you've got to be a champion. That was a very smooth take-off. So, now that we're in the air, tell me more about yourself."

"Well, let's see, where do I begin? I separated from my wife, Patricia, early last summer. Our divorce was final the week before Christmas. I gave her a healthy settlement in order to get it over, you know, so I could get on with my life. She's getting' married again in June. I've even filed the papers to have the marriage annulled through the Church."

"Oh, you're Catholic, too?"

"Yes, Father Thomas doesn't think it is a problem since we were not married in the Church, and because of the circumstances that caused our divorce—her infidelity. She actually confessed it to him in the disillusionment papers she filled out for the church. It was a real shocker for me to find out the first time she stepped out on me was while we were practically on our honeymoon. She admitted to Father Thomas that she has a sexual addiction."

"I see."

"Ben and his wife, Lynne, are upset with me because the divorce has split up our foursome. We have a reputation for being 'fuddy-duddies'."

"Fuddy-duddies?" What's that?"

"You know the type, skip the constant realm of parties, won't tolerate drugs or heavy drinking in our crew, and never mess around on our wives. You get the picture. Just normal, boring people... like most of the drivers you'll meet this weekend."

"I see...go on."

"Well, Pat, my ex-wife, got it into her head that she didn't want to be my wife any longer. She said I was married to my race car. I took it pretty hard; but, in reality, and just between you and me, things hadn't been so good between us for a long time."

"I'm sorry, Dave."

"We went through the motions, pretending to be happy. Unfortunately, because of the split, things have changed between my partner and me as well. Lynne, Ben's wife, wouldn't come on this trip because of it. Ben blames me for her not coming."

"In all these years, you were never untrue to your wife, Dave?"

Dave glanced into the back of the airplane. Jake, Ben and Lee were sitting in the rear of the airplane, laughing and talking. The Mayor and her husband were sitting side by side, in the middle of the plane, holding hands, talking quietly.

Since everyone was laughing, and having a good time, oblivious to their conversation, Dave knew he could speak freely, without being overheard.

"No, never. Pat and I married young. She's been the only girl in my life. When she turned forty, something happened. She wanted more of my time than I could give her. We were having mechanical problems up the 'kazoo,' and our sponsors were threatening to quit sending their checks. Finally, the pressure got to us, and we split up; but, we both knew it was all over except for the 'shoutin'.'"

"I'm sorry things didn't work out. Life's not easy, is it?"

"No, it's not. Confidentially, I've been thinking about dissolving my partnership with Ben, you know, buy his share of this plane, and let him have the race cars. I could just walk away; find something else to do with my life. I need a change."

"What would you do if you didn't race?"

"There's plenty of opportunities. I've been offered a sports broadcasting job; or, I could do commercials and endorsements, or maybe just test cars. I'd be happy just being a mechanic again. I could be

Ben's Crew Chief, call the shots for him. I'd still be a part of the team; but I wouldn't race at all.

"Do you mind me asking how old you are, Dave?" she asked.

"I was forty-five last April...and you?"

"I'll be forty-three in July."

"You don't look it! I don't see one gray hair. I would've guessed you to be in your early thirties." he said.

"Really? Well, I guess I'm lucky. I don't dye my hair, though. I've inherited my Dad's hair. He was seventy years old when he died last year, and his hair was still brown."

"Oh, I'm sure I'll be completely gray soon 'cause it's turning fast. Would you believe, I didn't have a gray hair before the divorce?"

"Well, in my opinion, your hair looks great. When my hair turns gray, I'd want it to be like yours. It's coarse and thick, isn't it?" she said as she touched his hair. Then, embarrassed by the tingling sensation that radiated through her body when she touched him, she pulled her hand away.

Dave grabbed her hand in mid-air, and put it to his mouth, kissing it gently. "Thanks, I'm glad you like my hair. Yours is pretty, too. I like long hair. Your curls hang down almost to your waist."

"I've always worn my hard long; although, I usually wear it up when I work. I guess the only complaint I have about myself is my weight. We're never happy with ourselves, are we? Well, I've done everything I can to lose weight; but, since my problem stems from a metabolic problem, nothing seems to work. Watson Clinic told me I'd have to drop to two hundred calories a day in order to lose weight; but they also said I'd die before I lost the weight. Used to be, I hated to go to the doctor because they would hassle me about my weight. The doctor I'm seeing now is okay with it. I have convinced him that I've tried everything to lose weight. I stay in shape by doing aerobics and taking fast walks; but, unfortunately, no matter what, I can't seem to lose weight. You look great, though, Dave. You must work out."

"Yes, I do whenever I can. Driving a race car takes a lot of stamina. But, back to your situation regarding your weight, Millie, and I'm not just saying this to make you feel good. I have to admit that I actually prefer a woman with a little extra meat on her bones. I equate it with a bald man trying to grow hair, or a short person trying to go taller. Same scenario. You know, there are men who prefer heavy-set women. I've never really been interested in the skinny, superficial types. Pat was thin when we split up; but she wasn't when we first met. Although she had several miscarriages, we never had children. I guess I wanted a son for all the usual reasons; but it wasn't meant to be. That's enough about me, though, what about you? How long have you been a widow?"

"Seven years—my husband was killed in the line of duty. He was a Florida State Highway patrolman, who was killed by a drunk driver who fell asleep at the wheel, and crossed the median on I-4. The impact of the crash cut my husband's car in half. The drunkard, of course, was able to walk away from the scene while Jacob lay dying on the road. They prosecuted, of course, and found him guilty of manslaughter. He served his time; but he's out of prison now."

"That's terrible, Millie. I'm so sorry."

She continued. "Jake's decision to go into the legal profession stemmed from our ordeal with the trial, and the devastation of our loss. The life insurance and settlement money helps to pay Jake's tuition; but he also received a scholarship because of his good grades. With the life insurance, besides Jake's tuition, I was able to pay off the mortgage on our home, and put a little in the bank. I haven't had to worry about money since Jacob's death; but the money can't keep me company. It can't take away the loneliness I feel. I'd much rather have Jacob than all the money in the world."

"He'd be proud of you. You've done a good job with Jake. He seems to be a fine young man."

"Sure, he'll make a good, conscientious attorney. When he passes the bar exam, he'll be on his own."

"And you, Millie, what about you? What kind of future do you have?"

"Lonely, I guess. I wish we'd had more children; but something happened when Jake was born. The doctor said I'd probably never be able to have another baby. We talked about adoption, but never got around to it before Jacob died."

"Do you date much? Have a lot of friends?" he asked.

"Yes, I have a lot of friends; but to be honest, Dave, this is my first date since Jacob died. I'm scared to death 'cause this date's going to last three days! I'm afraid I'll bore you to death."

"No way, I'm not the least bit bored. I'm glad you felt comfortable enough with me to say that. We'll have fun, you'll see!" he assured her. "I like you, Millie. Your natural charm is refreshing."

Ben came to the cockpit to get their empty Coke cans. "Hey, Masden," he challenged, "Lee dares you to do a loop-de-loop before we land in Daytona. I've bet him a ten-spot that you won't 'cause of your lady friend here. The Mayor said it's okay with her! I dare you! In fact, I double-dare you!"

Dave didn't say a word. He sat quietly until Ben had returned to his seat and fastened his seat belt. Then, with a twinkle in his eye, he winked at Millie, and proceeded to maneuver the silver aircraft into a perfect loop-de-loop. Everyone roared and cheered as the horizon suddenly turned "upside down".

Millie became light-headed, and felt a little queasy as they returned to an upright flying position. She swallowed hard, and managed to smile at Dave.

"Pay the man, Ben! You lost your bet." Dave said.

Everyone laughed as Ben grumbled and handed Lee Henderson a ten-dollar bill.

"Hey, Dave, this ten-spot is yours if you'll do it again!" Lee challenged.

Dave looked at Millie. "Are you up for it?"

"What the heck .... go for it!" she said, trying to sound cheerful.

"All right, everyone, hang on. Here we go..." Dave instructed as he once again performed a perfect loop-de-loop. Their passengers, including the Mayor, clapped as they returned to an upright flying position. She took the ten-dollar bill from Lee's hand and passed it up to the cockpit.

"Here, Millie, hang onto this for me. We're approaching the runway for Daytona, and should be on the ground in about five minutes. Are you glad you came?"

"Yes, Dave, I am .... I certainly am. This is fun."

"Great! I'm glad you came, too."

Chapter Three

When they arrived at the airport terminal, Dave ushered Millie and Jake to a van that was parked on the grounds, while Ben ushered the others into a second one. While Ben anchored the airplane, Dave removed the groceries they had purchased earlier that day, which were now inside a large red cooler, and placed them in Ben's van. He also removed a large package, wrapped in brown craft paper, and put it in the van. Dave got into their van on the driver's side, to make conversation with Millie and Jake until Ben was ready to leave.

"Was that the groceries you bought this morning?" Millie asked.

"Yes, we've had them under ice. They're for the fridge in the trailer so the guys will have something to eat when they're too busy to go to a restaurant. The other package was something we picked up for Dale Earnhardt."

Ben walked over to their van and said, "Dave, I called the track. I can take some practice laps now. Why don't you take your guests to the condo and get them settled in? Then, come on down to the track so we can pace the car. Charlie'll run laps with me 'til you get there."

"Fine," Dave replied. "We'll see you in an hour or so." He started the van and shifted the gear to drive, pulling away.

Once they had left the airport parking lot, Dave noticed Millie had a surprised look on her face. "If I may ask, Millie, what's that look mean?"

"You have a condo in Daytona? I'm surprised. I assumed you stay in motels."

"Well, when we were winning big, we needed a tax deferment. Real estate was an easy option. We bought this condo because we spend several weeks here, preparing for this first race; and, we then come back for another race in July. It gives us a place to come to when we need to get away."

"Are you guys Snowbirds?"

"Snowbirds?" he asked.

"Yeah, you know, come to Florida in the wintertime to escape the cold weather?"

"No, not really. Once in a while, though, Ben comes down. As for me, I kinda like wintertime."

"Do you have trouble with your fans? Don't they sometimes get overly aggressive?"

"Well, we don't have much privacy when we stay at a hotel, but, please don't misunderstand my words. We never get tired of our fans. We appreciate them because they made us what we are today. They normally just want to talk for a minute, get an autograph, you know, the usual fanfare stuff. They feel as if they know us just because they see us on television or at the track. This first race at Daytona is the kick-off for the season. It's considered to be the Superbowl of racing."

"Hum-m-m, I see."

"Hey, Dave, what are your chances for this race?" Jake asked.

"Well, we didn't get a favorable pole position. While we were gone, the crews' been making some adjustments on the engine. Hopefully, we'll do better in the race tomorrow. Stock cars are built to perform equally; but these minor adjustments can make a difference. You'll see, later, when we test the car."

"I didn't think you were allowed to make changes to the basic stock car." Jake said, surprising Millie with his knowledge.

"Well, everything must be approved by NASCAR before the race. They are pretty strict. Minor adjustments, as minute as air pressure in the tires, can definitely make a difference."

"Do you think I could drive the car?"

"No, Son, I rather doubt it. We're not supposed to let anyone even *ride* in the car. Once in a while, when there's no one around, we'll take someone out for a few laps. There's a slim chance that I might be able to take you for a lap or two on Monday, or maybe tomorrow evening, after the race."

"Oh, God, that would be awesome!" Jake exclaimed, letting his guard down, exposing his excitement at the possibility. "I'd love it!"

"Well, we'll see. Ben's a fanatic about the cars, especially before a race. If the car makes it through the race without mishap, I'll see what I can do to take you for a spin. What about you, Millie, would you like to go a few laps in the car, too?"

"Sure, I've always liked race cars."

"You'll see an entirely different view from the car. I warn you, though; it's addictive, something you'll never forget. Racing gets in your blood, so to speak."

Millie smiled; but, in the back of her mind, she was thinking about getting into the car through the window with everyone watching. She wondered what would happen if she didn't fit, or, God-forbid, got stuck!?

Evidently she had a peculiar expression on her face, because Dave asked, "What does that look mean?"

"Well, there aren't any doors, are there? Isn't it difficult to get into the car?"

Dave laughed out loud. "Well, it's not as easy as getting into this van; but, I'll help you. You'll do great! You're so funny. You have such a natural charm."

"Mom!" Jake smirked, somewhat embarrassed. "We'll get you a step ladder and push!"

"She'll do great, Son." Dave said, taking her hand, defending her.

"The name's 'Jake'. Don't call me 'Son,'" he said sarcastically, regaining his spoiled-brat attitude.

Dave pulled into the driveway of a beautiful adobe-like condo in a secluded neighborhood. After helping Millie get out, Dave unlocked the front door, using a key from his key ring.

Millie gasped with amazement when she stepped inside. The condo was larger than it appeared from the street. The living room was two stories high, with a stairway coming down both sides. The predominant living room wall contained a massive stone fireplace with a majestic marble hearth.

The room was exquisitely decorated using a colorful southwestern motif. A large Navajo blanket was neatly positioned at an angle, on the stone wall above the fireplace. The living room furniture was in earth tones, over-stuffed and comfortable looking. Decorative area rugs and a large, long-haired, bearskin rug were lying on the floor in front of the fireplace, accenting the stone flooring. There were massive antique brass candelabras on each side of the thick wooden mantel.

Off to the right, there was a dining room, with seating at the table for ten people. A large, well-kept, well-stocked, kitchen was located behind the dining room. The kitchen cabinets were oak, with glass fronts, and colorful etchings.

A half-bath and recreation room circled back to the living room. There was a magnificent oak pool table in the center of the recreation room. A large-screen television and several over-stuffed chairs were situated around an oak game table in the corner. A fully stocked bar was situated next to the pool table.

"Dave, this is more beautiful than I could ever imagine. I feel like I've just walked into the pages of a magazine."

"Well, essentially, Millie, that's what you did. We bought this condo, like I said, when we were winning big. Lynne, Ben's wife, asked a decorator to duplicate a picture she saw in a magazine. Come on, I'll show you the upstairs."

"Did your ex-wife help with the decorating?"

"No, she wasn't much interested in things like that...."

Dave showed Millie and Jake two of the four bedrooms, each decorated exquisitely. Each bedroom had its own bathroom. The first of the bedrooms was very masculine in decor, with large oak furnishings, continuing the southwestern motif. The other bedroom was totally feminine, with colonial-style furniture, which looked as if it had come from Ethan Allen Gallery.

"How many people will be staying in this condo, Dave?" Millie asked.

"Just the four of us. You two can use these two rooms. My bedroom's to the left and Ben's is across the hall." he said, pointing towards both rooms. "The reason we have four bedrooms is because our parents used to come down for the race; or, sometimes, Ben's children come down. This trip, though, it's just me and Ben."

"Why didn't Ben's wife come?"

Dave didn't say anything at first, just looked at the floor. "She's got her nose out of joint because Pat and I split up. Things became real tense before the season ended last year. I mentioned that while we were on the plane, didn't I?"

She could tell Dave was troubled because Lynne had not come with Ben on that trip. "Oh, I'm sorry, of course, you did."

Then, to change the subject, Millie said jokingly, "Hey, I want to see your bedroom, Dave. Is it clean?"

"No, I'm a slob! I guess you can take a look." he sighed.

Dave opened the door to his bedroom, and they walked in. The room was immaculate. The bed was made, Dave's clothes were neatly hung in the open closet, and his shoes were placed, side-by-side, on the floor of the closet. Then he showed them his bathroom. His shaving kit was sitting on the vanity.

Even though Millie could tell the towels had been used, they were neatly hung on the towel rack.

"Oh, yeah, Man, you're a real slob!" Jake smirked. "I wish my room was this clean! My dorm at school's a mess. Mom'd have a fit if she saw it."

Millie chidingly glared at Jake, and then smiled at Dave. "Did you just get here today?"

"No, we came down a week ago last Tuesday."

"A real slob, huh?" she teased. "This room looks pretty clean to me."

Dave smiled proudly.

"Hey, Mom, you take the bedroom with the ruffles. I sure don't like ruffles; but, you love them." Jake suggested. Millie nodded her head in agreement.

Still carrying his overnight bag, Jake left the room, leaving Dave and Millie alone in his bedroom.

"You call this sloppy?" she teased.

"Well, we have a maid who comes in once a day. She must have straightened up a bit...." he said with a smirky smile.

"I don't think she did. I think you're a neat-nik. You seem like the type. This condo makes my house look like a cabin. It is really breath taking. It's hard for me to imagine living like you do. Isn't it hard, having to travel so much? Do you have condos in any other cities where you race?"

"No, but Daytona's one of our favorite places. We have a time-share in Arizona, with the week blocked out for when we race there. Its only once a year. Most of the time we get motel rooms. Sometimes, we bunk in one of the trailers. A lot depends on how well we're doing in the circuit. If we do well, the sponsors'll pick up the tab for a lot of things. When I was married, though, we always got rooms, no matter what."

"Well, I can understand that...."

"In the divorce settlement, I gave up our cedar home in North Carolina in exchange for her share in this condo. I've got to make some decisions regarding my life, because I'm still living in temporary housing. I inherited a piece of property from my Dad. If I decide to stay in North Carolina, I'll probably build a house on that land. We'll see. One thing I'm sure of, I'm glad you decided to come with me. I'm enjoying getting to know you, Millie."

Suddenly serious, Millie could tell by Dave's demeanor that he was thinking about trying to kiss her. Since she wasn't ready for him to make a move, she turned to walk around his room.

The king-size bed had a massive oak headboard, with matching nightstands and majestic lamps. "This is a very masculine room, Dave. It suits you."

The comforter on the bed had a dark green background with a black-and-brown geometric print. Dark green mini-blinds, with a coordinating cornice board, decorated the large window. There was an entertainment center in the corner, which contained a 24-inch television with built-in VCR. Millie noticed the movies on the shelf were about racing, or westerns, science fiction, and action varieties. Dave came up behind her as she read the titles, and slipped his arms around her waist.

"Do you want to watch a movie?" he whispered.

"No, I'm discovering things about you. You said you might dissolve your partnership. Do you think you'll be happy if you're not driving a race car?"

"I won't know 'til I try. If I take the sports broadcasting job, I'll still be at the track, be able to see my friends, and would still be an important part of the NASCAR scene. At some point, I have to quit driving, or wait for a wreck to kill me."

"Have you ever had any serious wrecks?"

"Two years ago, Butch Smith, another driver, lost control on turn four at Charlotte and smashed into me. My car became airborne. I'll never forget being inside that tumbling car. An on-board camera captured the whole thing. I've got it on tape here somewhere."

"Were you seriously hurt?" she asked.

"No, luckily, I walked away with a few scratches and bruises, a mild concussion, and a broken arm."

"Were you hospitalized?" she asked.

"Yeah, for two days. I hated it! It was a precaution because of my concussion. I'll admit that racing hasn't been the same for me since that wreck. Ben says that I've lost what they call the 'competitive edge.'

He says that I'm too cautious now … not willing to take unnecessary chances. That's yet another reason to bow out now, while I can, step aside so I won't hold him back."

"A wreck like that would be detrimental for anyone. I couldn't even get into a car for several months after Jacob's wreck. His car was a twisted mess, and his blood was splattered everywhere. Dave, he was almost decapitated."

"Oh, you poor thing. I'm so sorry."

"They told me not to go see the car; but, I had to. My life had changed dramatically and I had lost the love of my life. I guess my life kind of ended that day, too. This is the first time I've felt alive since then." she whispered, more to herself than to Dave, a revelation.

"What a tragedy…." Dave whispered, putting his hands on her shoulders to turn her around to face him.

"Well, enough about that, Dave, have you driven very much since then? Won a race?" she asked.

"No, Ben's been doing most of the driving since then. He's won a couple races, though."

"You're probably suffering from an understandable confidence problem. Don't you think you'll be fine once you win another race?"

"Maybe. How about you? Have you ever *really* gotten over your husband's death? It must have been very hard for you, Millie." Dave said sympathetically as he gently pulled her into his arms and held her.

Millie didn't know how to respond. She wondered if he was asking her the question, or trying to find an answer to the question for himself. Wonder if he's ever gotten over his wreck, she thought to herself, deciding not to say anything.

"You need someone to hold you, to let you know everything's okay. You need to know how special you are. Everyone does." Dave whispered as he gently held her in his arms.

"I guess I didn't realize it; but, you're probably right."

Millie could feel Dave's heart beating rapidly. She could sense his loneliness, an emptiness she knew so well herself. She realized he could make a difference in her life before the weekend was over, provided he wasn't a phony ... only saying what he thought she wanted to hear just to get close to her.

"No one escapes from life without a certain amount of pain. Everyone needs someone to help them through the rough times," he assured her. "Millie, everything's going to be fine if we'll just be patient. I can sense it, can't you?"

Dave's arms felt wonderful. Millie's mind was racing, trying to think of something to say. Things were happening too fast. Millie felt inadequate to handle the charms of Mr. Dave Masden. She would be in serious emotional trouble if he continued to hold her in his arms.

Jake walked into the bedroom, interrupting them by loudly clearing his throat. "Uh...hum."

"Dave, why don't you challenge Jake to a game of pool?" Millie suggested, as she pulled away. "I'll unpack, freshen-up, and join you guys in a few minutes. It's almost three-thirty. Don't we have to be at the track soon?"

"Yes, but we've still got a few minutes. Come on, Son; let's see if you know how to use a cue stick." Dave challenged.

"I told you not to call me 'Son'!" Jake said, as they bounded down the stairs, two at a time. Dave turned back to look back at Millie and winked.

Millie went into the bedroom which had been assigned to her, and closed the door. Yes, she and Dave have the potential to develop a relationship, provided he was being honest. If his words weren't a come-on, their lives *could definitely* change before their date ended on Monday.

She knew Jake still had reservations about Dave. She wondered if his reservations had merit; or, if he was simply being overly protective of her. Jake's hostility could be a major obstacle, but, very often, time has a way of taking care of things.

Could she be patient? She wondered. Would Dave be patient with her? She said a silent prayer, asking for God's will for the weekend. "If it is meant to be, it will be." she prayed.

Chapter Four

The mattress on the bed in Millie's room was so high; she had to use the decorative footstool that was near the bed to sit down. She lay down to relax a few minutes, to clear her mind and gather her thoughts.

She was surprised to discover the bed had a waterbed mattress … the cylindrical, wave-less kind. She had always been curious how it would be to sleep on a waterbed. She couldn't help but wonder if Dave's bed had the same kind of mattress; then she chastised herself for thinking about his bed.

The bedspread ensemble consisted of a white cut-Battenberg lace with embroidered coverlet, and an eyelet dust ruffle. There was a large rocking chair in the corner, and an entertainment center, similar to the one in Dave's room. She got off the bed and walked across the room to see what movies were on the shelf. These were more traditional in nature: "*Gone with the Wind*," "*Dr. Zhivago*," "*The Thornbirds*," "*The Goodbye Girl*." …. Romantic titles.

Millie quickly hung up her clothes in the empty closet and placed her boots on the closet floor. She took her cosmetic case to the bathroom, and put her things in the empty medicine chest.

The bathroom was tastefully, but femininely decorated. Millie placed her hair dryer and hot comb in the vanity, checked her make-up, and changed into the skirt and boots, which were a nice compliment to the black embellished sweater she was wearing. By changing clothes, she'd be ready for whatever lay ahead for the evening. After all, Dave had mentioned a party earlier.

Millie could hear Dave and Jake laughing as she walked down the stairs. She eased into the black leather chair near the door, and watched them play. Soon, they were all laughing at Dave's pool-playing antics.

Noticing Millie had changed clothes, Dave said with a wink, "Wow, you looked good at the airport, but I can't resist a lady who wears boots. You look fantastic!"

His compliment in front of Jake embarrassed Millie and she blushed. "Thanks, Dave, I like boots, too." She stammered.

"All right, Dave," Jake said smartly, "Take your turn and quit trying to make time with my Mom. I'm warning you, I'm watching you."

Dave wasn't sure if Jake was kidding or not, but he chose to laugh off the remark. "Well, don't worry about your Mom, Jake; she's in good hands.... You worry about how to get your cue-stick to work right! I'm going to clear the board with this shot!"

"Well, I'm not worried about the cue-ball. Using a play on words, I'm more concerned about the hands.... your hands! You remember to keep your hands on the cue-stick and off my Mom." Jake smirked with a grin, thinking his smart-aleck remark was clever.

Millie, who was somewhat perturbed by Jake's remark, picked up a small pillow from the chair and threw it across the room. The pillow hit Jake in the head, and then bounced off, striking Dave in the face, causing him to miss his shot. "I can take care of myself, Jake Greene. Will you two lighten up and play pool?" At this remark, everyone laughed.

"Boy, Jake, she got us both with one throw. We'd better get on with this game before she uses more drastic ammunition. I think she's getting' mad at us...."

Jake looked intently at his Mom, and then looked at Dave, "Nah, Man, she's kiddin'. She's not ready to bring out the heavy artillery yet."

"Take your turn, then before she throws another pillow. She sure messed up my shot!" Dave instructed, as he gave Millie a beaming smile.

He knew he was beginning to gain Jake's trust. He hoped for Millie's as well.

"Mom, I'm glad Dave asked me to come along. I've been studying too hard lately. I needed to cut loose and have some fun."

"Me, too, Jake…. Me, too." Millie agreed.

Dave smiled but didn't say anything. He mouthed the words…."Me, too," as he shook his head affirmatively and pointed a finger at his chest. Then, glancing at his watch, he said, "It's four fifteen. Ready to go to the track?"

"Sure, let's go…."

When they arrived at the large track, they drove directly into the infield, and stopped in front of an area which displayed the lightning bolt emblem. Ben was stomping around the outside of the racecar, cursing under his breath.

"Dam-mit, Masden, it's about time you got here! There's somethin' wrong with this god-damn car. I'm not getting' enough power. You figure it out. You're the mechanical genius! Will you take it a couple laps to see what the hell's the matter…?"

"Sure, can I take Millie or Jake with me? I don't see any other drivers on the track, he asked.

"Dam-mit, Man, what did I tell you this morning about getting distracted?" He said angrily.

The tension was obvious as Millie glanced around at the pit crew. She knew not to "rock the boat."

"Dave," she said, "Why don't you take the car out alone? Ben needs your help. After all, you are his partner."

"He's been meaner than a grizzly bear in heat lately. Okay, I'll be back in a few minutes." He said, as he climbed into the car.

Dave hit the starter switch and the engine of the shiny red race car roared into action. Dave cut the motor and carefully listened as he hit the starter button again, and then again. Finally, he slowly pulled the car onto the race track, and rapidly increased its speed.

The bright red race car sported a large "19" on the top and both sides, and carried a large Coca-Cola decal on its hood. It was moving so fast around the track that Millie could no longer read the number.

After several laps, Dave slowed the pace and returned to the garage area. He cut the motor and listened intently as he hit the starter switch again.

Looking a Charlie, the crew chief, Dave instructed, "Check out the ignition wiring. Something's not right. I'd hate for the starter to go out during the race tomorrow."

"Right away, Boss, we'll rewire the whole system. You know, the wire seemed a little brittle when we wired in the new switch this mornin'."

Charlie motioned for the mechanics, and the crew began to make the repair immediately.

"This should only take a few minutes, Millie," Dave explained, "Then we'll lap the car again."

While the crew worked, Millie observed the area around them. Dave explained to her what was happening, and told her the names of the other people who were standing around.

Rusty Wallace and Dale Earnhardt were talking in the garage next to them. Down the road, Pat Patterson, the sports announcer, was talking to David Green, Terry LaBonte and Jimmy Hensley. Sterling Marlin was having his photograph taken in front of his car. Neil Bonnett was walking across the track, talking to Ned Jarrett and his son, Dale. "Handsome" Harry Gant and Ernie Irvan were taking a few laps around the track in their cars. Activity was abundant at the track as each crew prepared for the big race.

After the repair had been completed, Ben drove the car around the track as Dave paced him, using the headset. The car lapped at 152.9, which meant it was in a-one condition, ready for the competitiveness of the next day's race.

"Hey, Ben," Dave suggested, "You need to get away from here for awhile.... Let's go down the street, blow off some steam and get some steaks and cold brews..."

"Hell, no, I'm doing fine. I have to stay here until the car's perfect," he smirked.

"Stop being so hyper, Colson, the car IS perfect. Do I have to call Lynne and have her come down here? She'll calm you down."

"No, way, Jose, she's been in a bitchy mood lately. I don't want her around. I'll be okay. Hell, I'm always okay. I'm not hungry, but I guess you're right, Pard. But, why don't I ask one of those little cuties over them by the fence to join us?" Ben said, pointing to a group of young-looking women who frequented the track.

"My God, Ben, what in the world are you talkin' about? Now I know you've lost your marbles.... You don't need that!"

"Well, Masden, if you can do it, I can do it!"

"Hey, there's a big difference. I'm freaking divorced! Need I remind you that you are still married, to a very special lady? Thank about Lynne and the kids. Come on, Man, let's get some grub."

"Oh, okay."

They all got into the van and went to the Race Track Lounge across from the track. The steaks were scrumptious, thick, and cooked to perfection. Their conversation consisted of Ben's constant boasting about their past victories, and his hopes for winning the race. Millie sensed desperation in his voice, a need to win.

Millie wasn't sure she liked Ben Colson.... and she knew he didn't care much for her. He was skinny and quick-tempered, an agitated-type personality.

After Dave paid their check, he suggested, "Let's all go to Kyle's party. We can kick up our heels and do the Texas two-step."

"You know god-damn well I don't dance, Masden." Ben smirked sarcastically.

"Well, everyone we know'll be there. Lee's supposed to sing, too. You like to talk to him. Come on, Man, unwind and have some good clean fun. If you ask, and won't step on her toes, Millie might dance with you."

Ben surveyed Millie's face, which was devoid of expression. "Well, okay, let's go. I don't know about dancin' but I can get drunk...."

"I hate to be a wet blanket, Ben, but you know that's not a good idea either. Sure, you can have a couple of beers, but unless you want me to drive tomorrow, you'd better not have too much to drink...." Dave warned.

"Nan, Man, I'm drivin' tomorrow! We've gotta win. Get offa my back. You've been naggin' like a fishwife this trip. Did Lynne put you up to it?"

"Get off it! I haven't talked to Lynne since Christmas. What in the world's gotten into you Ben? You're actin' crazy!" Dave said, genuinely concerned for his long-time partner.

"Oh, hell, forget it.... Let's just go!"

The drive to the party was somber. Every time Dave and Ben looked at each other, Ben glared. When they finally arrived at the lounge, it was a relief to get out of the van, because the tension had been so thick you could "see" it in the air.

From the outside of the building, it appeared as if the lounge was closed. They walked inside and towards the back of the building. Millie could hear music and people laughing. The air was filled with cigarette smoke.

Ben immediately disappeared into the crowd of people who were gathered there. Dave introduced Jake and Millie to some of the drivers and their wives ... Bobby Hamilton, Kyle Petty, Davey Allison, Alan Kulwicki, and Morgan Shepherd.

The band was loud. Dave and Millie danced a couple of fast numbers, and then the music slowed. Dave pulled her into his arms and their bodies seemed to mesh together into a dancing embrace. Millie could feel his muscles flex as they twirled around the dance floor. She could smell his musky cologne, and felt weak because their bodies were pressed so closely together.

At first, Dave held Millie's hand in a traditional waltz style, and then he moved her hand to his waist and put his arms around her, pulling her even closer to him. When the dance had ended, they were breathless, shaken with emotion.

"You're a great dancer, Millie." Dave whispered.

"So are you, Dave."

The band emcee said, "Let's have a 'change partners' dance. Take your best date out to the floor. When the music stops, change partners with the couple on your right. We'll continue this until you get back to your original partner."

Dave and Millie obediently went to the dance floor. When the music started, Dave gently glided Millie across the floor. The music stopped and Millie found herself dancing with Darrell Waltrip. The music stopped again, and she was dancing with Bill Elliott. The next time the music stopped, she danced with Ben. He was very quiet during the dance, unlike the other partners she'd had. When the dance finally ended, Dave quickly rejoined Millie, and Ben walked away without saying anything to her.

"Dave, it's so smoky in here. Can we step outside for some fresh air?"

"Sure, that's a good idea. The smoke is bothering me, too."

"Have you seen Jake? I've lost track of him."

"Well, I saw him dancing a few minutes ago with a cute little blonde. He looked like he was enjoying himself. Quit worrying, Mill, he'll be okay." Dave kidded her.

As they stepped outside, Dave put his arm around her. She laid her head against his shoulder and took a deep breath. Neither said anything, enjoying the cool fresh air, and the quietness. The moon was full, and the sky was filled with beautiful bright stars. They enjoyed their moment of silence…. The silence before the storm!

The door swung open roughly and Ben came out with his arm around a slim redhead. He was surprised to see Dave and Millie standing outside. He had a guilty look about him.

"Don't wait up for me, Partner. Don't worry, though, I'm not getting drunk, I'm gettin' laid!"

Dave shook his head in wonderment. "I'm sorry, Millie. I don't know what's gotten into him. He's never acted like this before. As far as I know, he's never been with anyone but Lynne. Maybe I should go after him...."

"Whatever you think...."

Dave started to follow Ben, and then stopped. He turned around and looked at Millie. "Oh, hell with him! This gives me yet another reason to end this partnership. Everything's changing so quickly. Let's forget about him and go back inside. He's making a big mistake, though, I just know it!"

"This could really mess up his life, Dave." Millie sympathized. "Hopefully his wife won't find out about it...."

"Let's try to forget him." Dave said as he took her hand. Millie saw Dave turn around again out of the corner of her eye, looking in Ben's direction. She turned to look, too, and Ben had completely disappeared. As they walked back into the lounge, Millie knew Dave was deeply concerned for his partner.

Jake approached them to introduce them to a cute little brunette. "Mom, this is Paula Brown. She's in my political science class. We were surprised to run into each other here...."

"Hi, Paula, it's nice to meet you." Millie said. "This is Dave Masden..."

"Hi, Mrs. Greene. Hi, Dave." Paula said shyly. "Good luck in the race tomorrow."

"Mom, we're going to take a ride down the beach in her car. I'll see you later. Lee Henderson's getting ready to sing. You'll wantta see that...." Jake said.

"Are you sure you can find your way back to the condo, Jake?" Millie asked.

Oh, quit worrying, Mom. I'll find my way back..." Jake assured her as they walked away. "The condo's just down the street, right, Dave?"

"Yes, Son, go back down A-1-A and turn on Jefferson. You guys go on, have a nice ride...."

"Well, Dave, we've both been deserted. Let's go in to listen to Lee's mellow tunes. Maybe he'll do my favorite song." Millie suggested.

"What did you say it was?" Dave asked.

"Well, I cry every time I hear 'God Bless the USA' but my all-time favorite is 'You've got a Good Love Comin'.'"

"Tell you what, you stay right here and watch. I'm going to make a pit-stop and I'll be right back. Would you like something cold to drink?" he asked.

"Sure, that sounds great... anything in the soft drink line."

Millie was standing to the right of the stage with an unobstructed view as Lee Henderson began his act. In a few minutes, Dave returned holding a beer in one hand, and a Coke in the other. Millie took the Coke and thanked him. Dave put his arm around her waist, and took a long drink of his beer. Millie enjoyed Dave's closeness as she leaned against him, relishing in his masculinity, realizing how hungry she was for a man's touch.

Lee Henderson ended his first song, a fast ballad, and started to talk.... "I have a special request for Millie...."

He started to sing...."*You've got a good love comin' from me tonight.....*"

Millie gasped and looked at Dave in amazement as Lee stepped off the stage and walked over to where they were standing. He sang the entire song to Millie. Miraculously, she managed to remain calm, enjoying the attention, as she continued to hug Dave with one arm.

When the song had ended, Lee said into the microphone..."I understand this is your first date with this guy. Do you think he'll be able to take care of you tonight?"

The crowd wildly started to tease them. Millie knew Lee was kidding, and it was all in good fun. She also knew, though, that everyone was listening for her answer to Lee's questions especially Dave.

"Yes, Lee," she whispered, "I think he can handle it..."

The crowd cheered and yelled as they both blushed.

"Well, Millie, if he can't, you let me know!" Lee teased, as he turned and walked back onto the stage. He began the first line to another song...."*Well, she'll turn into a lean, mean, lovin' machine... better than a centerfold in any magazine.*"

Relieved that the spotlight followed Lee back to the stage, Millie and Dave now stood in darkness as the group continued to tease them playfully. Millie turned to Dave and buried her face in the nape of his neck.

"Did you do that?" she asked

"Well, you said you like the song.... and it seems to fit! We both need something good in our lives, don't you think? Did I embarrass you?"

"I can handle that kind of embarrassment. You're really a special man, Dave. You're the one I'm not sure I can handle! You deserve to be loved."

"So do you, Millie.... So do you! I'm a good judge of character. Your sweetness spoke to me this morning at the store. You knocked me for a loop!"

They began to sway in a dancing movement as Lee sang his next song.... "*I Don't Want to Wake You...*"

As they danced, Dave whispered, "God, are you listening to the words of that song? I'm starting to care for you already. What's happening between us? Do you feel it, too? Whatever it is, it feels so good...."

Millie decided she'd better not reply to his questions. She responded by running her hands across his back, and squeezed him gently.

At the end of Lee's concert, he sang "*God Bless the USA*" as a finale. While they watched him sing, Dave stood behind Millie with his arms resting on her shoulder in a semi-hug. She hugged his arms and rested the back of her head and shoulders against his chest.

When the song ended, Millie had tears in her eyes. She was amazed at how dramatically her life had changed in just twenty-four hours. Dave gently turned her around to face him, and wiped a tear from her cheek.

Millie turned back around to face the stage as Lee took a final bow. He looked over at them and gave them a "thumbs-up" signal.

"Why don't we go back to the condo and relax, Millie? We'll build a fire in the fireplace, watch a movie, talk, and get to know each other a little better. I'll behave …. that is, if you want me to behave." Dave suggested.

"Okay, all this cigarette smoke is starting to bother me…."

Kyle Petty and his wife were standing at the door when they left. "Thanks, Man, you throw a great party." Dave said as he shook his hand.

As they were leaving, Dave Earnhardt, Kix Brooks, and Rusty Wallace were arriving with their wives. Dave introduced Millie to the group. Then, they excused themselves and walked outside, arm-in-arm.

On the way back to the condo, Dave held Millie's hand as they listened to the soft country music that was playing on the van's stereo.

Chapter Five

Once they'd gotten back to the condo, Dave asked Millie if she'd like a fire in the fireplace. Since the night was chilly, she nodded her head affirmatively.

"Watch this.... I'll amaze you with this feat of magic!" He joked mysteriously as he walked to the fireplace. "Wa-lah, Alla-kazam," he said as he flipped a switch that was located near the mantle, causing the fireplace to burst into radiant flames.

"That's amazing! I have a fireplace at home; I should get one of those. Fireplaces are too hard to clean. Is it gas?"

"Yes, like having the real thing only there's no mess to clean. All you have to do is remember to pay the gas bill!" he joked. "Are you hungry?"

"No, I don't think so. Are you?"

Dave thought for a moment, putting his hand on his stomach. He shook his head. "How about a nightcap? A glass of wine?" He suggested.

"Sure, that'll be great. Maybe we can talk and get to know each other better."

"Make yourself comfortable," he instructed, "I'll be right back."

In a few minutes, Dave returned to the living room carrying a bottle of wine and two glasses. He also had a small tray containing assorted chunks of fresh fruit and cheese.

"I'm impressed! You did this in just those few minutes?"

"I wish I could take the credit; but, it was the maid. She leaves the fridge filled with the things we like...."

"Does this maid actually exist?" she asked.

Dave smiled, not saying anything as he poured the wine and handed her a glass. He sat down next to her on the sofa. "Here's to the race tomorrow." he toasted, holding his glass up. "No, wait, here's to tomorrow's race and to new beginnings; getting to know you better."

Their glasses clinked and they took a sip of wine. The silence was a little uncomfortable. They were preoccupied with their thoughts regarding the evening's potential, and dealing with the questions and answers that could change their lives forever. Millie knew she had to do something or she'd be in his arms. Dave Masden was much too attractive, irresistible.

"Have you and Ben been with NASCAR very long?" Millie asked, relieved to break the silence.

"I started out as a mechanic in a service station in Durham, North Carolina. It wasn't long before I became interested in racing and started to repair race cars. The first crew I worked on was Lee Petty's gang, in the late sixties. I worked for several different drivers until Ben and I met at Daytona in 1972. The race was won that year by A. J. Foyt."

"Wait, isn't he an Indy-car driver?"

"Yeah, but he also got involved with Winston Cup. Well, anyway, since Ben and I had saved most of the money we'd made in racing, we were able to purchase a rookie's assets when he wanted out of the business. Although we've never won at Daytona, we're dying to win. Like I said, it's considered the 'best of the best' and kicks-off the season. It more or less sets the pace for the rest of the circuit."

"What about your spare time? What do you like to do then? I'm assuming you get some spare time outside of racing."

"Well, believe it or not, we don't have much spare time. Racers are a close-knit bunch. We hunt together, fish, play a round or two of golf... the usual things, when we're not racing. Several of us have Harleys, we'll take a ride. There are a couple drivers who are involved in hang-gliding and free-falling. All in all, we're friends. One of the reasons we were in Brandon was to pick up a shotgun for Dale Earnhardt. Did you know there are a lot of gun collectors in your area?"

"No, I never thought about it. Wait a minute, you're all friends??!!? You don't act like it when you're racing."

"Well, there are a few rivalries. The rookie who caused my wreck, Butch Smith, and I have had some bad blood pass between us. I don't know it for a fact; but I think he's partially responsible for my marriage breaking-up. The competition you see between drivers on the track is real. Mostly, we want to run a good, safe race without anyone getting hurt. Butch is too aggressive, even more so than Dale Earnhardt. When a driver's too aggressive, they actually cause wrecks. Butch takes unnecessary chances. I don't want to see anyone end up getting killed because of his foolishness."

"I don't think I know anything about him."

"He was at the party tonight; but, I didn't feel like speaking to him. I'm usually pretty friendly with all the guys; but, I've not seen him since I heard he's engaged to my ex-wife. She wasn't there, though. As far as I know, he was alone. He gets around, if you know what I mean..."

"You mentioned getting hurt in a wreck. Has Ben had any serious wrecks?"

"He's been luckier than me, just some fender-benders. He always seems to have mechanical problems; but sometimes those can be dangerous. Cars spin around the track at a very fast pace. If a car stalls, and can't move out of the way fast enough, it could get smashed."

"You guys have been through a lot together."

"Yes, we have. He's been like a brother... that is, until last year. Oh, I don't know, Ben and I may be coming to the end of an era. I can't complain because, all in all, the sponsors have been good to us. I've made enough money to be set for life; but money doesn't mean much to me. My needs are simple. I keep thinking about what you said today...about when Jacob died. Since my divorce, and even a couple years before that, I've not been able to get the pieces of my life to fit together."

"I know what you mean. It's like you were a complete person; but, suddenly, you lose your arms and legs. Life doesn't seem to be worth living. There's a large ache in the middle of your chest." Millie sympathized, hitting the middle of her chest lightly with her fist.

"Do you suppose that's what attracted us to each other this morning at the store? You knocked me for a loop the first time I saw you. Your big blue eyes got to me the first time you smiled.... Let's see, what did you say? *They give you too many choices, don't they?* I knew I had to find a way to talk to you.... I had to get to know you better." He said, as he stroked her arm. He picked up a strawberry from the plate and put it in her mouth.

"How sweet, Dave. Well, I told you this is the first time I've been remotely interested in another man since my husband's death. You can imagine the mental anguish I've put myself through to justify allowing you to pick me up, so to speak. I caught a lot of flack from Jake because of it. I've never been 'picked up' in my life. I've led a very sheltered life."

"I don't think I picked you up; our spirits brought us together. I want to know everything about you. Nothing you have said or done so far has scared me, or angered me. I haven't seen any red flags in this relationship so far. I think we're having a good beginning, don't you? Maybe this is answered prayer?"

"Maybe, if we can get past the animosity from Jake and Ben! Have you noticed they seem to be trying to keep us apart?" she asked.

"I sure have and I try to ignore it. I can bring Ben around; and, Jake's opinion will change once I prove to him, and to you, that I'm not just looking for company for the weekend. I want this to work out between us."

"Well, I guess I'm open to it, too."

"You know, Millie, men and women aren't so different. We both need to be loved, to be needed, to be appreciated. Our basic needs are the same. Men and women need to appreciate each other's strengths, and accept each other's weaknesses. Having a 'significant other', so to speak, makes life more enjoyable. What did Joyce Brothers say? Something about how many hugs we need every day. I think it was six a day are needed in order to be mentally healthy."

"Well, then, why don't you put your arms around me. My quota for hugs is mighty low. You've changed my life in such a short time," she whispered, "It scares me."

They enjoy a gentle embrace. Silence again.... a very uncomfortable silence, as they glanced at each other randomly, then quickly looking away.

"Well, while you drink your wine, why don't I put on some music and dim the lights? It's too bright in here. I like the glow of the fireplace," he suggested.

"I've heard the glow from a candle or fire compliments a woman's complexion. At my age," Millie joked. "I need all the help I can get."

"You look great! Why don't we move closer to the fire," he suggested. "Come on, let's sit by the fire..." he said as he grabbed two large pillows from the sofa and placed them on the bearskin rug in front of the fireplace.

Millie was apprehensive; but she couldn't help herself. She was curious to see what the evening had in store. She walked to the fireplace while Dave dimmed the lights and started some CD's to play on the stereo.

Her mind was racing at an incredible speed. This is happening too fast, she thought. How can I slow it down? Do I want to slow it down? She wrestled with her thoughts, consumed by desire...a deep need to know this man intimately.

Dave pulled her into his arms as she stood by the fire and gently kissed her. His lips were soft and inviting. The roughness of his 'five o'clock shadow' ravaged her delicate skin.

She wanted to lose herself in his arms. Thrills swept through her body. Tears welled in her eyes.

When the kiss broke, he held her in his arms, whispering in her ear, "I've wanted to do that ever since I met you."

She couldn't speak.

As he kissed her neck, he whispered, "That was nice...you certainly know how to kiss. Can I have another one?"

She looked at him through her tears and stroked his lips with her fingertip. She responded to his question by putting her arms around him as they kissed again and again.... passionate, yearning kisses that left them breathless.

Realizing her futile loneliness, she surrendered to her need to cry. She trembled as sobs racked her body, almost out of control.

Dave didn't know why she was crying. He held her tightly in his arms, searching his mind to understand the workings of the intrinsic feminine mind.

"Millie, what's wrong?" he whispered.

"I'm sorry, Dave. It's not your fault. I forgot how good it feels to be held. I've missed being hugged. Sometimes I go for days, weeks, even years without having anyone hug me...or touch me. Your arms feel too good. This is happening too fast. Please forgive my emotional display. I'm so sorry."

"Millie, you don't have to apologize. I'm touched. I've felt so lonely myself ... lately; I thought I was going crazy. I know exactly what you mean about going so long without a human touch. I actually prayed a few days ago for the Lord to allow me to love again. Lately, Jesus is the only friend I can trust. I get so tense, especially before a race. I want you, Millie. I want to touch you, to make love to you; but I know it's too soon. We don't want to mess up a good thing by trying to rush it," he told her as he placed his hands on her face, savoring the softness of her skin. "Besides, I happen to think there's a lot to be said for waiting... not rushing a physical relationship. We will both know when the time is right...."

"I'm glad you feel that way. Me, too. I can't believe I'm crying."

"I think it's sweet. At first, I didn't understand; but, now, I'm really touched. Boy, for a few minutes, I was pretty tense 'cause I thought I'd done something wrong."

"No, you didn't; but, I've got an idea that will help you relax," she said mysteriously, "If I can remember how to do it!"

She sat down on the bearskin rug in front of the fire. Looking at Dave, she patted one of the pillows, "Come on, and lay down. I'll help you relax."

"What are you up to?" he asked, somewhat leery, following her instructions.

"Just trust me... You do trust me, don't you?"

"Sure."

"Well, then, lean back and relax. Get as comfortable as possible." she instructed.

"I'm as comfortable as I'm going to get, not knowing what you're going to do!" he said. "Whatever it is, I think I'm gonna like it!"

"Then, close your eyes and don't say another word."

Millie started to caress his face..... gentle, soothing strokes with just the tips of her fingers and fingernails. She continued the facial massage until the tension left Dave's face.

"This is great...." he whispered. "Where did you learn to do this?"

"Remember, I was married to a cop. Policemen have a high divorce rate because they're under so much stress. Jacob would be so tense when he came home from work; and, we started to have some problems in our marriage. I didn't want a divorce so I studied massage.... to help him relax after a stressful day at work. I learned the art of massage from a book."

"You're my kind of woman. I've practically gotten a college degree from reading books."

"Sh-h-h, just be quiet and relax...." she instructed as she continued the massage. Within minutes, Dave became relaxed to the degree that he fell asleep.

Millie sat up and leaned against the coffee table. She sipped the wine and watched the fire, allowing Dave to sleep for a few minutes. She closed her eyes, savoring the memory of Dave's lips against hers. Then she stared at the flames in the fireplace, thinking, as she gently rubbed her fingers across her lips, pensively, savoring the feel of his lips against hers.

"God, you're beautiful," Dave whispered, as he sat up to kiss her tenderly. "I've been laying here watching you stare into the fire. You're as beautiful on the inside as you are on the outside. That facial massage was incredible! I can't believe I was so relaxed that I fell asleep. Forgive me... some date I've turned out to be, huh!"

"You're a good date. There's no need to apologize. The fact you fell asleep lets me know I've still got the touch. I've been told I give a 'pretty mean' back massage, too," she told him, "but, I don't know you well enough for that yet."

"'Yet' being the key word! I'll have that to look forward to..." he whispered as he kissed her again.

Their kisses once again grew intense, as they clung to each other in a passionate embrace, body to body, clinging to each other as they rolled on the bearskin rug. In the back of her mind, Millie struggled with the morality question she had deep within her psyche. She couldn't allow their passion to get out of control. It was too soon. She broke away from Dave's embrace and straightened her clothes, pulled her skirt down.

"Dave, here we go again. This is happening too fast. I'm not ready to go any further. You don't think I'm terrible, do you? Leading you on or anything?"

"I could never think that. I'm sorry. Yes, again, things <u>are</u> moving too fast. I agree completely. This feels like a beautiful dream. You're right, Millie, let's slow down a little; not spoil this good thing that's happening between us. One more little kiss and we'll call it a night. After all, I have to be at the track at seven in the morning."

He kissed her gently and stood to his feet. Taking her hands in his, he helped her get up. Then, pulling her into his arms, he kissed her again. The doorbell rang.

"I know this sounds corny, Dave, but we're saved by the bell!" she kidded. "That's probably Jake."

Dave walked to the door, unlocked and opened it. "What are you doing here?" he said.

"I decided I'd better come down. I know how crazy Ben gets before a race. Is he already in bed?"

"No, Lynne, I don't know where he is. This is a friend of mine.... Millie Greene. We went to a party tonight and just got home. There's no one here but us."

"Oh, hi, Millie." Lynne said nonchalantly, looking at her quizzically. "I'm sorry for the intrusion but I didn't have the door keys. I'll wait for Ben upstairs. I'm sure he'll be home soon. It was a tiring trip; I hate to fly commercial airlines ....." Lynne said, looking at her watch. "Goodnight. It was nice meeting you.... did you say, 'Millie'?"

"Yes, Lynne, Millie Greene .... with an 'e'. Goodnight. I'm sure Ben will be home soon." she said, trying to sound confident that he would, in fact, be home soon.

Lynne didn't respond. She glanced around the room, noticing the wine and cheese, the glowing fire. Then she looked at Dave..."I guess this is what life's all about .... change."

"Goodnight, Lynne. It's good to see you. Maybe tomorrow, after the race, we can have a long talk." Dave said as he watched her ascend the stairs.

After he heard the bedroom door close, Dave whispered. "I'll call around and see if I can find Ben. Why don't you sit down and relax. Have some more wine. I'll just be a few minutes."

While Dave went into the kitchen to make the calls, Millie sat down on the sofa and sipped her wine, savoring the memory of Dave's arms. But, she couldn't help but wonder if Dave was handing her a line, saying whatever he thought she wanted to hear to get close to her.

After a few minutes, Millie gathered their dishes and took them to the kitchen. Dave was standing by the telephone, shaking his head, deep in thought. He looked concerned.

"No one knows where Ben is. Harry Gant said he saw him an hour ago. He said Ben was drinking. I wish I knew where he was. This could cause some serious trouble between him and Lynne.... and NASCAR."

"Do you want to go look for him? I'll go with you."

"No, if he doesn't want to be found, we won't find him. I don't even know the woman he left with. This is my fault."

"Your fault! How could it be your fault? You had nothing to do with Ben leaving the party with that woman."

"Yes, but...if Patricia and I hadn't split up, we would've all been here tonight...relaxing, getting ready for the race. We all go back a long way. He would never have gone to that party if I hadn't suggested it. This can't be easily erased."

"Is that what you want? For Patricia to be here?"

"No, that's behind me. Please believe me; I'm glad you're here. You're right, Ben's messin' things up for himself, without my help!"

"I'm just as much at blame as you are. If I hadn't come with you this weekend, you probably wouldn't have gone to the party tonight. Right?"

"I might have. The loneliness has really gotten to me lately. None of the blame belongs to you."

"Well, then, think positive. Maybe he's somewhere sleeping it off. He'll be home soon. From what you told me, they've been together a long time. If they have a strong relationship, they'll weather this storm. After all, a love that inhibits is not actually love. Love involves allowing your lover to have a certain amount of freedom. You know the old adage, *'If you love something, set it free. If it comes back to you, it's yours forever. If it doesn't come back, it wasn't what it was supposed to be in the first place...'* That's a paraphrase, but you get the idea, don't you, Dave?" He nodded his head in agreement.

They walked back into the living room. "Yes, now, let's have a goodnight kiss and hit the sheets; well, I mean, you in your bedroom and me in mine—but, who knows, maybe it won't always be that way."

"Goodnight, Dave. This has been a great date."

"Goodnight, Mil', it's been my pleasure. But the date's not over until I take you home to Brandon, remember that!" He cuddled her in his arms and kissed her, leaving them with a hunger to extinguish the passionate fire that was igniting deep within their souls.

"Oh, God, Dave, are you for real? This isn't a game you're playing with my emotions, is it?"

"No way! I hope I'm not coming across as phony. It's not in my nature to be manipulative. What you see is what you get—if you're willing to take a chance...." he challenged.

The front door opened. "My God, Mom! What are you doing? You just met him." Jake shouted as he surveyed the room with its dimmed lights, the romantic music, and the glowing fire. "What would Dad say about this?"

"Jake, your Dad is dead! He's been dead for <u>seven</u> years. I've not done anything to be ashamed of tonight...now, say goodnight before you embarrass yourself further."

"Son, I could never hurt your Mother. She's a good woman. I'm very interested in her. She deserves to have a life outside of you, don't you think?"

"I told you not to call me 'Son!' I don't want to see Mom get hurt, that's all."

"Hopefully, I won't hurt her but, you need to back off, Jake, give her a little credit. I'm telling you, she can handle herself. She's a lady!"

"And, I'm warning you, Dave Masden, you'd better not hurt her or you'll answer to me."

Dave didn't respond to his angry threats.

"Goodnight, Jake!" Millie instructed. "This is none of your business."

Jake knew by the tone of her voice that she wouldn't allow him to continue the discussion further.

"I'll see you tomorrow." Millie said.

"Oh, goodnight!" Jake said, as he ran up the stairs, three steps at a time.

At first Dave and Millie didn't say anything. They looked at each other and smiled. The smile became laughter. "Oh, Lord, Dave, I've created a monster. Do you think our relationship will survive our friends and family?"

Dave pulled Millie close and kissed her gently. "You've done a great job with that boy. I'd be the same under similar circumstances. Everything'll work out, you'll see."

Dave turned off the fireplace, locked the front door and they walked upstairs, arm-in-arm.

"What about the stereo?" she asked.

"It shuts off automatically."

They stopped outside her bedroom door and kissed again ... a sweet, gentle, goodnight kiss.

"See you in the morning." Dave whispered, putting his finger to his lips in a silent kiss. He gave her a sensuous, approving look and made a sexy growling sound...."Wow!"

"Goodnight, Dave." She said as she closed the bedroom door.

Millie went into the bathroom. She washed her face and brushed her teeth. She put on her new floor-length nightgown, a feminine cotton eyelet fabric with small lace insets with tiny blue ribbons, sewn bodice pleats and a ruffled flounce.

She folded back the beautiful bedspread and climbed into bed. The satin sheets on the waterbed felt luxurious. What a treat, she thought. Her body tingled. Every erogenous zone in her body screamed for attention in the luxurious-feeling bed. She hadn't allowed herself to feel sensual since the night before Jacob was killed.

She closed her eyes, remembering how wonderful she'd felt in Dave's arms. Now she knew how much she needed a man in her life. She needed to love and be loved. She needed to make love, and have a wonderful man make love to her. She plumped one of the pillows until it felt like Dave's shoulder. She prayed, thanking God for the wonderful day. She prayed for God's will to be done in their relationship.

After tossing and turning for over an hour, she fell asleep; but kept waking throughout the night. Each time she awoke, she had a tingling sensation in her body...like the first time Jacob had excited her when they were mere teenagers, initially exploring love.

What does the weekend have in store for her and Dave Masden, she wondered. Passion? Anger? Frustration? Sex? Being hurt because he'd forget her when the weekend was over? Their passion was building too fast. Could she refuse him tomorrow night... after the race? She wanted him.......bad. True love waits. Could their love wait? Could she wait?

Chapter Six

Early the next morning, a gentle tap at the door awoke Millie. At first she forgot where she was; but, then, suddenly remembering, she jumped out of bed and ran to the door. It was still dark outside and she stubbed her toe on the footstool. She thought it was still the middle of the night when she opened the door.

"Good mornin', Darlin'," Dave whispered. "I thought I'd let you know I'm going to the track. Ben still isn't home, so Lynne's going to be pretty mad when she gets up. I'm sorry that I have to leave you here alone with her. When you're ready to come to the track, call this phone number," he instructed, handing her a piece of paper. "I'll have someone pick you up. Try to be there by ten o'clock. God, Millie, you look incredible this early in the mornin'."

"I must look a mess," she said, trying to straighten her hair.

"No way, you look fantastic! Do you need anything before I leave?"

"No, I'll manage, thanks, but what about you? Do you want me to fix you some breakfast, make some coffee?"

"No, that's sweet, but I need to leave in about ten minutes; but why don't you come down and have a cup of coffee with me? It's already made."

"Oh, that sounds wonderful. I need some caffeine! I'll grab a robe and be right down," she replied.

"Okay, see ya," he said as he started down the stairs.

Millie ran to the bathroom and splashed some cold water in her face. She quickly combed her hair, and did the best she could with her make-up in the minute she'd allotted herself to get ready. She put on the matching robe to her nightgown, and pulled some socks onto her feet.

As she bounded down the steps, somewhat frazzled and shaky, she heard Dave's voice. She stopped in her tracks and listened to see who he was talking with. Then, Millie realized Dave was talking to Ben.

"Hey, Man, where in the hell have you been?"

"You know, Masden, you saw me leave with her." Ben smirked.

"Do you know Lynne's upstairs in your bedroom? She got here last night. We told her we didn't know where you were; and, come to think of it, that wasn't a lie."

"Really, Lynne's here? Boy, she's going to be pissed. Who would've guessed? Well, I may be facing a divorce myself! I did a really stupid thing this time. I'm outta control, running on empty, so to speak." Ben said, "There's too many changes, too much pressure, time's running out for us, for me. Why do things have to change, Dave? I want to be a champion at the track, and I want Lynne by my side. Oh, shit, she's here. I'm surprised she changed her mind.... But I'm glad she's here."

"For Pete's sake, Ben, get a grip. Were you careful last night? There's a lot of diseases out there, you know. You don't know anything about her or where she's been. Lynne would never forgive you if you gave her some sexually-transmitted disease. Correct me if I'm wrong, Ben, but you've never been with another woman since you two got married, right?"

"A man doesn't mess with a good thing. God, you know the ironic thing? Hell, I couldn't do it! I slept with the chick, but I couldn't... uh, rise to the occasion, so to speak. Maybe it was the booze, or maybe it was the woman. I've never had THAT problem before. Isn't it a crock?"

The stair made a loud creaking noise when Millie turned to go back upstairs. She felt like an intruder and had turned to return to her bedroom so they could continue to talk without her overhearing them.

Dave walked over and saw her, "Mil', come on down and have some coffee with us…" he suggested.

"No, I'll go back upstairs so you guys can talk. It sounds like you need to talk about … things…." she retorted, embarrassed at what she had already heard.

"Come on down and have some coffee with us…" Ben confirmed, as he poured her a cup of coffee. "I take it you met Lynne last night?"

"Well, yes, just for a minute. We'll probably have a chance to talk today during the race." She said nervously, then to change the subject… "I guess you're pretty excited about the race today?"

"Excited isn't exactly the word for it. I'm a little hung over, and I didn't get much sleep last night." Ben stated, shaking his head in disbelief.

His remark embarrassed Millie so she broke eye contact with him and looked to the floor. "Will you be okay to drive today, she asked.

"After I down about four pots of black coffee. I've been up the night before a race before; but then it was because of a mechanical problem with the car. Once the caffeine and adrenaline kicks in, I'll be fine. How's everything going between you two?" Ben asked, as he gave Millie a knowing look, assuming they'd spent the night together.

"Man, she's a doll … a real doll! I couldn't ask for a better date." Dave said, smiling at Millie. "I asked her to come down for coffee. Get your mind out of the gutter, Ben. We didn't sleep together last night. Don't assume anything else because it's not true. Millie's a nice girl. I've got my work cut out for me in this relationship. So far, we've had to deal with my hostile partner, a hostile friend, and her hostile son."

"Well, I'll try not to be so hostile from now on. I've had my teeth kicked in, so to speak, and I have no right to judge anyone. Excuse me, Millie, for jumping to conclusions. Hopefully, I'll be able to patch things up with Lynne 'cause I sure don't want a divorce. Boy, she's going to be pis…s" Ben stopped and slapped his hand over his mouth. "Sorry, I mean she's going to be real mad."

Glancing at his watch, Dave said, "Ben, we'd better hit the road. Do you have everything you need?"

"Yeah, let's go."

Turning to Millie, Dave said, "I'll see you at the track about nine-thirty or ten. There'll be a big crowd, and I'll be busy most of the time, but I'll try to spend a few minutes with you before the race."

"I'll be fine; you just do a good job and you two win this race!" She retorted.

"We will. Who knows, Lee Henderson might be there. You'll probably like it if he sits with you…." Dave teased, "He'd better not try to steal my girl, though!"

"Ha ha, real funny, Dave."

"Since Ben has come home, you guys can use the other van. Here's the keys," Dave said, handing them to her. "Lynne knows the routine."

Dave kissed Millie gently, and she watched as they left the condo, locking the door behind them. The room was suddenly quiet, empty, and vacated…. Lonely. Millie refilled her coffee cup and went into the living room. Since it was chilly that morning, she hit the button to start the fireplace, and sat down on the footstool in front of the fire to warm herself. She sipped the strong black coffee, and thought about the drastic changes that had occurred in her life in the past twenty-four hours — she had to shake her head when she realized that it had been less than twenty-four hours since she'd met Dave.

After about twenty minutes of prayer and meditation, Millie's serenity was challenged because Lynne came downstairs.

"O-o-h, that coffee smells good. Do you mind if I join you?"

"No, of course not. It's your condo. I'm just a guest here…" Millie said, unsure of how she felt about Lynne Colson.

Lynne went into the kitchen and returned carrying a cup, and the coffeepot. She topped off Millie's cup, poured her own coffee, and sat down on the hearth. "Did Ben come in?"

"Yes, they left for the track a few minutes ago. I understand we'll join them later…."

"Yes, we will. I'm sorry; I've forgotten your name."

"It's Millie Greene.... With an 'e'. Dave and I just met; last night was our first date."

"Millie, I apologize for my rudeness last night. I was shocked that Ben wasn't home when I got here. He likes to go to bed early the night before a race. I thought he wanted me here with him. Maybe I was wrong. The only time I've missed one of his races is when I was real pregnant, and ready to push out the kid...."

"That's pretty remarkable, to never miss a race."

"When Dave and Pat were together, we had so much fun." Lynne said wistfully, causing Millie to feel uncomfortable, confirming her doubts about Lynne's acceptance of her in Dave's life.

"In your opinion, Lynne, why did they break up?"

"I guess Dave was spending too much time at the track, working on the cars. Pat is a high-maintenance person, if you know what I mean. She demanded too much of his time. She never understood that he had to spend so much time working on the cars. Dave's not been the same since he crashed a couple years ago. There was a lot of tension between him and Pat even before they split up; but I think their problems stemmed from that crash."

"Yes, Dave told me about the accident. Was it really bad?"

"Don't get me wrong, Dave's a great guy. As far as I know, he's never screwed around. Pat broke up their marriage when she started to run around on him. She even tried to pull me into her deception."

"That's a shame. I wonder if she regrets breaking up with him. Have you seen her since they split up?"

"Oh, sure, I've seen her around town a few times, but our friendship's over. If I have to choose between them, I'd choose to maintain my friendship with Dave."

"Dave's quite a guy, isn't he?" Millie smiled.

"I tell you, that man is one mechanical genius. Ben's probably the better driver of the two because his senses are still razor sharp during a race. Dave, though, he can tell what's wrong with a car just by listening to the motor."

"I witnessed that at the track yesterday." Millie said.

"Hum… now I wonder if it's our turn, mine and Ben's, to split up. I wonder if MY man's been messin' around."

"Why do you think that?"

"Because he wasn't home last night. When you have been married to someone as long as I have, you have a second sense about these things. If we split up, our kids would be devastated."

"Do you want to break up?"

"If he's messin' around on me, maybe. I told him a long time ago that I'd never tolerate it. I said I'd leave him in a heartbeat if he even made me think he was out with someone else. Well, last night, I think he was out with another woman or he would have been home. So, I may have to eat my words, or stand up to them…." She said wistfully.

"Well, maybe he stayed somewhere else because of me…" Millie said, pointing to herself. "Maybe he assumed that Dave and I wanted to be alone and he stayed with the guys at the track. In other words, there could have been a reason why he wasn't here last night."

"Well, I guess it's possible…. but not probable. Ben would have just gone to bed and left you guys alone. He's a sound sleeper; he wouldn't have heard a thing!"

"Even if he did something last night, surely you could forgive him one indiscretion. Relationships aren't easy; and if you have one that works, it would be a mistake to walk out because of one mistake. Infidelity is merely a symptom of something going wrong in a marriage. That is, unless you are looking for an excuse to walk away….."

Lynne didn't say anything, staring into the fireplace at the flames, thinking about what Millie has said. Then she stared at Millie, and then stared at the floor. Looking back at Millie, she said, "I don't know you. Why am I talking to you about this?"

Millie calmly replied, "Because it's easier to talk to a stranger than to a loved one. I'll be your sounding board if that's what you need, but I've got to tell you, my husband, Jacob, and I had a terrific marriage. One morning, he left for work and never came home. I received a call from the morgue to identify his body, what was left of it. You and Ben have something to work with here… It's not hard to forgive someone if you really love them. You know, the kind of love that extends beyond the bedroom."

"Oh, I'm sorry, your husband was killed! When?"

"Seven years ago. Dave's the first man I've dated since then. Frankly, Lynne, I'm scared to death. Today's dating world is crazy. There's so many diseases, so many head games. I wonder if I'll ever see Dave again after the weekend's over."

"Oh, I think you will, Millie. Again, I'm sorry I was so rude last night. Will you sit with me during the race so we can cheer our men to victory, and get to know each other better?"

"Sure, I'd like that…."

"Dave's job today is as important as Ben's because he has to talk Ben through wrecks so he won't become a part of them…"

"Do you still miss Pat?"

"Sure, I guess, but to be honest with you, she could really be a bitch sometimes. Everything always had to be HER way. We went where SHE wanted to go… you get the picture. Dave's a gem. He loved her no matter what she did. He was devastated by the divorce."

"I sensed that yesterday…."

"Last night, though, he looked like the old Dave. He was smiling, happy for the first time in a long time. You are good for him, Millie."

"Thanks, he's good for me, too."

"He's been mad at me ever since the divorce because I'm always trying to fix him up with somebody. Finally, he just quit coming around to see us. This is the first time I've seen him since Christmas. I used to see him every day!"

"He's certainly been good for me so far, Lynne. Here, let me refill your cup." Millie said, picking up the coffeepot.

"I need something a little more substantial. I think I saw some fresh pastry in the breadbox." Lynne said, as she disappeared into the kitchen. "They'll go great with this coffee."

"Dave gave me the keys to the van outside so we can come to the track. He said he'd like us to be there about nine-thirty."

"Yeah, we'll get ready as soon as we eat this luscious pastry." Lynne replied as she handed Millie a slice of warm apple strudel.

"Ben likes for me to be at the track before a race, to give him a good-luck kiss and hug. Talking to you has really helped me, Millie. I'm glad you're here."

"Me, too, Lynne; but I'm not alone. My son, Jake, is upstairs asleep. He'll want to go to the track with us."

"How old is he?"

"He's twenty-four ... a pre-law student at Stetson."

"You have a twenty-four year old son?"

"I'm afraid I have a hostile twenty-four year old son. He's giving Dave a hard time, becoming very protective of me, if you know what I mean...."

"Geez, don't worry, Dave'll win him over."

While they ate their pastry and sipped their coffee, Millie couldn't help but notice Lynne's natural beauty. She was tall and slim, a natural blonde if there ever was one, whose haircut made her look somewhat like Princess Diana of Wales.

A few minutes later, Jake came bouncing down the stairs. Millie quickly introduced him to Lynne.

"Hi, ya, Lynne, nice to meet you. Where is everyone?"

"Well, Ben and Dave went to the track a while ago."

"Shoot, I would've liked to go with them. Can I have some of that coffee?" Jake mumbled, trying to wake up.

"Sure, but it's almost gone. Look in the cabinet next to the sink for a coffee mug. There's sugar and creamer on the counter, and the pastry's in the breadbox. Please help yourself. You can warm it up in the microwave." Lynne told him, smiling at Millie, and mouthing, "He's cute...."

Jake returned carrying a coffee mug and two pieces of strudel. Lynne drained the pot into his mug, which almost filled it.

"Is that enough coffee, or should I make another pot?" she asked.

"No, this is fine. I don't usually drink a lot of coffee."

"Jake, have you been to the Daytona 500 before?" Lynne asked.

"No, all I've done for the past six years is study... learning as much as I can until I take the bar exam. I've challenged myself to pass it the first time I take the test...."

"Well, maybe the excitement of the race will help you forget about studying for a while. You'll never forget the powerful sound of all those engines when they start their motors. Are you going to sit with your Mom and me?"

"I don't know yet. Dave said something about putting me to work in the pit."

"Yeah, he likes to do that. Watch out, though, because racing'll get in your blood if you're not careful. If racing fuel gets in your nostrils, it stays in your veins forever; and then, you'll have a need to be at every race in the circuit. We have two sons; and although they're not interested in racing right now, I expect they'll follow in their father's footsteps, and maybe our daughter, too!"

"Oh, I don't think there's a chance of that happening with me. I've got other plans for my life. Although, if everything goes well in the race today, Dave said he might take me for a ride in the race car. I would like that!"

"Dave's a good man, and he usually keeps his word. He'll take you for a lap or two if he can, I'm sure." Lynne assured him.

Glancing at the clock, she said, "We'd better get dressed and get down to that track before they send the bloodhounds after us...." Lynne quirked. "It's going to be chilly at the track. Do you guys have warm clothes to wear?"

"I think so…." Millie said.

"Come on with me," Lynne instructed, "I'll get you both a jumpsuit so everyone will know you are part of the Colson-Masden team."

"Well, Dave gave us jackets. I assumed that would be sufficient." Jake said.

"No way, come with me," Lynne motioned, walking towards the laundry room behind the kitchen. She pulled two red jumpsuits from the rack and handed them to Jake and Millie. "We only have two sizes, but I assure you they'll fit!"

"Thanks, Lynne, we'll give them back to you after the race." Millie said.

"Oh, no you won't! Besides, Millie, I have a feeling you'll be needing them again." Lynne said, smiling knowingly. "Let's get ready to go. We need to leave in about forty-five minutes. Can you be ready by then?"

"Sure, no problem."

The trio went upstairs and into their respective bedrooms, showered and got dressed to go to the racetrack. After Millie pulled on the jumpsuit, she stared at herself in the full-length mirror and smiled. She looked much better than she thought she would; and, today she wanted to look great!

Millie dried and styled her hair – she was having a "good" hair day. Her hair was perfect, hanging in ringlet curls down her back. Luckily she had a red headband that completed the look she was trying to achieve.

The bright red jumpsuit was a perfect fit. Her hair was perfect. She felt confident, and ready to charm the world … especially the magnificent Dave Masden!

On the way to the track, they stopped briefly at a Chapel to pray, and receive communion. They prayed for the safety of all the drivers.

As they neared the track, Lynne asked, "Millie, do you work?"

"I assist an interior decorator, and my specialty is unique antique furniture and country decorating," she replied.

"No kiddin'! Hey, this is great. I love to dabble in antiques. That's how I usually spend my time when we're in all the different cities. I'll find some out-of-the-way antique shop, and I'm in virtual seventh heaven. Pat hated searching for antiques. Hey, this is perfect. I'm really glad you met Dave."

Jake took a deep breath and sighed…. "Oh, Lord…"

"What's wrong with that?" Lynne asked him.

"Nothing, I guess. You guys're a perfect match. Mom's a fanatic when it comes to an antique."

The two women smiled at each other. Lynne winked at Millie and whispered, "Don't worry, Dave'll win him over. I bet you an antique he will."

"It's a bet!" Millie chuckled.

The track was crowded when they parked the van in the infield. Ben saw Lynne immediately and thought she was acting angry. He stuck his head under the hood of the race car, trying to ignore his seemingly-angry wife.

Lynne walked over to Ben and said, "Ben Colson, where were you last night," she demanded, hands on her hips in a threatening manner.

"Slept at the track in Charlie's trailer….." he mumbled.

"I don't believe you. Turn around here, Ben, look at me!"

Ben turned around, trying to feign a calmness, hoping the crew wasn't listening or paying attention to Lynne. He knew he was in trouble.

"This is for good luck in today's race, Hon. We'll talk about last night later, after the race. No more lies, though. I want the truth!" Lynne said as she put her arms around Ben and kissed him. Then she whispered in his ear, "I've missed you…. Can hardly wait until tonight….!"

Ben put his head down and rested it on his wife's shoulder. "Oh, God, Lynne, I'm sorry about last night. You know I love you; I really do. Please forgive me for not being there when you got home. I'm glad you're here, Sweetheart. I've missed you so much."

"Me, too, Ben. This is the longest we've ever been separated. I'm sorry I didn't come with you last week. I should have......let's never spend another night apart!"

"Oh, Honey, thanks for understanding. I didn't want to think about the possibility of losing you during the running of this race. It's all I've thought about....."

"We'll talk later," she whispered, putting her fingers to his lips to stop the words he was trying to say. "Right now, don't think about anything but winning this race. Are you sure you're okay? Your eyes are kinda bloodshot. Didn't you get any sleep last night?"

"I'm a fool... a stupid fool. I've been downing coffee all morning. Dave said he'd drive, but you know I'll be okay. If Dave takes over now, we'll have to take a provisional starting position because he didn't get qualified. We don't need to start dead last. If I start to feel rough, Dave'll take over after the race starts. If necessary, he can take over after a few laps. We've already cleared it with NASCAR."

"You guys are a winning team in my book; remember that, no matter where you start. Maybe you'd better bite the bullet, step aside and let Dave take over." Lynne suggested.

"No, I'll be fine. I promise." Ben assured Lynne, giving her a hug that let her know he was glad to be back in her arms.

At first Dave hadn't noticed that Millie had arrived at the track. When he saw Ben and Lynne embracing, he surveyed the crowd of people standing in their pit area. Millie saw Dave and watched him visually search the crowd, knowing he was looking for her. When their eyes met, she smiled at him and waved. He motioned for her to come to him, to see what he was doing.

As she walked over, Dave gave her an approving look that sent thrills throughout her body. "You look sensational! Red is certainly your color. I could use a good-luck kiss, too."

"You've got it!" Millie said, stretching to throw her arms around his neck. When their kiss broke, he pulled her against him and kissed her again, more passionately. The guys in the crew cheered. Dave and Ben were both getting good-luck kisses. How could they possibly lose today? Jake, however, wasn't at all happy about the romantic display of affection, which was taking place between his mother and Dave Masden.

"Come on, Millie," Lynne yelled, "We'll have to wait 'til after the race for a victory kiss. I usually sit across the tracks in the special viewing section so I won't get trapped in the infield, in case something would happen."

"What do you mean?"

"In case of an accident… They medi-vac the driver out; but they forget about the wife. At some tracks, once the race starts you can't leave the infield until the race has ended. Of course, you also can't get back into the infield once the race starts. Some tracks have tunnels so you can go back and forth; but Daytona doesn't have a tunnel. They'll be closing the track to traffic soon. Let's go…."

"Jake, why don't you stay here…" Dave suggested. "You can be my assistant in case I need something during the race. You'll have a good view of the race, and know what's happening every second."

Jake nodded his head affirmatively and followed Dave, smiling to himself as he walked. He felt as if he was a part of the team. The feeling surprised him.

"Let's run by the trailer and get a Coke on the way…" Lynne suggested, "We gotta support our sponsors while we're in public.

The rig (trailer) was huge. "Wow, this is really equipped. I never dreamed a semi could house so much equipment!"

"We carry two full cars, plus spare parts for another one. There are four sleeping berths, a bathroom, and a small kitchenette, too."

"A virtual home away from home…" Millie remarked as she took the can of ice-cold Coca-Cola from Lynne. They rushed across the track just prior to the gate being closed.

When they arrived at the special viewing section, Lynne introduced Millie to some of the people in the stand. Ernie Irvan's wife was there, as well as Clint Black and Lisa Hartman. Lee Henderson came in and spoke to them.

"Well, Millie, it's a pleasure to see you again. I'm curious, did he take care of you last night?" he teased.

"That's none of your business, Lee Henderson!" She quipped teasing her new friend. "It's too soon to answer that question. You know it was our first date."

"Ah ha, then I've still got a chance," he joked.

"NOT!" Lynne interjected. "If you're not careful, Dave'll get you for hittin' on his woman."

They all laughed, knowing it was all in fun …. A tension breaker.

"Is it okay if I sit with you guys?"

"Sure, you know it is…." They answered

A few minutes later, a man and woman stepped in front of them so they could sit at the end of their row. At first Millie didn't say anything. She stared at the couple in wonder. Is that who she thinks it is? Finally, she nudged Lynne and asked…"Who is that?"

"Who do you think it is?" Lynne said, jokingly.

"Paul Newman and Joanne Woodward?"

"Bingo. Would you like to be introduced?

"Maybe later. I can't believe it! Paul Newman's butt was only two inches from me and I didn't even know it!"

"I saw Sammy Kershaw and Tracy Lawrence come in a few minutes ago. You know, the country singers. Wantta meet them?"

"Maybe, I heard Tracy's getting a race team up, and Sammy's doing some sponsoring. Is that right?"

"Uh-m-m, yes, I think so."

"How soon does the race begin?"

"About fifteen minutes or so. See, all the cars are lined up. There's our #19. Ben is standing beside the car, talking to Dave and Jake. We're in the eighth row outside. The two men talking to Dale Earnhardt in the #3 car is Dr. Jerry Punch and Randy Pemberton. They're sportscasters. Jerry Punch is actually a doctor. Up in the booth, you see Neil Bonnett and Ned Jarrett. I have a couple of headsets in my purse so we can listen to their commentary during the race. The earphones also protect our ears from the loud noise of the race.

The crowd cheered as each driver was introduced to the crowd. Some drivers received a louder cheer than others. When Ben's name was called, Lynne, Millie and Lee jumped to their feet to applaud and cheer their favorite team.

As the National Anthem was sung, the excitement and anticipation was more than Millie could stand. Dave looked so handsome as he prepared for the race. The shiny red Coca-Cola sponsored car was gleaming in the bright sun. Jake was shaking hands with Sterling Marlin and Michael Waltrip. Everyone was primed and ready for a magical day

Chapter Seven

Excitement ran rampant throughout the standing-room-only grandstand, and in the gathering of friends and families that were waiting for the race to begin in the special viewing arena.

Millie noticed Ben was now sitting inside the race car. Dave and Jake stood side-by-side in the pit area, wearing headsets, and looking very handsome in their jumpsuits. The pit crew was standing on the concrete wall next to their pit, anxiously awaiting the start.

"Hey, Ben," Dave said into the two-way radio. "How do you feel? Are you primed and ready to win this race?"

"Right on, Partner. This is going to be a very special race. I can feel it in my bones. Let's pray to finish with both me and this car intact. The sponsor'll pick up the tab if I can at least finish the race."

"Well, we're ready for a victory in the pit. You've got a good car under you. Stay focused, and I'll let you know what's happening around you on the track. Our spotters are in place, ready to watch you win this race, too. By the way, Man, I'm glad Lynne came down for the race. She and Millie seem to be hittin' it off, don't they? I don't know what happened; but I'm glad. I've got a good feeling about Millie. She may be the one for me."

"I would never have admitted it; but so do I. I was jealous 'cause you were able to explore the world of women – and you, you fool, wouldn't even date – that is until you saw her in the store yesterday. I wouldn't have given her a second glance; but you evidently saw something special. You've not been the same since."

"Man, I'm tellin' you, she's an answer to a prayer!"

"I hope I can work things out with Lynne, too … you know, make up for some things. Well, this mornin' I thought we were history. Lynne told me she'd walk if she ever caught me with another woman. Right now, I'm on top of the world, ready for this victory. Something's gonna happen, Dave. I know it!"

"Well, stay focused and I'll do the same. After this race is over, we can pick up where we left off with the women in our lives. Right now, we can't think about anything but what's happening on the track. Smith's right behind you in the pack."

The crowd cheered as Richard Petty walked to the microphone to officially start the race, when he loudly said into the microphone: "Gentlemen, start your engines!"

The crowd roared and jumped to its feet as the finely tuned racing machines cranked to full power. Although tremendously exciting, the sound was deafening. Goose bumps prickled Millie's arms as the glorious racing machines circled the oval track. She immediately said a silent prayer for God's protection for all the drivers, and asked for God's will for the race. Then, she obediently put on the headset that Lynne handed her, to discover that she had been right. It definitely helped distort the loud noise of the track.

The pace car finally pulled away and the green flag was waved to signal the start of the race. Millie knew at that moment she would never forget the sound of the motors roaring into action, and the sound of the tires on the pavement. The ground literally vibrated from their horsepower.

Millie glanced across the track to the pit area. Jake was watching the race with his mouth open, totally engrossed by the fast action on the track. Dave was rapidly talking into the headset. The pit crews were standing on the concrete wall. The crowd cheered as Kyle Petty's #43 car took the lead.

Ut oh, a yellow flag was waved. A car was having trouble and had to leave the race after only two laps. Tough break! The mighty cars slowed their pace until Dick Trickle's disabled car could be removed from the track with a blown engine. When the green flag waved again, the drivers picked up the pace and roared into immediate action.

Except for a few position changes, the race remained unchanged for the next twenty laps; then the yellow flag was waved again.

"Ben, go low. You'll miss the crash if you go low, into the grass if you have to…." Dave told Ben. His instructions enabled him to clear the crash, even though he couldn't see two feet in front of him because of smoke. A tire had blown on Dave Marcis' car, causing him to lose control and hit the wall, collecting Bobby Hillin and Kyle Petty's car in the melee.

Kyle Petty was so angry; he tried to fight with Bobby Hillin. Although their anger was real, their antics were amusing to the crowd as Kyle threw his helmet at Bobby.

Several lead cars came into the pit for service while the track was being cleared of debris. Rusty Wallace, Dale Earnhardt, Dale Jarrett, Geoff Bodine and Mark Martin refueled and changed all four tires. Then #19 came into the pit for the same.

"Thanks, Dave, and thank the spotter. I'd never have made it through that mess if it wasn't for your instructions. It was a close call."

"No problem – that's what you pay me for! Ha ha. How's the car running?"

"It seems a little tight in the corners. I'm having Charlie take out a round or two. Tires feel great. Car's performin' at its peak. First class……"

The green flag was waved to signal the approval to resume the racing speed once again. The powerful engines met the challenge and roared into action. Ben managed to gain a position and was now in fifth place. The cars were huddled dangerously close together. No one would give an inch in their positions, as they continued to speed around the track at 175 mph. Butch Smith was drafting Ben, much too close for comfort, trying to cause him to get loose so he could take his position.

Suddenly a turn four, dust and smoke filled the air once again. Al Unser, Jr., had lost control and bounced off the wall, gathering Bobby Hamilton in the process. Luckily, Ben was on the other side of the track at the time. Debris flew everywhere, and the drivers slowed their pace before they reached the crash site – everyone, that is, except Butch Smith, who forced his way around the leaders of the race so he'd be in first place when they got to the line. Ben shook his head at Butch's obvious stupidity. Why didn't NASCAR see his dangerous move, he wondered.

Al Unser, Jr. had an injured foot and had to be helped from his car and into the ambulance. Neil Bonnett announced that the injury was not serious enough for hospitalization.

Ben made another pit stop while the track was being cleared. Millie watched from across the track as the crew quickly jacked the car, changed the tires, cleaned the windshield, and refueled #19. She saw Jake hand Ben some Gatorade, and was pleased that the weekend was working out so well for him ... that he was able to experience the excitement of the race, first hand.

In a record few minutes, Ben returned to the racetrack, maintaining his position in sixth place. Butch Smith was still in first place, followed by Dale Jarrett, Rusty Wallace and Dale Earnhardt.

Lee bought Lynne and Millie a hot dog from a vendor, and got them a fresh can of Coca-Cola because the excitement had caused them to work up an appetite.

"Why do hotdogs always taste so much better at the track?" Lynne asked him.

Lee shrugged his shoulders... "Beats me?"

Millie and Lynne thanked Lee for their lunch.

The green flag was waved again, and since they had new tires, the race continued at an even-faster pace, as they circled the track repeatedly, lap-after-lap. The front runners struggled to maintain their positions. Ben was able to gain a position, and was now happily in fourth place, with some tough competition ahead of him. The space separating the leaders was minimal.

Butch Smith, Dale Earnhardt, Rusty Wallace, and Ben Colson, in that order, zipped around the track, making the profession of Winston Cup racing look incredibly easy. They knew, however, that tragedy could break at any second.

Dale Earnhardt tapped Butch's bumper to signal that he wanted to pass. Butch stubbornly held his position while Dale continued to draft his car until Butch's car finally got loose, causing him to move to the top of the racetrack to keep his vehicle under control. Dale, Rusty and Ben zipped past him quickly.

Ben had to swerve to maintain his position as Smith rejoined the line-up. It was obvious that Smith was angry, hell-bent on regaining the lead.

At lap 179, Rusty Wallace's car slid sideways, but then dug into the grass, launching it end-over-end twice before it did six barrel rolls. It came to rest in an upright position, utterly destroyed. Millie immediately prayed for his safety.

Everyone held their breath, fearing for Rusty's life. As soon as Neil Bonnett announced that Rusty was okay, the crowd cheered loudly. To their amazement, Rusty climbed out of the car and walked to the in-field ambulance. He waved to the crowd as he stepped into the van.

After the caution, with only six laps to go, Butch Smith was determined to win the race. He drafted Ben, dangerously close, then rammed into the rear end of the #19, causing Ben to swerve, and rub the front of the avenging car. Both cars spun out of control, crashed into each other, and veered away, directly into the wall. Ben had crashed the rear of his car into the wall, causing the front end to come off the track. The #19 then flipped and came to rest directly in front of their pit area. The fuel cell had burst, and the #19 was now upside down, and in flames. The crowd held its breath, watching, fearing for the worst. Many prayed silently as they watched in horror as the inbuilt fire extinguishers in the car were bringing the flames under control.

Inside the car, Ben could feel liquid spilling all over him. By the odor, he knew immediately it was fuel. He quickly broke away the steering wheel and unfastened his safety harness, trying to get out of the car as quickly as possible. The car sparked and again burst into flames. Ben was mesmerized, unable to move. The flames were incredibly hot and Ben couldn't breathe. His life flashed before his eyes… then everything went black.

Without a moment's notice, Dave jumped over the fence at the pit and ran to their car. His only thought was for Ben's safety.

Two members of Hut Stricklin's crew tackled him, trying to keep him from rushing to the burning car. Dave jerked away. Although the fire was intense, he could see Ben moving. He had to get him out of the inferno as quickly as possible – or he would die a certain death in the car.

The ambulance and fire truck were parked on the other end of the track. Dave knew Ben's jumpsuit was flame-resistant; but unless he was pulled out of the car quickly, he would literally cook inside the suit and helmet.

Every second counted in this race for life. Dave pulled away again and ducked into the flames. At first the fire kept him from reaching Ben. Then, there was an instantaneous break in the flames, caused by one of the inbuilt fire extinguishers spraying the car.

Dave moved forward and grabbed at the lifeless form in the race car. He felt Ben's shoulders through the flames; and with an unbelievable burst of adrenaline, he jerked Ben from the blazing vehicle.

In the grandstands, Lee grabbed Lynne, who had turned white as a sheet as she watched what was happening in front of her. He was afraid she was going to faint when she saw the flames overtake Ben's racecar.

As Dave dragged Ben's lifeless body to the grass, the ambulance and fire truck arrived at the crash site. Dave felt the cold blast of a fire extinguisher as one of Alan Kulwicki's crew sprayed him, trying to extinguish the flames of his burning jumpsuit. His suit, which wasn't flame resistant, was still on fire. He rolled in the grass to extinguish the flames, oblivious to the pain he felt. He allowed the cool liquid being sprayed from the extinguisher to ease the pain; but still, his only thought was about Ben. Was he alive?

Ignoring his pain, Dave pulled the helmet from Ben's head and unzipped the collar or his jumpsuit. Ben wasn't moving. The ambulance crew had already started to work on him, trying to resuscitate him with oxygen. Dave could tell by the look on the paramedic's face that it didn't look good for his partner.

Dave felt an oxygen mask being strapped on his face as another paramedic started to work on him. Dave glanced up at the people who were gathered around them. They were all pointing at him.

He searched the crowd for Millie. He saw Charlie. He saw Jake. Where was Millie, he wondered. His hands were starting to hurt, a deep intense pain like none other he'd ever experienced. He held his arms up into the air to see what was causing the pain. Shocked at what he saw, his hands and forearms were charred black.

Dave lost consciousness as they were being loaded into an infield ambulance. Since their injuries were so serious, they were taken to the helicopter to be immediately removed to the local hospital.

Lynne was hysterical. Millie and Lee tried to comfort her, as Millie tried to ignore her own anxiety. After all, she'd lost her husband in a horrible crash. Was she a jinx, she wondered. A million thoughts permeated her mind. She began to cry, wiping away her tears as Lee helped her and Lynne get into his car, which luckily was parked nearby, so they could go to the hospital.

"Now, Ladies, remember, these men are professional athletes. They know what they're doing," he said, trying to comfort them, to reassure them to hope for the best. "We have to pray, and believe they are going to be okay. Come on, let's get to the hospital. You'll see for yourselves."

The short drive to the hospital seemed to take hours, although in reality only took a few minutes. The ride was somber, as each passenger said their silent prayers, anticipating their arrival at the hospital.

When they arrived, they were instructed by the emergency room personnel to sit down in the waiting room. "You can't see them now. They just got here. We'll let you know as soon as we know anything."

"You can't tell us anything?" Lynne demanded of the nurse.

"I can only tell you they are both alive. That is all I can say at this time. Now, please, sit down and let us do our job. If you pray, this is the time to do it. We'll call you as soon as we know anything," the young doctor instructed as he rushed down the hallway.

Lynne, Millie and Lee were ushered into a private waiting room so they could avoid the deluge of reporters that had arrived at the hospital. Lee hugged them, trying to comfort them. Millie pulled some tissues from her purse and handed some to Lynne.

Lee said every comforting thing he could think of… "These men are the best of the best, in first-rate condition. They'll be fine. We've got to believe that!" Finally, running out of comforting words, they all sat quietly, praying, crying softly.

"Oh, I can't go through this again. I lost my husband this way. Because of this accident, I'm now having to re-live that horror. I'm afraid for Dave and Ben." Millie sobbed.

"I know, Millie," Lynne said, "I've never been through anything like this before. I'm glad I made up with Ben before the race. I'm so afraid he's not going to survive this thing… Can you believe Dave's bravery? If he hadn't pulled Ben out of that car, he surely would have died on the spot."

"Now, Ladies, really, they could be fine…. Just a few burns and scrapes." Lee said, trying to again assure them. "Calm down. Let's try to remember, no news could be good news. Just because we haven't heard anything doesn't mean we are going to hear bad news. Let's hope for the best."

Jake and Charlie arrived at the hospital, along with several members of the crew. They were also shown to the private waiting room. "Are they okay?" They asked, almost in unison.

"We don't know yet…." Millie said as Jake hugged her. "All the doctors have told us is that they are still alive." Succumbing to the tears, she buried her face in Jake's shoulder and sobbed. "It's like re-living the horror of your dad's crash, Jake."

"I know, Mom, that's why I didn't want you to get involved with Dave Masden. He's a risk-taker. Dad was a risk-taker, too. If Dave's okay, I don't want you to see him again, okay, Mom? I can't stand the thought of you being hurt again."

"Let's not talk about that right now, Jake. Dave's become very dear to me. I didn't know how much I needed to have a good man in my life. Dave's a good man. After your father died, I closed myself up, ignoring life and love. That's not good."

"I know you did, Mom."

"Everyone needs to be loved. I thought I was unlovable because of my weight problem. Dave doesn't care about the extra weight. He sees beyond the physical and touches a spot so deep inside me. I pray he'll be okay so I can tell him. By his acceptance of me, he gives me the freedom to be me" she said, as she wiped away a tear.

"Oh, Mom, what am I going to do with you," he said, shaking his head.

"Help me heal those emotional scars so I can love again. Pray for complete recovery for Dave."

They sat down again on the large couch that dominated the small room. No one said anything. Almost in unison, they would look at their watches, then glance at the clock on the wall, sigh, and close their eyes in a silent prayer. The minutes seemed like hours as they waited, hoping to hear some good news.

Millie pulled some Rosary beads out of her purse and prayed silently, as each member of their party waited, silently, watching Millie finger the beads, praying with her under their breath.

"Son," Lee said to Jake, unable to stand the quiet any longer, "Why don't we find a coffee machine. We might be here for awhile, and I think we could all use a cup."

They walked to the reception desk and asked for directions to the coffee machine. Then, they got the steaming cups of coffee and returned to the private room.

After what seemed like hours, but in reality was only an hour and a half, Ben came walking down the hallway, assisted by the young doctor. He was wearing only a hospital gown and his socks. When Lynne saw Ben, she got up and ran to him. They embraced, and everyone sighed with relief.

"I didn't think I'd get to do this again. I was so afraid you were dead." Lynne said as she embraced Ben.

"Not me, I'm too mean to die," he joked to ease the tension. "Where's Dave? If it hadn't been for him, I'd be pushin' up daisies right now. Doc says I'm gonna be fine; said I could go home if I'm careful… and if I can find something to wear."

Looking around again, he said, "Where's Dave?"

"He's still in there! He was hurt pretty bad, too." Lynne explained. "His suit caught on fire."

"Doc, you've got to find out about him. He's my partner, and my best friend. I heard he saved my life…. He's got to be okay!" Ben said to the young doctor who stood near him.

"Another team's been working on him. I'll see if I can find out anything about his condition. You sit down, though, you're still pretty shaky. You've had a massive shock to your nervous system, and swallowed a lot of smoke."

"I'll take care of him, Doctor," Lynne said, sitting down on the sofa with Ben.

Ben looked over and nodded his head to acknowledge Lee and Charlie. He avoided making eye contact with Jake and Millie, who were sitting on the opposite end of the L-shaped couch. He couldn't face the questions in Millie's eyes, or the pain.

Jake walked over and shook Ben's hand. "I'm glad you're going to be okay, Ben. I've never seen anything like that. The way he grabbed you and pulled you outta that car, just like you were a rag doll or something. It was incredible."

"He's strong, that's for sure! I'm glad he is… my life was passing in front of my eyes." Then, looking at Lynne, "You were in every scene,

Honey. I was afraid I was losing you. You and the kids are my life. Maybe its time to put the cars out to pasture, so to speak, put them in "park" permanently."

"Nah, come on, Man, shake it off." Charlie interspersed. "You'll feel different tomorrow. Sure, you had a close call; but you've got what it takes to make it in the long run. We were close to the finish of this race. The sponsor'll be happy tomorrow because you ran a good race. You would've ended up in the top five if it hadn't been for the fool Smith."

"Is he okay?" Ben asked, "Did he get hurt in the crash?"

"Hell, no, Ben," Charlie said, "He walked away. NASCAR's going to have a talk with him, though. He'll get a big fine over this fiasco."

"Who won the race?" Ben asked.

"Dale Jarrett, followed closely by Dale Earnhardt. Smith got a D-N-F, too!"

"Ben," Lee interrupted, "You and Dave have always impressed me with your professionalism. That's one reason why I've followed your career, and put money into your team. I consider you both to be friends…. And winners. True Winners. Like Charlie said, shake it off. Give it some time. Everything'll look different tomorrow. You'll see."

"I just hope I have a partner tomorrow. Where's that doctor?" He finally glanced at Millie, who was staring down the hallway in the direction the young doctor had taken. She looked so frail and fragile, so vulnerable, so afraid, as she continued to finger the Rosary beads.

About five minutes later, the doctor returned. "He's going to be fine! He has some nasty burns; but he'll make it with very little permanent damage. He wants to see someone named Millie, alone."

"I'm Millie," Millie jumped up, pointing to herself.

"Then come with me, Miss." He instructed. Millie followed him down the hallway to a room just off the corridor. She was apprehensive, and excited at the same time. She wondered what Dave would say to her; and she wondered what she would say to him. Would she end their affair before it had a chance to begin?

She also wondered how Dave would look ... how serious his burns were. She had to see him to chase away her apprehensions, to tell him she cared.

Chapter Eight

At first, Dave didn't realize that Millie had walked into his hospital room. He was lying in his bed, eyes closed, feeling the effects of the drugs they had given him to relax. Both arms were covered with thick bandages from his forearm to the tips of his fingers. His arms were positioned on pillows to ease his pain. He face was bright red as if he had a bad sunburn. His hair, eyebrows and eyelashes were singed, and almost non-existent. Since Millie thought he was sleeping, she eased into the chair beside him. She closed her eyes and silently prayed for Dave, while observing his obvious injuries.

Sensing her presence, Dave opened his eyes, which were bloodshot and irritated from the smoke and flames. He blinked his eyes several times, trying to focus. Finally, he saw a clear vision of his Millie, and she looked like an angel to him. Her face was devoid of expression or emotion, as she silently prayed, thinking he was asleep. Her hands were folded, and her eyes were closed.

Dave waited patiently, noticing how lovely she looked as she said her prayers. He felt privileged that she would take the time to pray for him. After she finished, he tried to smile at her, and finally managed to whisper, "Hi, Millie."

"Hi, yourself, Dave, what a heroic thing to do, grabbing Ben from that car without thinking about your own safety. It's the bravest thing I've ever seen." She said appreciatively.

"Stupid's probably a better word for it…" he whispered in his raspy voice. "I didn't really think about it. I knew the fuel cell had exploded on impact, and the automatic extinguishers didn't seem to be working. There was only a few seconds to save his life. In spite of our problems of late, he's still my best friend. I love him like a brother. Is he doing okay?"

"Oh, yes, he's sitting out in the waiting room, chomping at the bit to get to see you. They've treated him, and are going to release him to go home. They said he's a little shaken; but he's going to be fine, thanks to you. He wants to see you."

"In a few minutes, okay. I just want to spend a minute with you; after all, you're my date. Some date, huh?"

"Well, one thing's for certain, it's like nothing I've ever known before …" She replied, trying to lighten the seriousness of the conversation. "Can I do anything for you, Dave? Are you in pain?"

"Well, it's pretty bad, but the pain killers are kickin' in. Fortunately, I've got a high tolerance for pain. Can I have a drink of water, my throat is so dry."

Millie picked up the pitcher of water by his bedside and poured some into a glass. She opened a straw that was lying on the table and held it so he could drink the water.

"Oh, that's much better; but it hurts, too. My throat is pretty sore from all the fire I swallowed," he said. "The doctor says I'll have a few scars but that I should recover completely. I have to stay overnight; but after he checks me tomorrow, I may get to go home to my doctor in North Carolina. If there's no sign of infection, I can go home….."

"I'm so glad you're going to be okay, Dave. I was scared…. Really scared for you. It was like re-living Jacob's death." Millie said as her voice cracked and tears welled in her eyes. Her breathing became labored as she fought the tears, trying to control her anxiety.

"I'm so sorry, Millie," he whispered, "I'd never want to cause you pain. I know it's a little soon in our relationship to be serious; but from the first time I saw you in that store, I saw something special in your eyes. Didn't you feel it, too?"

"Yes, and it scared me to death!" She said, trying to chuckle through her seriousness.

"That's what life is all about, Mil'…. Taking chances. When we were flying to Daytona, I realized that you have closed yourself up to life. You're your husband got killed, you hung it up, so to speak. You're too vital and vibrant to give up on life. You've taken time to mourn; but it's time to begin to heal, to live again, and to love again. I'm sure it's what your husband would want; and, I'm going to do everything I can, Millie Greene with an 'e', to make you fall in love with me. I accept you, unconditionally, one-hundred percent, just the way you are! No lies, no phoniness, no head games. I thank God for His gift of saving me today, and for giving me this opportunity, this chance to love again, to love you, Millie!"

"Oh, Dave," she said, touching his shoulder, "What a wonderful compliment. You're so brave! Honestly, the way you saved Ben's life without a selfish thought for your own safety. Sure, it caused me to re-live Jacob's death, but I also realized that you are a lot alike. I don't know if I have it in me to give love another chance, especially with someone as dynamic and daring as you are. I realize I need someone in my life, though. Sure, I manage to stay busy; but in essence, I lead a very empty life emotionally. I want to put Jacob's death behind me, once and for all, and live life to the fullest for as long as God allows me to live. I'm just not sure that you're the kind of man I need….."

"My life's empty, too, Millie, but we can change all that. What happened today reinforces my feelings. I meet a lot of women. I've had plenty of chances to date; but none of them interested me like you do. You definitely have my full attention. Something happened to us both in that store yesterday. Let's see what it is. Let's give God a chance to work a miracle in our lives. Regardless of what you say, I'm exactly the kind of man you need….."

"Well, I admit I've built a wall around myself, my emotions… a safe haven so to speak. I've filled the empty caverns of my life by staying busy, ignoring love and romance. Yes, I'll admit, you interest me. Jacob would not have wanted me to withdraw from life like I have. He would want me to get on with my life once my time of grief was over. He would want me to have a life. If the situation were reversed, I would want him to find someone to love again. We had a terrific marriage, but HAD is the key word. He's gone, God bless his soul. He can't hold me in his arms anymore. Remember how I almost came unglued the first time you kissed me….?"

"Yes, I sure do. I was deeply touched. This accident has accelerated our relationship somewhat, and caused us to dig deeply inside our feelings. Will you give me a chance? Let me prove it to you…" he dared.

"Oh, you! Okay, Dave, I surrender. I'll try to put my anxieties behind me and give us a chance; but I can't make any promises – not yet!"

"Good, that's all I ask. I know this is happening fast; but life is so fragile. I'm not afraid to let you know that I'm falling for you … hook, line and sinker. The amazing thing is, I'm not sure you even had bait on your hook. Didn't stop me, did it? You must admit, though, our lives are much more exciting today than they were yesterday morning. Heck, I love to fish…. I'm casting my line in the water right now, hoping for a nibble, a prize catch, so to speak."

"How did you get so smart, Dave Masden?"

"Well, I haven't had my head stuck under the hood of the race car ALL my life. Once in a while I wash the grease off my hands and read a book, see a play, watch a movie, taste and test life. I can't wait to see what's in store for us in this relationship."

"Very philosophical…."

"How about a kiss, Millie Greene with an 'e'? I think it would be quite appropriate right now. I could use one…."

"Will I hurt you?"

Dave shook his head and Millie bent across the bed and kissed him lightly on the lips. She could feel the heat, like a sunburn, emanating from his skin. "Here's to discovering the mystery of life according to Dave Masden," she whispered, as she kissed him again.

"Um-m-m, here's to discovering the mystery of Millie. You're such an interesting, Lady. We're the pawns in this game of love, a game that is impossible to predict or understand. I loved watching you come to life again. There's nothing wrong with waiting. Hell, I'm glad you waited – that I'm the lucky guy who gets to watch you blossom and grow..." he said smugly.

"You're embarrassing me, Dave."

"Hey, you continued to live life... although not fully. You're self-assured, and know how to handle yourself."

"I'm not so sure about that!"

"Oh, yes you are, you just don't know it. I was watching you while you kidded around with Lee Henderson. You kept your cool at the party last night. I also noticed you in the grandstand today, joking and meeting those stars. You didn't let them shake you. You're exactly the kind of woman I need...."

"What kind of woman is that?"

"Oh, I don't know .... You know, soft, gentle, feminine, sexy, independent, caring, cool and relaxed. I'm basically hyper before a race, especially if I'm driving. I need a woman who'll help me stay focused, to encourage me, to have a calming effect on me. You aren't at all self-centered, but you are self-assured. You genuinely care about people and it shows. But, you're not easy.... You are definitely a challenge."

"Hey, let's lighten up. You're scaring me with all this serious talk. I've never known anyone who came on so fast. Remember that I've not had a 'first' date since I was sixteen years old. Let's take it slow...."

"As soon as I get these bandages off, I'm going to take you on the date of your life. In fact, we're still on our first date, right? Our first date will last until I take you home! Boy, I've got to get these bandages off .... fast!"

"Is that so? Well, I'm not going anywhere – besides, as I recall you brought me here by airplane. You promised to see me safely back home. I don't think you can fly that plane right now...."

"Well, Ben could probably fly you home, if you really want to go," he teased.

"Well," she teased, kissing him gently, "I prefer to go home with the guy who brought me...."

"Speaking of Ben, you'd better let him come in now. He doesn't have my patience. He's probably pacing the waiting room floor, wondering if I'm fried to a crisp. How about another drink of water, and then let him come in...."

Millie held the glass so Dave could drink some more water, then said, "I'll be right back, then. I'll give you and Ben a few minutes to talk alone, if you want."

"No, I want you right here by my side. Who else is in the waiting room? Are there any reporters?"

"Well, when I came in here, Ben, Lynne, Jake and Lee Henderson – he drove us to the hospital. Charlie's out there, too. He's pretty shaken by the accident, and a few of the pit crew are there as well. There are some reporters outside; but the hospital won't let them come in."

"Oh, let's get this over fast. Have them all come in at the same time. That way, they can all say what they need to say and get outta here. Ben and Lynne need to go off and talk somewhere, spend some time together."

"I know they do, but I think everything is going to be okay between them, Dave. Lynne and I had a little talk this morning at the condo."

"I kinda thought you did .... Like I said, you're my kinda woman!"

"I'll be right back with them," she said.

"I look forward to that...." He said, giving her an approving look that sent thrills throughout her body.

Millie walked to the lobby, smiling. She felt as if she had just been handed the world, or won the Lottery. How wonderful, she thought to herself, that such a handsome man is interested in me – IN ME! I'm definitely interested in him although I have to take it slow. He is such a blessing. "Thank you, Lord," she whispered, "for everything!"

As soon as Millie walked into the private waiting room, everyone stood up. "He wants to see all of you," she said. "He's going to be just fine. His arms and legs are bandaged, his face is a little burned, his hair's singed; but he's going to be okay. He has to stay here tonight. If the hospital will allow it, he wants to see all of you at the same time....."

"Hell, they'll allow it!" Ben said, taking long strides down the hallway to Dave's room. "Let's go, Gang."

Lynne walked beside Millie and whispered, "Are you okay?"

"Yes, thanks, I'm fine. By the way, I see you found something for Ben to wear...."

"Yeah, Charlie had that sweat suit in his truck. After all, I couldn't very well let him roam around the hospital with his tushy hanging out, could I?" Lynne said. They chuckled, easing the tension of the moment. As they walked into Dave's room, they heard Ben talking....

"Man, how can I ever thank you? They said I'd a' been a goner if it hadn't been for you. How in the hell did you get me outta that car? I thought a steel crane had grabbed me. Man, you have a strong grip. My shoulders ache from being jerked outta that car. Maybe someday, somehow, I'll find a way to repay you for what you did for me."

"No repayment necessary. If the situation had been reversed, you'd have done the same thing for me. Besides, I couldn't have done it if you hadn't already broken-away the steering wheel and unfastened your safety harness."

"I can tell you this much, I saw my life pass before my eyes, that's for sure. You grabbed me from the jaws of death. What a friend you've been, Dave, Partner."

"That's what friendship's all about, Ben." Dave said.

"I'm afraid I've not been much of a friend lately. I remember flying through the air and coming to a sudden stop. I pushed the button to move the steering wheel, and flipped the buckle on the safety harness, trying to move – then everything went black. It was incredible. I had no idea you were so strong...."

"No problem, Man, really. I may be out of commission for a few weeks, though. You may have to fly the plane AND drive the racecar."

"I will, gladly, because I can. I'm alive, thanks to you – we're both alive. Thank God!"

"Dave," Charlie said, "That was incredible. I saw it with my own eyes and still don't believe what I saw."

"Hey, I lived it, and I don't believe it either!" Dave joked, trying to lighten the mood of the room. He didn't like playing the hero … getting so much attention from so many people for doing something anyone would have done if placed in that position.

Dave looked at Lynne, who was smiling, standing quietly, listening to everything being said. She shook her head when they made eye contact, walked over to his bed and kissed him on the cheek. "Thanks for saving my man, Dave, for giving him back to me."

"No problem – you can have him!" Dave joked.

"By the way," she whispered, "At first, I didn't think much of your new girlfriend, but she's really nice. I'm sorry I gave you so much flack over your divorce. I should've been more supportive."

"Forget it, Lynne," he said assuredly, glancing at Millie. She had a hunch they were talking about her since they both suddenly looked at her, but she had no idea what was being said.

"Dave," Jake said, clearing his throat, "That was awesome! When we met, you had two strikes against you. First, you weren't my Dad, and second, I thought you were trying to take advantage of my Mom. I didn't want to see her get hurt. I'm sorry I misjudged you."

"I could never intentionally hurt your Mom, Son. I like your Mom. She can take care of herself, Jake. She's really something!" Dave replied, smiling at Millie. She smiled and looked away as she felt tears well in her eyes.

"I know that now, Dave. I think you'll be good for Mom; but you've got to win her over yourself! That's not going to be easy, I warn you!"

"Good, I love a challenge," he said, winking at Millie. "I wouldn't have it any other way. Don't forget, I owe you a ride in the race car, Jake."

"Awesome! Maybe there'll be another chance … another time … another race."

"I hope so…." Dave replied.

Lynne pulled Millie aside and whispered, "I think you owe me an antique!" They both laughed, remembering their bet from earlier that morning that Dave would win Jake over.

"Oh, Mom," Jake said, looking at Millie, "Paula's going back to Stetson tonight. I'll catch a ride with her. That way, I can get some studying done before class on Tuesday."

"Did you call her?"

"Yes, she's on the way to the hospital now. I'll call home in a few days to see how Dave's doing."

"Hey, Jake, when Paula gets here, why don't we all go out to dinner, my treat." Ben suggested, "Then you can go back to the condo and get your stuff."

"Okay, that sounds fine with me. I'll check with Paula when she gets here."

"Millie," Ben said, "Would you like to join us for dinner? I don't think Dave's in any condition to take you out….."

"No, absolutely not," Dave protested loudly, "She's havin' dinner with me… that is, if she wants to…. We'll have the nurse order you a dinner tray, Millie. Stay with me, please."

"Okay, after all, you ARE my date!"

"Whew…. She likes me! Anyone who'd pass up a good steak dinner to eat hospital food has got to care. Do they provide candlelight and champagne in a hospital?" he joked. "After all, this is a private room!" Everyone laughed as Millie blushed.

The nurse heard their laughter and entered the room, giving them a disgruntled look, with her hands on her hips. "There are too many people in this room. Out, everybody out! I've got to take vitals…" she demanded, waving her arms.

"Dave," Millie said, "I'll be back in a few minutes. I'll walk them out and tell Jake goodbye."

Dave nodded his head but couldn't speak because the nurse had stuck a thermometer in his mouth.

Lee Henderson, who had been standing quietly in the back of the room waiting his turn to speak to Dave, walked over to him and whispered, "That was fantastic, Man. You let me know if you need anything! It seems as if you're in good hands, though. Millie's really nice."

Dave still couldn't speak. He just nodded affirmatively as Lee left the room.

Millie put her arm around Jake as they walked down the hallway, "Jake, I'm sorry your weekend has been so crazy. You came home for some peace and quiet, so you could study. I bet you haven't been able to study at all!"

"I've been studying too much, Mom. I needed a break. I'm not at all sorry we came, Mom. It's time you get over Dad's accident and get on with your life. I like Dave. We both need to get on with life, Mom. Look, there's Paula. Isn't she pretty, Mom?"

Millie answered his question by nodding her head affirmatively and held out her hand to Paula.

"Hi, Paula, it's sweet of you to drive Jake back to school. Can I give you some gas money?" Millie asked.

"Come on, Mom, I'll give her some gas money. I've got cash. Don't embarrass me…." Jake said, taking Paula's hand.

"Well, you guys have a good time. Bye, Jake, I'll see you for Spring break, right?"

"I don't know, Mom but I'll let you know when I call home. Bye, Mom." Jake said as he kissed Millie goodbye. "I love you."

"I love you, too, Son."

"Millie," Ben said, "Call us when you're ready to come home and I'll pick you up. Dave has the phone number for the condo. We'll probably see you later." Ben instructed, totally in charge of the group. "Come on, Lee, Charlie, Paula, Jake, let's go eat, my treat. The steaks are on me, and I'm hungry enough to tear into a big juicy steak or two."

A deluge of reporters ran up to Ben when they walked outside. He said, "I'll make a simple statement. I'm fine, thanks to my partner and best friend, Dave Masden. His burns are pretty serious, but he's going to be fine. I'll never be able to rightfully thank him for pulling me from that car. He saved my life. He's truly an American hero."

Ben waved away their additional questions as he and Lynne got into Lee's car. He motioned for Jake and Paula to follow him as they all drove away.

Millie went to the ladies room to refresh her make-up, comb her hair, and to spray on some cologne. Dave was resting when she returned to his room.

She positioned herself in the chair beside his bed and waited quietly, noticing again how handsome Dave was. Her head was spinning. She was so hungry to love again, and their relationship was feeling really good so far. Exploring the possibility of a romance with Dave Masden would be her ultimate challenge. She had suffered far too long from acute loneliness.

Maybe, like Dave said, he saw her need. She felt something the first time he looked into her eyes. Theirs could be a very unique, unusual relationship, indeed; a true gift from God. Was Dave her soon-to-be lover, she wondered. The thought scared her a little, but excited her immensely. She sighed and Dave opened his eyes, to smile at her, and give her the look she loved so much.

"I took the liberty to order your dinner, Millie." Dave said. "It'll be here in a few minutes. We're having the same thing, by the way, hospital food!" She chucked at his joke.

"It'll be just fine, I'm sure. After all, where could I find better company?"

"There's a problem, though," he said, with a smirk-y crooked smile, "I just realized your date can't feed himself."

"Well, I think I can handle that problem…. I always wanted to be a nurse…"

"You're so sweet, Millie. Do you think I can have another kiss?"

"Oh, I don't know, Dave, this could become addictive." She teased.

"Sounds good to me…."

Dale Earnhardt and Rusty Wallace interrupted their kiss. "Hey, we don't want to break in on this special moment. We stopped by to see how you're doing." Dale said, "Hi, Millie, I think we met last night."

"Yes, we did. I'm fine, Dale." She replied.

"Hey, did you win the race today?"

"No, that Jarrett gave me a good run and finally beat me." Dale said, "More than I could handle today. Jarrett definitely had the strongest engine out there today. He got under me, and got me a little loose in turns three and four. I don't know what it'll take for me to get a win at Daytona! But, I let them know 'black is back!' We stopped by because we're concerned about you and Ben."

"We're both fine." Dave replied. "Rusty, that was a spectacular crash you had today. Are you okay?"

"I'm a little sore. When we were running, I was saying to myself, 'Man, this is great!'" Rusty said, "I'm finally going to get a good Daytona 500 finish' .... Then it happened. Awh, I have a couple stitches in my chin, and I hurt my wrist; but I'll be in the next race, you can bet on it!"

"Good, I'm glad you weren't hurt. It was spectacular the way your car took off. I counted two flips and five barrel rolls." Dave said.

"I felt every one of them, too. I was running in a tight pack and Michael Waltrip got tapped and went into a spin. He hit me and I took off. I radioed my crew right away that I was okay."

"Incredible!" Millie said. "I couldn't believe you walked away from that mess. I couldn't get my breath for at least five minutes...."

"It kinda took my breath away, too. But, I have to tell you, it was fun!"

Millie got a strange look on her face, and Dave knew he'd better change the subject fast.....

"Dale, the gun you asked me to pick up in Brandon is at the condo. Ben'll get it for you if you stop by later."

"Good, thanks for pickin' it up for me. I'll let you fire it the next time we go huntin'. Do you think you'll make it to Rockingham?"

"Next race, in two weeks? I don't know how long these bandages will be on; but I'll definitely be at the race track, that's for sure, if NASCAR will let me." Dave retorted.

"Good." Rusty said. "Well, our wives are waiting in the car outside. We wanted to stop by before we headed out of town to make sure you were okay. Let us know if you need anything, okay?"

"I'm covered, thanks. I'll see you guys at Rockingham. Thanks for stoppin' by."

Dinner was as expected. Millie fed Dave two bites of his food, and then she'd take one bite of hers. They joked about the "mystery meat." The mood in the room was relaxed, quite jovial, considering the circumstances.

They were interrupted again when Darrell Waltrip, Morgan Shepherd and Bill Elliott stopped by to see Dave.

Just as they were leaving, Butch Smith walked in with Patricia, Dave's ex-wife. They totally ignored Millie, who was surprised when Pat gave her a mean look, and almost sneered at her.

Patricia was a very slim, anorexic-looking, cheaply-dressed woman, who had bright red, obviously-dyed hair. She was wearing a black leather jacket, a tank top and jeans that were so tight; Millie wondered how she got them zipped. She looked so cheap, not at all what she expected Dave's ex-wife to look like.

"Hey, Guy, I hope there are no hard feelings," Butch said, "Pat wanted to make sure you're okay."

"I'm fine, Pat, no need to worry about me. I'm too mean to die!"

"Well, I worry; you know I still care for you," she purred.

Dave started to retaliate but decided it would be to no avail. He was surprised to see Pat with Butch. He didn't want to start an argument in front of Millie. He just wanted them to leave but not until they had acknowledged Millie.

"I'd like you both to meet my girlfriend, Millie Greene.... With an 'e'."

"Hi, Millie," they said in unison.

Millie acknowledged and returned their "hello.'

The situation was strained, awkward. Millie stammered for words, she usually had a gift of gab and could talk to anyone, but she was speechless. Finally, Butch broke the silence.

"Well, we're not staying. Got things to do and places to go. It's nice meeting you, Millie. See you in Rockingham, Dave. Get well, Man."

"You can count on it, Butch."

He started to say something else, to release his anger, but decided against it.

Dave waited for them to leave the room, and then smirked: "That rumor I heard is true. She really is going with him. Did you see how she was hanging all over him? Did you see the way she looked? She used to be a nice country girl. Our marriage is really over."

"You didn't think it was?" Millie whispered, surprised by his remark.

"I believe in the sanctity of marriage. It takes two people, working together, to make it work. Unfortunately, my marriage ended a long time ago. If God allows it, we can start fresh, Millie. Are you willing to take a chance?" Dave whispered.

"Visiting hours are almost over, Dave. They'll be throwing me out of here soon. If you'll give me the phone number, I'll call the condo and have Ben pick me up."

"Why don't you stay with me? You can sleep here...."

"No, I'd better not."

"Ben and Lynne need time to be alone... to work out a few problems."

"Well, there's a motel next door. Maybe I'll be able to get a room there, now that the race is over." She suggested.

"I don't want you to leave, Millie. That chair you're sitting in becomes a recliner. Why don't you just stay with me? The hospital won't mind. I've already asked them. I'm not ready for our date to end. How about it?"

"Oh, I don't think so; but I will see if I can get a room next door, so Ben and Lynne can have a quiet evening at the condo."

"They need to talk. Jake and Paula are leaving tonight. Why don't you just stay here with me, please?"

"No, I'll get a room next door."

"Well, then, call them," he said, "But, I bet they won't have a room. Since it's a long weekend, people won't be checking out until tomorrow morning."

"You're probably right," she surmised. "Well, okay, I guess I can sleep here. I never sleep very well anyway. Sure, Dave, I'll be your private duty nurse tonight, but I warn you, I'm not always going to give in this easily to your pleadings. It'll give Ben and Lynne a chance to be alone. Like you said, they need to talk things out. I don't want to be a bother to anyone."

"You can bother me anytime…." Dave smirked, victoriously.

Several more visitors were received and introduced to Millie that evening, including: Wally Dallenbach, Jeff Gordon, Rick Mast, Neil Bonnett, Ken Schrader, Harry Gant, Bobby and Terry Labonte, and the Bodine brothers.

During the evening, every NASCAR driver either visited or called to see how Dave was feeling … to make sure he had everything he needed. His room was filled with flower arrangements and boxes of candy. Millie answered the telephone so much, she felt like his secretary.

"Never before have I met so many famous people in such a short time. They are, like you said, just regular people. You all care about each other….. It's remarkable!"

"Well, it's good to see them. That is, except for Butch Smith and my ex… I could have passed on that!"

"You handled the visit pretty well, Dave."

"So did you, Millie. She looks like crap. She used to have beautiful light brown curly hair, and dressed very conservatively. I don't know what's happened to her. She's lost a lot of weight. I wonder if she's even eating…."

"I'm sure the divorce has been hard on her, too. She'll be fine once she adjusts to her lifestyle changes."

"We're gonna be fine, too, aren't we?" he asked.

"I feel good about the direction our relationship is taking. I look forward to the road that lies ahead, Dave, what about you?"

"I feel just great about us. Remember, though, I travel that 'road' at a fast pace; but I have a hunch you won't have any problem keeping up with me...."

"I'll keep up with you if you hold my hand," she challenged. "Will you take me by the hand and show me the way?"

"No problem, I'll hold your hand very tightly just as soon as I get these bandages off!"

Chapter Nine

"I'm glad Millie called to say she's staying at the hospital tonight, Lynne. There's a few things I'd like to say. First of all, I'm very sorry about last night. I've learned my lesson well. I thought I was losing you, and that thought scared me to death. It scared me more than the wreck today. Can you find it in your heart to forgive me?" Ben pleaded as he poured Lynne a glass of Sangria, and flipped the switch to turn on the automatic fireplace.

"Do you deserve to be forgiven?"

"Everyone is entitled to make a mistake once in a while. I was confused. I can only say I'm sorry, and promise that it won't happen again."

"Where were you last night?" Lynne asked.

"Don't ask me for details. I'll admit I came really close to messin' up, big-time; but nothing really happened. Can we get past this and get on with our lives? This wreck has put everything in its proper perspective again. We're all back on track and you're my first priority from now on. You and the kids are all that matters in life. From now on, racing will take a back burner. I'm not going to make the same mistake that Dave did in his marriage."

"Dave's a good guy, Ben. I was with Pat when she started to flirt around with other men. I was as surprised as you were. It takes two people to make a relationship work. You can't blame Dave for everything.

Imagine me, defending a man in this scenario," Lynne remarked, "Don't men usually stick together?"

"Not always. I'm afraid I've not been a very good friend to Dave lately. I was ready to throw in the towel in our friendship and our partnership. We can surely get off track, can't we, even on a race track!"

"You've not exactly been my friend lately, either." Lynne whispered. "Do you still love me?"

"Oh, God, yes, I don't think I could go on if I didn't have you. At the end of the season, maybe we can take a second honeymoon. You pick the spot. Let's start fresh… can we do that, Honey?"

Well, I don't know that we can start fresh, but we can both work at it. If we are both determined to make it work, we'll find a way. It's not too late, Ben. The kids and I need you, now more than ever."

"Oh, Honey, I need you, too. If I didn't have you, I'd just find me a hole and crawl into it. I would cease to exist. When Dave lost Pat, I was panic-stricken that I'd lose you, too."

"That is never going to happen, Ben," Lynne assured him as she leaned towards him to receive a kiss.

Ben and Lynne renewed their commitment to each other, agreed to be true to each other, to work things out always – no matter what. They made love on the bearskin run in front of the roaring fire. Everything was right with the world.

At the hospital, Millie was tired but she couldn't sleep. She listened to the reassuring sounds of Dave's breathing as he peacefully slept. He was smiling in his sleep, probably dreaming a beautiful dream. Millie wondered what he was dreaming about.

Two days ago, she thought, she wouldn't allow herself to think about love, romance, sex, life, and togetherness. Now, it was all she could think about. The happenstance of meeting Dave Masden has initiated the return of sensual stirrings and had awakened passions within her, passions she has denied for the past seven years—seven years! Passion had returned like an avalanche, totally enveloping a mountain cabin. The mountain cabin was her heart and the avalanche was sleeping peacefully in the hospital bed next to her.

Millie studied Dave and began to fantasize about how it would feel to make love with him. Since their first meeting, Dave's eyes had communicated that he wanted things to work out between them. Could she keep up with him, she wondered. After all, she's nothing but a simple country bumpkin who has withdrawn from life. Oh, yes, she remembers what it was like to make love. Would she be so passionate when or if they made love that she might scare him away, she wondered, like an avalanche, rolling and tumbling out of control.

She closed her eyes and slid down in the chair, trying to get comfortable enough to go to sleep. She remembered Dave mentioning that he had asked God to allow him to love again. He actually gives God the credit for their being together. That thought was incredible to her, as she silently asked God to allow herself to love again, and to love Dave if it fit into God's plan for their lives. How marvelous to be so blessed by God.

Dave Masden is an amazing individual, she reasoned, a good man who is spiritual as well as sensual. She included a prayer of thanksgiving, not only for Dave and Ben being saved in the wreck, but also for allowing this promise of love to spring forth between them.

Dave mumbled in his medication-induced sleep. Millie watched him for a few minutes. Then, she couldn't help but notice the sudden bulge between Dave's legs, beneath the thin bed sheet. She couldn't take her eyes off his erection, which was thankfully covered by the sheet on the bed.

Millie leaned back in her chair and forced her eyes not to stare at Dave's well-endowed physique. She smiled and sighed, trying to think about something else. She fanned herself with her hand. After all, she couldn't let herself think about making love to Dave right then. They were, after all, in a hospital, and his arms and hands were bundled in thick cotton bandages.

Since she felt the need to go to the bathroom, Millie got up quietly and tiptoed out of the room to use the public restroom down the hallway.

Afterwards, she stopped by the nurses' station and talked to them for a few minutes. They gave her a Tylenol PM so she could get some sleep. When she returned to Dave's room, he was awake.

"Where did you go?" he asked.

"I had to go to the bathroom and I stopped to talk to the nurses for a few minutes. They gave me something to help me sleep. Did I wake you? Are you in pain," she asked.

"No, not too much; but I woke up and discovered you were gone. I wondered where you were. Why can't you sleep?"

"I don't know. I always have a problem sleeping, but I did fall asleep for a few minutes. I'm sure the Tylenol the nurse gave me will do the trick."

The nurse interrupted them when she came into the room to take Dave's vitals. She gave Dave another injection through his IV.

"What's in the shot?" He asked.

"It's an antibiotic to fight infection, and something to help with the pain. It'll help you sleep, too." She replied.

After the nurse had left and closed the door, Dave moved over in his bed and said: "Get your blanket and get in here with me. We'll snuggle and talk until we fall back to sleep. That chair's probably not too comfortable."

"No way, I'm afraid I'll hurt you, Dave. Really, this chair's fine."

"Get over here, Millie. I'd love to feel you sleeping next to me. I won't even feel the pain if you're in here with me."

Reluctantly, Millie did as Dave insisted and got into his bed with him. After all, she reasoned, what could it possibly hurt? She was fully clothed and planned to stay that way. She lay down on top of his covers and pulled the blanket over her to cover them both. Then she gently laid her head on his upper chest.

"Am I hurting you?" She whispered.

"Nothing I can't live with. I hurt no matter what; but I'm fine, really. You know, Millie, in a lot of ways, ours doesn't feel like a new relationship.

It's so, how do I say this, comfortable. I thought I'd be nervous when I met someone new, but I'm not. I appreciate your flexibility, your calmness."

"I don't feel so calm now, Dave, I'm scared. Scared for you and what you do for a living, scared for me because this is happening so fast. I'm afraid this will end as quickly as it began. Then, where will we be? Do you understand what I mean? You're breaking down my brick wall! It's perfectly okay that you've come crashing through my solid brick wall of emotions; but what happens if this doesn't work out between us. I'd never want to hurt you in any way."

"Hey, we'll survive. For a long time now, I've not been living life to the fullest. When it's time to die, I want to know that I've lived a full life … not just been waiting to die. Life's far too short. You're too pretty to hang it up, Millie."

"Thank you, Kind Sir. I admit that you're breaking down my resistance."

"Good! Oh, my God, this feel good, doesn't it? You here beside me? Your head on my shoulder? It's a feeling that I could get used to really quick. As far as tomorrow comes, let's take it one step at a time, and enjoy the walk. Let's live a good life, and live it to the fullest extent possible. We can do that. We have that potential."

At first Millie didn't say anything, contemplating his words. "You're right, of course. I was simply existing … waiting to die. I wasn't really living, only going through the motions. But, listen, that's enough serious talk for tonight. You need your rest. Goodnight, Dave. Sweet dreams!"

"My dream's here with me. Tonight, I had a beautiful dream about us. The moment we met, I started to day dream about us being together like this," he whispered.

"Like this? In a hospital," she joked.

"Oh, you know what I mean, silly." Let's pretend that we're back at the condo, curled up in each other's arms, without a care in the world. Now that's a dream we can live with, isn't it?"

"You're so sweet, Dave. Will you always be like this? You're being so complimentary? So sensuous? Making me feel so precious to you? You know exactly what to say to get to me…"

"Oh, I hope so, Millie, I hope so." Dave whispered, as he kissed her on the forehead. Then he positioned his arms so he felt as little pain as possible and soon they were both sound asleep.

"Gud mornin' Meester Masden! Are you ready fer ye bath?" asked Helga, a large German nurse who was standing precariously over them. "Meeses Masden, you shouldn't be in his bed. It's against hospital rules. You could've hurt his wounds, yeah, that's a fact."

Embarrassed, Millie quickly got off the bed, folded the blanket and watched the nurse get Dave out of bed. Then she walked him to the bathroom, dragging the IV stand behind them. He turned and winked at Millie, just before the nurse closed the bathroom door.

Millie picked up her purse and walked down the hallway to use the public restroom. She washed her face, and applied fresh make-up. Finally, she brushed her hair and pulled it into a perky ponytail. By the time she returned to Dave's room, he'd been bathed. He smiled at her as soon as she walked in.

"Don't you look cute, Meeses Masden…. Just like a teenager." Dave teased her using a phony German accent. "H-um, you smell great. What is your cologne? I've never smelled it before."

"It's French. The translation means 'Private Moments'. Believe it or not, I order it from Q-V-C, the shopping channel on cable television. How do you feel? Are you hungry?

"Well, I have to tell you, I feel much better since Helga took out the catheter tube. Yes, I'm starving. Where's breakfast?"

"I'm sure it'll be here in a few minutes. Did I hurt you last night?"

"No, not at all. You didn't hurt me one bit. I loved sleeping next to you. Hopefully, there will be more nights…"

Dave's arduous expression embarrassed Millie and she broke eye contact and looked down at the floor just as the breakfast tray was brought in…

"I had the nurse order one for you, too, Millie, but they said it'll take a few minutes to get here. We'll both eat mine; and then, when yours gets here, we'll both eat it, too. Okay," he suggested.

"We'll see," she said as she uncovered the breakfast tray, which the orderly had placed in front of Dave. "This looks pretty good."

"How about a sip of coffee first? My throat still hurts and the warm liquid might help."

Millie poured Dave's coffee, placed an ice cube in it to cool it down a little, and held it to his mouth so he could take a sip. "Watch out, it's still pretty hot."

She sat the coffee down and pierced some sausage and scrambled egg with a fork. She put the food in Dave's mouth.

"It needs salt and pepper." Dave mumbled.

Millie opened the little containers of salt and pepper to season his eggs. Soon his breakfast tray was clean. Millie put a clean straw in Dave's orange juice and held it so he could drink it. She topped off his meal with the rest of the coffee.

When the second breakfast tray was delivered, Millie fed most of that food to Dave as well. He seemed to have an insatiable appetite. She drank some of the orange juice, and ate a piece of buttered toast. After Dave drank most of her coffee, she finished it.

The doctor came in to examine Dave and asked Millie to wait in the hallway until he told her it was okay to return. Since she knew it would take a few minutes, Millie walked to the lobby and sat down. She couldn't help but notice a newspaper that was lying on the table near her. She opened the paper to the sports section and found an article on the front page regarding the previous day's wreck. Ben's quote about Dave's being "*a true American hero*" was the headlines on the sports page.

Dave's bravery during the rescue of Ben from the race car was being touted as heroism. There was a blurb on the front page of the paper regarding the race, and the spectacular events that ensued.

Millie retrieved a quarter from her purse and walked to the newspaper machine outside the hospital to buy a copy she could keep. Then, she sat down in the lobby to re-read the article.

About a half-hour passed before she saw the doctor come out of Dave's room. After the doctor gave her the signal that it was okay to return to his room, Millie folded the paper and put it under her arm, thinking Dave would want to see the article. When she re-entered his room, he was somber. His mood was subdued.

"I thought you'd like to see this article..." she said, holding up the paper. "They're calling you a hero, Hero."

Dave didn't say anything. He looked at the article for a brief second, and then looked away sullenly.

"What did the doctor say? Do you still get to go home?"

"Yeah, call Ben and have him bring me something to wear. Sweat pants and a tank top will be okay. I can leave as soon as he gets here."

Millie picked up the phone and dialed the number Dave had given her the night before so she could let Ben and Lynne know she was going to stay at the hospital. Ben answered, and Millie relayed Dave's message to him.

"Tell Dave I'll be there in a few minutes," Ben confirmed. He hung up without saying goodbye, but Millie knew he was elated with the news.

"What did the doctor say, Dave," Millie insisted.

"He said I'll have to wear these bandages for several weeks. I have to see my doctor as soon as I get home, and he said I might need to be hospitalized when I get there. The burns are worse than I thought, Millie. I'm not in a lot of pain; so I assumed the burns weren't so bad.... I guess I'm just feelin' sorry for myself."

"Hey, Dave, you're going to be fine, right? Positive thinking is nine-tenths of the battle. Let's face the facts. You could have been killed in that wreck. You said you have a high tolerance for pain. Well, prove it to me. Come on, cheer up! I challenge you to grit your teeth and hang on. In a few minutes, you'll be relaxing at the condo, with everyone fussin' over you, spoiling you to death."

"You want the truth? I've enjoyed you fussin' over me…. Having you all to myself. I won't soon forget it!"

"I won't either, Dave. It's nice to have someone to do things for again. Where's that fabulous smile I like so much. Maybe a kiss? Have we had a good morning kiss? I don't think so," she joked, trying to get Dave to smile.

Finally, her pleadings worked and Dave smiled at her. He moved over to make it easier for her to kiss him. "Thanks for being there for me, Millie. I really appreciate it!"

Within minutes, Ben came charging into the room, much like a herd of buffalo, with Dave's clothes tucked under his arm. "Let's get you checked outta this high-priced motel and get you home. Nurse! Where's that nurse? Let's get you dressed and get your butt outta here."

Millie walked down the hallway to get the nurse. While she was gone, Dave confessed to Ben that he was concerned about being able to care for himself once they left the hospital. He was embarrassed that he wouldn't be able to use his hands for anything.

"Hey, Ben, maybe I'd better stay here until we're ready to fly home. Man, my hands are worse than my arms. I can't use them at all! I can't even go to the john by myself…"

"Hey, don't worry, Pard, your ole buddy'll take care of you. After what you did for me yesterday, if I have to, I'll wipe your furry butt a few times. Just don't tell any of the guys about it! And, I promise, I'll try not to embarrass you in front of your lady…." Ben kidded.

"You'd better not!"

"Seriously, Man, I don't want you to stay here. If we can't manage, I'll hire a nurse. The sooner we get you outta here, the sooner you'll be well."

"Can you imagine trying to go to the bathroom with your hands tied behind your back? That's exactly how I feel…."

"I'll take care of you, don't worry." Ben assured him.

"Before I can race again, I have to get a doctor's release."

"Well, we'll cross that bridge when we come to it, just one step at a time. You'll be just fine." Ben said, "I'm just thankful we BOTH get another chance."

Millie came back into the room, followed closely by the nurse, who suggested they wait outside while she got Dave dressed. After they sat down in the lobby, Millie showed Ben the newspaper article.

"You know, Millie, it's a horrible thing to say; but this could be the best thing that's happened for our career. What's important, though, is that Dave's going to be okay. It may be tough for a few weeks, but he's a champion through and through."

"Well, how about you, Ben? Are you feeling okay today?" She asked.

"Great, one-hundred percent. I'm still a little shaky, a little stiff and sore – and my shoulders are killin' me where he grabbed me and yanked me outta that car, but I'm lucky to be alive. I know that."

"Dave said his burns are much worse than he thought. Are you going to be okay to fly him home?"

"Sure, you bet, no problem. If it's okay with you, we'll go back to the condo to see how well Dave can maneuver with his bandages. If he gets along okay, I'll fly you back to Brandon and then fly us on home."

"Sure, that's fine, but we could all take a commercial flight back to Tampa."

"Dave'd never hear of that. He always takes care of his friends. Wait, let me correct that statement; we always take care of our friends. Millie, I consider you a friend. Lynne does, too. We told the mayor and her husband that we'd get them back home, too."

"Thanks, Ben."

"Well, then, it's settled." Ben insisted.

They all spent a relaxing afternoon at the condo; but the first time Ben had to help Dave in the bathroom, Lynne and Millie almost rolled on the floor with laughter. They could not refrain from laughing at the antics they overheard coming from the bathroom. It was hilarious.

After the bathroom fiasco, when Dave and Ben returned to the living room, try as they might, Millie and Lynne couldn't keep a straight face. Finally, although they were embarrassed, Dave and Ben had to laugh, too.

"Dave, you have such a good sense of humor. You'll be able to handle this little inconvenience if you'll let us help you. Don't let our kidding upset you. Being able to laugh at ourselves will help us all get through this. We all think you're great, and feel you're going just fine the way things are now." Lynne assured him.

Millie fed Dave a light lunch, and then went upstairs to take a shower and pack her things. She helped Lynne pack Dave's suitcase. When she returned to the living room, she sat down on the sofa, enabling Dave to rest his head in her lap, with his arms resting on pillows. With the help of one of her facial massages, Dave was able to take a nap.

"You're good for Dave, Millie." Ben said.

"Thanks, Ben. He's good for me, too."

"Listen, if you don't have to get home in a hurry, we'll let him sleep for awhile. I'll call and make arrangements to fly back to Brandon at five this afternoon. We'll just pick up some pizza and soft drinks for supper .... Have it on the plane."

"That sounds like a good plan to me, Ben." Millie whispered, so she wouldn't wake Dave.

"How's everything going between you two? Everything okay?" Ben asked.

"Great! But, maybe you should ask Dave that question. I personally think things are progressing very well between us."

"Good!" Lynne interspersed, "I look forward to seeing you again, Millie. Maybe you can come to North Carolina for the next race. It is in two weeks, right Ben?"

"Yeah, Rockingham."

"That's practically at our back door, Millie. You can stay with us at our house if you'd like…."

"We'll see, after all, Dave may not want me there…"

"Oh, he'll want you there. I'd place a bet on it." Ben assured her. At that moment, Dave's eyes opened and he smiled at her, and nodded his head affirmatively.

"Yes, I'll definitely want you there…." he whispered.

"We thought you were asleep…." Millie said.

"I know," he said, smiling.

They picked up the pizzas and soft drinks on the way to the airport. Millie helped Dave get comfortable on the plane, and fed him some supper. Then, she helped Lynne serve soft drinks and pizza to their guests before the plane left the ground.

The return flight was quiet. Lynne put some continuous-play CD's on the stereo. Unlike their flight to Daytona, everyone was now subdued …. concerned about Dave's injuries.

Millie took Ben and Lynne another can of Coca-Cola; then sat down beside Dave on the couch in the rear of the airplane – the most comfortable seat on the medium-sized plane.

Dave raised his arm and rested it on top of the couch so Millie could snuggle close to him, and put her head on his shoulder. Since they were so tired, the hum of the airplane engine, and the soft music playing on the stereo, lulled them to sleep.

After they landed, Millie helped the the Mayor get their luggage. She helped Lynne clear the Pizza debris from the airplane trash cans while Ben went to make arrangements for refueling, and to file a flight plan to go home. Dave sat quietly, watching the two ladies scurry about the airplane. He was dreading the moment he'd have to tell Millie goodbye… after all, she'd be leaving soon.

Ben came aboard, shaking his head. "Well, Folks, there's a storm front passing over Georgia. We have a two-hour delay before we're cleared for take-off."

"Well, then, why don't you come to my house?" Millie suggested. "I'll make some coffee. I'd like you to see my cabin!"

"Didn't you tell me you're a country decorator?"" Lynne exclaimed. "Oh, Ben, I'd love to see her house."

"What?" Dave said, somewhat confused, "Millie, I didn't know that you had a cabin."

"Well, there are still a few things you don't know about me. It just never came up in the conversation…."

They got into Millie's cougar and she drove towards South Brandon, and turned down a tree-lined driveway, stopping in front of a rustic-looking log cabin.

"I'm still in shock, Millie; I thought you were kidding when you said the condo made your house look like a log cabin," Dave exclaimed. "You rascal."

Millie glanced across the car to the passenger side where Dave was sitting. He stared at the cabin, then at her.

"Ah ha, gotcha!" she kidded him. "I love that look of surprise."

"I'm impressed, Millie. Why didn't you tell me you were a decorator? That you actually lived in a log cabin?"

"Like I said, Dave, it just never came up in the conversation. Come on in… let me show you MY place," she boasted confidently.

As they walked into the cabin, Dave said, "Talk about walking into the pages of a magazine, this is beautiful. You did this? You did the decorating? I love it. It seems like everyone I know wants a log cabin retreat in the mountains. I bet you stay pretty busy."

"Well, if you remember, I told you I manage to stay busy. Jacob and I bought the shell for this cabin; but we finished the inside ourselves. I went to Interior Design school, and took some basic southern architecture classes so we could keep it rustic. Jacob worked on the floorboards for hours until he got them to creak. It took years to find exactly what we wanted to put in every nook and cranny," she joked, using a phony southern accent.

The focal point of the living room was a large stone, log-burning fireplace. The log-beamed cathedral ceiling added to the ambiance. The furniture included a federal blue plaid couch with wooden trim accents, and two antique trunks for end tables. The slab coffee table contained a gorgeous silk floral arrangement with small American flag accents. It was sitting on top of a sampler that resembled a Confederate flag.

Early American accents were tastefully placed throughout the room, including a large wooden flag on the wall, and a bowl of red wooden apples sat on one of the tables. An afghan was draped carefully across an antique rocking chair, and a large handmade rag doll was leaning against it.

Millie ushered them into the dining room. "This is an 18th Century French country table and chair set that I found at an estate sale. I took an old quilt and made the table runner and placemats. This chandelier came from an old building that was being renovated downtown. The light bulbs look like burning candles. I thought I'd have a real problem finding replacement bulbs, but I finally found a supplier."

She continued to the kitchen: "The kitchen's a little more modern, as you can see; but we built in the appliances so they're almost invisible. The stove looks like an antique Franklin; but it has modern electric burners and convection oven. The top contains a microwave. Pretty sneaky, isn't' it?"

Millie showed them Jake's bedroom next. He bed had been hand-fashioned from pieces of logs that were strapped together with rawhide strips. His bedspread was an antique quilt. The matching nightstand and chest looked as if it was handmade as well.

"Did you make the furniture?" Lynne asked

"No, you'll be surprised to learn that these are open-stock pieces form Bauer in Seattle. I've used this bed in many of the cabins I've decorated. It's my best seller."

The guest bathroom in the hallway contained an old-fashioned footed bathtub. It was accented with amusing porcelain dolls. One was sitting on a tiny commode reading a book, and another was a small boy in pajamas, running away with a tiny roll of toilet paper. On a small shelf next to the bathtub, a small boy was fishing. His line contained several porcelain fish, and a big pot of silk daisies was sitting in the corner of the bathroom.

"This bathroom's too pretty to use…" Lynne said.

"Well, it doesn't get much use because Jake and I both have our own bathrooms. This room always gets included in magazine articles because it's so unusual." Millie explained.

She took them to her bedroom: "My bedroom furniture was made by the same manufacturer as Jake's but you see, it's quite different."

**** Next sentence needs changing *****

Millie's bed was fashioned from massive, twisted-twig, heart-shaped motif, four-poster bed with a ruffled spread and pillow shams. The room was rustic looking, but oozed with femininity.

Millie showed them her bathroom that contained an old-fashioned footed tub, and pull-chain commode. "When you open this door," she demonstrated, "You'll find a modern shower. We converted a linen closet into a shower stall."

"Boy, I can't believe this, Millie. You're somethin' else. I never dreamed you could do somethin' like this. I'm really impressed." Dave exclaimed, proud as a peacock.

"Well, you didn't ask, and I don't make it a habit to brag about myself." She explained.

"I apologize for not asking. When you said you usually wear your hair up when you work, I just assumed you work in an office. I should have asked. I have to hand it to you, though; this is a very pleasant surprise. This house definitely suits you."

"My cabin's been featured in several magazines; and the decorator I work with took a video of my cabin to show prospects who are interested in country decorating."

Dave noticed the phone on the nightstand. A red light was flashing on the answering machine. "It looks like you had a call, Millie."

Dave looked closer to the phone…. "I stand corrected. Your machine is flashing '22'. Does that mean you've had 22 calls since we left on Saturday?"

"Yes," she replied, a little concerned. "I hope nothing's happened to Jake."

She rewound the machine so they could hear the messages: "Millie, this is Lisa. I've got a V-I-P client who would like you to pull his new cabin together in two weeks. I told him we could do it. Call me as soon as you get this message."

The next six calls were from Lisa…"Millie, where are you?"

There were three calls from her neighbor, Roberta, and the final one from her was simply, "Well, since you're not home, I guess you decided to go to Daytona. Call me when you get home."

The next call was from Jake, letting her know he made it back to school okay.

The next four calls were from Lisa, each one more panicky: "This is a big commission, Millie, but we've got to hurry. Call me, please."

There were several hang-ups, and Lisa left several more messages, each sounding more desperate than the previous one. The last call was from Lisa: "I've put the blueprints and spec sheets in your mailbox. If I don't hear from you by 10:00 Tuesday morning, I'll give the job to someone else. I showed my client the video of your cabin, and he wants you to duplicate it if you can. Call me!"

"Well, as you can see, I'd better take a minute and call Lisa. Why don't you make yourself comfortable in the living room? I'll make some coffee and call her from the kitchen."

While the coffee perked, Millie called Lisa to tell her she would take the job. She gave her no explanation about her whereabouts for the weekend.

Going back to the living room, Millie said: "Excuse me for a minute while I run to the mailbox and pick up the specs. I'll be right back…"

"I'll walk with you, Millie, if it's okay." Dave said.

"Sure, but it's a long walk to the mailbox. Would you like me to drive the car back out to the mailbox, or are you up to walking?"

"No, I'd rather walk. I've been sittin' since the accident yesterday. It'll do me some good to stretch my legs. I'm not used to sittin' around."

As soon as Dave and Millie left to go to the mailbox, Lynne got up and walked around the cabin again. "She has real talent, Ben. This is really incredible. I bet she'd love to explore some of the antique shops we have back home. Maybe she'd help me with our place. There's something missing in our mumbled mess of country collectibles."

"Well, why don't we ask her to go back with us?" Ben suggested. "You two can work on her project while Dave and I get ready for the next race. Until he gets his medical release, though, he'll have to hang around with you guys."

"That's a great idea, Honey." Lynne said.

"I'll say something to Dave while you help Millie in the kitchen … make sure it's what he wants…."

They continue to walk around the cabin, looking at everything contained within the cabin. They're so many little tasteful knickknacks to see.

"Oh, everything smells so good, Ben. It's these little baskets of potpourri that she has sitting around. She doesn't need an associate. She should be doing this on her own."

On the way to the mailbox, Millie and Dave talked about the cabin, and how her career had evolved.

"It all began when my home was featured in the Tampa Tribune. Lisa called me as a result of the article and the rest is history. Since that time, I've decorated cabins in practically every state in America."

On the way back, Dave got serious, "Millie, it's been great being with you. Do you think we can stop walking long enough for a hug? I sure could use one...."

Millie stopped walking and stepped in front of him. Putting her arms around his waist, she laid her head on his chest and hugged him. Standing together, the top of her head barely came up to his chin. Dave rested his forearms gently on her shoulders to protect his bandaged arms. That was as close as he could come to returning the embrace.

"Oh, this feels so good, Millie." He said, closing his eyes, savoring the warmth of her much-needed embrace.

"This feels even better!" she whispered as she carefully put her arms around his neck. Standing on her tiptoes, she kissed Dave. Gently at first, but then with more passion.

"Thanks for a wonderful weekend, Dave. I'll never forget it. I may not get a chance to give you a goodbye kiss before you leave – at least, not a good one."

"I don't want our weekend to end, Millie. I'm angry with myself for getting hurt because I can't even touch you. Can't you come with us? Can't you decorate this cabin from Southern Pines? We have antique shops and country decorating stores. Who knows, you may even find a new merchandiser. You can express ship everything directly to the cabin." He pleaded emotionally.

"The cabin's located in a little town in Northeastern Georgia. North Carolina is much closer to the cabin than Brandon is...." she reasoned. "I'm intrigued by your suggestion, Dave. I shouldn't admit it, but I'm not ready to say goodbye either.... not knowing when I'll see you again.... or if I'll see you again."

"Oh, I promise you, no matter what, you'll see me again," he assured her. "Come on; let's talk to Ben and Lynne. You can probably stay with them, or you can stay at my place."

Remembering his dilemma of not being able to use his hands, Dave said, "I could get you a room in my hotel; but I have to tell you, seeing your cabin has inspired me to get my own place. I have that property just sitting there. Maybe you'll help me build a log cabin and decorate it for me. I'll pay you whatever you want...."

"That would be fun. I'd love to help you with your place at cost. We can do it together. Oh, here we go again. You've given me a challenge to take a chance. Oh, Lord, what should I do?"

"What do you want to do, Millie? You know in your heart that there's only one answer.... You have to take a chance! ... a chance on me.... a chance on us."

"Oh, you, you're impossible. What should I do?

"Take a chance, Millie," he challenged, with a twinkle in his eye, self-confidently, knowing he would get his wish.

When they got back inside the cabin, Millie went directly to the kitchen to get the coffee, followed closely by Lynne. They put coffee cups and the coffeepot on the table. Millie put some homemade chocolate chip cookies on an earthenware plate, and put them on the table, too.

"Millie, the potpourri you use smells heavenly. Where do you get it?" Lynne asked.

"It's my own recipe. It's easy to make in the microwave. I'll be happy to show you how to do it sometime."

"How about coming with us, Millie? You can show me then... I have a microwave!" Lynne said excitedly, clasping her hands together with glee, like a small child.

Millie smiled and glanced at the table, seeing if everything was ready. As an afterthought, she got an antique metal straw from her utensil drawer and put it in one of the mugs so Dave could drink his coffee by himself. She didn't comment on what Lynne has suggested at that time.

Lynne called to Ben and Dave to join them in the dining room. When Dave saw the metal straw, he smiled. He walked over to Millie and kissed her on the cheek, thanking her for her thoughtfulness.

"You're the most thoughtful person I've ever met, Mil'. Thanks, I feel stupid not being able to do anything by myself. Do you think I can borrow this straw for a couple weeks?"

"Sure, you can."

Lynne couldn't wait any longer. "Millie, we want you to come to North Carolina with us! I'll show you around Southern Pines, and help you with this decorating project while the guys are getting ready for the next race. We'll all be together, can go out to eat together, and stuff like that. You know, just have fun and get to know each other better."

"Yeah, Millie," Ben piped in, "What do you say?"

"That's really funny, guys, because while Millie and I were walking to the mailbox, we already had this discussion."

"Tell you what," Millie said, "I need to spend a couple hours in the office tonight to do some preliminary work on this project, and gather some material that I'll need. Oh, I guess I didn't show you my office. It's the third bedroom, which I converted into an office. I didn't want to clutter up the house with paperwork and catalogues. If I get the basics started tonight, maybe I can go. Can we wait until early morning to leave? If not, I'll just take a commercial flight tomorrow."

"We wouldn't hear of you taking a commercial flight." Lynne said. "Ben, why don't you call the airport and change our take-off time."

Ben picked up the telephone without further discussion to put their plan into action, after finding the number in his little black address book. He called the airport to make the arrangements.

"It's settled then; we'll leave tomorrow morning." Ben said. "Lynne and I'll get a motel tonight. I'm sure there are some good ones in Brandon."

"Oh, no, you won't. I won't hear of it!" Millie protested. "I've got plenty of room here. You can have Jake's room. Dave can have my bedroom, and after I get my work done, I'll sleep on the couch. Okay, then, I guess I'll go with you!"

"GREAT!" they all said in unison. Millie glanced at Dave, who was so happy he glowed."

Chapter Ten

After enjoying their coffee and finalizing their plans for their upcoming trip, Millie and Lynne changed the sheets on Jake's bed and put clean towels in his bathroom.

Dave picked out the movie "*Robin Hood, Prince of Thieves*" with Kevin Costner to watch while Millie did her work. As soon as she had everyone comfortable, and the movie had started, she escaped to her office.

Using her computer, she created purchase orders for a bed, chest-on-chest, and matching nightstands. She printed and faxed the order to Bauer in Seattle with instructions to rush the order directly to the cabin.

She reviewed the color scheme and window sizes using the specs and photos. She chose curtains and shutters from the Laura Ashley catalog with coordinating bedspreads, tablecloths, towels, shower curtains and area rugs. She also ordered the curtain rods and accessories that would be needed. She printed and faxed the order to them with the same instructions regarding direct shipment to the cabin.

Millie glanced at her watch. It was ten-thirty. She decided to give Roberta a quick call. She dialed the number and her neighbor answered.

"Hi, Roberta, this is Millie. I thought I'd better call to let you know I'm still among the living...."

"Good, did you go to Daytona with that guy?"

"Yes, and I'm really glad I did. Everything's going great between us so far. Did you watch the race?"

"No."

"Oh, then you didn't see what happened. Dave saved Ben's life. He pulled him out of a burning car. Ben's okay; but Dave spent last night in the hospital. His arms and hands are badly burned. I'm going back to Southern Pines with them. Will you keep an eye on everything, and get my mail for me? I don't have time to get to the post office to stop mail delivery."

"Sure, I'll be glad to. You know, we did see the accident on the news last night. They gave it a lot of air time. The guy you had the date with was driving the car?"

"No, he's the one who pulled him from the car."

"You're kidding! What a brave thing to do. When do you think you'll be back?"

"Oh, probably a week or so... If you need anything, get in touch with Lisa. I'll call after we get there and give you a phone number, just in case there's some emergency."

"Okay. Well, good luck. I hope everything works out for you."

"Thanks, Roberta." The phone line went dead.

Millie quickly sketched her plans for each room on a sketchpad, based on window and door placement. Then she created and faxed another purchase order to Thomasville for living room furniture, similar in design to her own.

She created a work order for Lisa's work crew, specifying exactly what their work scope would include at the cabin and faxed it to Lisa.

As she was putting the information she'd need for her trip in a briefcase, Dave pushed open the door gently with his foot and said, "How much longer are you going to be? You must be exhausted."

She pulled her sketches out of the briefcase and showed them to Dave. He was impressed. "You could be an artist! These sketches are incredible."

"Thanks! The sketches allow me to 'look' at the room when I select the accessories and accent pieces. I've decided to go with an Early American accent, similar in nature to mine, with the flag accents and apples. I usually give my clients the sketches, along with a drawing of the outside of their cabin, if possible. Sometimes they frame the pictures. I don't always get to see the finished cabin, though. I probably won't get to see this one."

"I hope you'll get to see this cabin. It can't be far from Southern Pines."

"Well, we'll see. Sometimes Lisa doesn't want me to see the finished product. I enjoy decorating—the challenge to transform a humble cabin into a rustic masterpiece. I was just putting everything away. What are Ben and Lynne doing? Is the movie over yet?"

"Well, Lynne wanted to come in and help you; but, we wouldn't let her. They went to bed after the movie. I laid down on your bed; but it didn't feel right...with you in here working. Aren't you tired? It's almost one o'clock in the morning."

"You're kidding! I was so absorbed in my work I didn't keep track of the time. I'm sorry I abandoned you for so long. I guess that nap today messed up my sleeping pattern."

"No problem...just remember to be as forgiving when it's my turn. You'll need to give me the same freedom to work on the cars when I have to...all night, if necessary. There'll be times when you'll think the race car is my mistress, though, taking all my time. Besides keeping the cars in top condition, we have to appear at sponsor promos, make various personal appearances and interviews, practice runs, qualifying runs, final adjustments to make...there's a lot to do before a race. We have a tight schedule. We always have to look ahead and get prepared for races that are a couple weeks away.... plus be prepared for the race for the week. You get my drift?"

She nodded.

Dave continued, "We use a computer, too, looks about like yours. We keep files on all the different races, what worked, or didn't work, our stats the last time we raced at that track. We have short tracks, night races, tracks with horrendous turns and banks, road tracks.... every race is different. The car has to be set up depending on the track. Road tracks are totally different from race tracks."

"Aren't all races about the same, though? The cars are factory specials, right? You have basically the same equipment to work with.... the tracks are similar."

"Minor adjustments have to be made at each track, taking into consideration such things as weather conditions, track conditions and such. Small improvements can make all the difference. You'll see!" Dave replied.

"Well, right now, I'm exhausted and still have to pack before we leave in the morning. Do you know what time we're leaving?"

"I think Ben said ten o'clock."

"I'll set my alarm for seven in the morning. I'd like to fix your breakfast .... sausage, eggs, gravy, homemade biscuits, fresh Florida orange juice. I haven't fixed a big breakfast since Christmas when Jake was home. How's that sound?"

"Oh, be still my heart. All this and she cooks, too! That sounds scrumptious, Darlin'. It's been a long time since I've eaten a home cooked meal; but why don't you wait until next week? If you mess up your kitchen, you'll have to clean it before we leave, right? There may not be enough time. We have to be at the airport by nine-thirty."

"Ah, ha, you just proved you ARE a neat-nik. If you weren't, you'd have never thought about cleaning the kitchen!"

"Guilty as charged...but, I'll get a rain check on that breakfast?"

"You bet!"

"Come on, let's get to bed, okay?"

Millie went to the bathroom and changed into her nightgown while Dave lay down on her bed. Then, she set the alarm and turned off the light.

"Goodnight, Dave, I'll see you in the morning." she said as she started to leave the room.

"What... no goodnight kiss?" he asked.

"She obediently walked over and kissed him. Then she went into the living room and laid down on the couch. After just a few minutes, Dave got up and came to the doorway of the living room.

"Why don't you sleep in your bed? I can't stand to think of you having to sleep on that sofa."

"I'm fine! Really, it's comfortable. Goodnight, Dave, see you in the morning."

"Oh, come on, with these bulky bandages, what else could we do but sleep? Come on, get on here and sleep in your bed."

"I swear, Dave Masden, you have far too much control over me! What am I going to do with you? I'd better sleep on the couch tonight. I'll be fine. A lot of times I fall asleep here and end up spending the night on the couch. It's actually quite comfortable, honest. Sometimes I actually choose to sleep here."

"Yeah, but I won't be very comfortable knowing you're on the couch. Besides, I need you to keep me warm...." he teased.

"It sounds like you're warm enough for both of us!" she joked. She got up and walked across the room to where Dave was standing. She put her arms around his waist, laid her head against his chest, and hugged him. She could feel his heart pounding. It was beating in-sync with hers.

"Okay, Millie, I'll admit it. I want you with me," he whispered. "The pain is much worse at night...feels like a severe razor burn. I can't sleep."

"Did the doctor give you some pain pills?"

"We forgot to get the prescription filled."

"Good Lord, Dave, what am I going to do with you?"

"Be my friend, be my lover, whatever God will allow this love affair to become. I need you, Millie." he whispered, emotionally pleading. His voice was broken, his tone was sincere. His emotional display touched Millie as she snuggled against him.

Dave whispered, "I know things are happening fast. It's hard to believe I feel so close to you this soon in our relationship. But, something wonderful's happening here. Don't you feel it, too?"

"I haven't decided if it's wonderful or not. I've not had a good night's sleep since we met!"

"Really? Well, then, come on, lay down with me in your bed. You'll sleep better there."

"I surrender! If I plan to get any sleep tonight, I'd better lay down with you until you fall asleep." she said, somewhat exasperated...afraid to face the emotion she knew was building within her. "I'll get you some extra-strength Tylenol to help with the pain until we get your prescription filled."

She went to the bathroom, got three tablets and a glass of water. She helped Dave take the medication; then, plumped up the pillows and helped him get situated in her bed, using extra pillows to cushion his injuries.

She gently laid down beside him, and put her head on his shoulder. Soon Dave was asleep. Being totally exhausted, and emotionally spent, Millie moved over so she wouldn't hurt Dave; and, in only a few minutes, she was fast asleep.

Later that night, Dave cried out in pain, startling her.

"Dave, what's wrong?"

"My arms are burning like crazy. The doctor knew what he was talking about when he said the pain would get worse before it got better. I feel hot...almost as hot as the fire.... hot and cold at the same time."

Millie knew Dave was exhibiting signs of infection—feeling hot and cold at the same time. His forehead was beaded with perspiration. "What can I do to help you?"

"What can anyone do? Lord, it hurts. This is awful!"

"I'll get you some more Tylenol." Millie quickly went to the bathroom to get the pills and a glass of water. She also grabbed a clean washcloth and ran some cold water over it. "Why don't I wake up Ben and we'll take you to the hospital in Tampa? They specialize in burns."

"No, not another hospital; I'd rather wait until I get back home. Let's wait a few minutes to see if the Tylenol works." He suggested.

With her help, Dave swallowed the pills and drank about half a glass of water. Then he laid back on the bed and Millie sat down beside him. Using the cool washcloth, she wiped the perspiration from his forehead; then, folded the cloth after running cold water over it and placed it on his head.

"How about one of my facial massages...like I gave you the other night, Dave? Maybe it'll take your mind off the pain and help you relax enough to go back to sleep. You need your rest."

"That would be great. Would you mind? I know you're tired. You were sleeping peacefully, like a baby, gorgeous in the dim nightlight. I watched you for a few minutes, then I fell back to sleep."

"You've got your nerve, watching me sleep!"

"Wow, I'm tellin' you, my hands are killing me..." he said, changing the subject.

"A massage will help you relax until the Tylenol kicks in, you'll see. I'll help any way I can." she assured him.

"You're the kindest person I've ever met. It comes across so naturally. I've never known anyone like you. You are a gift... Thank you, God, for my gift..."

Millie gently massaged his face using only her fingertips.

"Oh, Millie, that feels so soothing." he said, welcoming the facial caress. She continued to caress his face until he had fallen asleep. Then, she went to the couch and laid down, leaving her bedroom door open so she could hear Dave if he awoke again. She was afraid to lay down with him because she didn't want to hurt him. Within seconds, she was asleep.

The next morning, Millie took a fast shower and styled her hair while Ben helped Dave in Jake's bathroom. Lynne helped Millie pack her clothes, making sure she'd take clothing for their colder weather.

"It'll be cold. Take your warmest sweaters, boots, and coat. Pack a couple of dresses, in case we want to go out to a nice restaurant, and to

Church. While we're shopping the antique stores, you'll need sweatshirts or warm sweaters and jeans. Bring a flannel gown to sleep in....but, then again, Dave's going to get well! You may want a sexy nightie, too." Lynne teased.

Millie blushed. "Lynne, this is happening too fast! My head's spinning. I keep asking myself if I know what I'm doing."

"Don't worry, Dave's a prize, a real life-sized prize. A lot of women would love to have a chance with him. I've tried to fix him up, too. He wanted nothing to do with them. I can tell he really likes you...."

"Did you and Ben work out your problems?"

"Yeah, I gave him a hard time, but forgave him. We've been together a long time. I'm not sure if anything happened the other night or not...."

"Maybe I shouldn't tell you this, Lynne, but I overheard them the morning of the race. Ben told Dave that nothing really happened. It was a close call, though, from what I gathered. They didn't know I was standing on the stairs."

"I'm glad you told me. We'll keep this as our little secret."

"Okay."

"You know, Millie, we're going to be good for each other. Sure, sometimes I miss Pat 'cause we were friends for a long time; but she's not nearly as nice as you are. She really put Dave through the trenches. I was with her when she got together with Butch Smith. I tried to talk her out of seeing him."

"How did they get together?"

"She pursued him, big time. I was embarrassed for her. He's the love 'em and leave 'em type! Nobody likes him—especially Dave. That's probably why she chased after him, to hurt Dave."

"Wonder why she would want him over Dave. Dave's so much better looking. I only met Butch Smith for a minute; but, he didn't impress me."

"Their affair started long before her marriage ended. Dave was heartbroken. He doesn't even know about the other men she dated. I talked to Pat 'til I was blue in the face. To be honest, I was sick of the deception."

"Do you think it's over between them? She came to the hospital the other night .... with Butch Smith. It made Dave angry."

"Believe me, it's over. Even though he's upset about the accident, I've never seen Dave this happy. He's glad he met you. I hope things work out for you two."

"Me, too. I don't know how I'll handle myself when those bandages come off. He wants me with him all the time. So far, nothing's happened; but the fires are starting to burn, if you know what I mean. I don't take lovemaking lightly.... When I make love, it's got to BE love. There's a lot to be said about waiting...."

"That's kind of old-fashioned thinking, isn't it?"

"No, it's God's thinking. Dave and I talked about it a little..... Well, we'll see." She sighed. "This is just another bridge that will have to be crossed when we come to it..."

"But, it's not like you're virgins. You're both single. Don't be afraid to take a chance, Girl. Dave's like the gold ring on the merry-go-round. Go for the golden ring and enjoy the ride. Life's a circus...a merry-go-round ride that's over before we know it."

"Lynne, I've not been with a man since my husband died. Our marriage was so wonderful; we could have written a manual for everyone to read on how to have a happy marriage. I'm afraid that I'll scare Dave to death the first time because I've got so much passion built up inside me." she laughed, surprised at her candor.

"Go for it. Grab that golden ring!"

After eating a quick breakfast at Grandy's, they arrived at the airport at nine twenty-five. The flight was smooth. Ben and Lynne sat in the cockpit. Dave and Millie sat in the back of the plane, listening to CD's on the stereo.

After they landed, Dave showed Millie his shiny black truck that was parked at the airport. He asked her to drive it to Ben's house. She agreed.

She had trouble, at first, with the gears. Dave patiently talked her through each shift until she mastered the transmission.

"I converted my transmission..." he explained. "It's like an old-fashioned gearshift, you know, probably what you drove when you were a teenager."

"Dave, I love a challenge. I'm not going to let these gears get the best of me. You have a nice truck; it suits you. Did you have this interior custom-made at the factory? Don't they call this upholstery 'tuck and roll?' It's pretty in red and black. I never dreamed a pick-up truck could be this nice."

"It was a special order from Ford."

"By the way, I've noticed your race cars are Fords."

"We've always driven Fords. Right now, we're driving Ford Thunderbirds. I don't even like to work on Chevy engines, let alone drive them. It's just a matter of preference. Some mechanics prefer Chevys; but, as for me, I've always preferred Fords."

"Nothin' wrong with that.... I drive a Cougar!"

"I noticed!"

They drove down a long lane to a beautiful cedar home situated on a large piece of land. As soon as they went in, Millie told Lynne...."This is lovely. Will you show me around?"

Lynne walked her through the large home that contained a two-story, open-air living room, a massive stone fireplace and huge windows with a breath-taking view of a wooded meadow. The over-stuffed conversation pit was dark brown with gold accent pieces.

"You've done a great job with your decorating. I find no fault. I wouldn't change a thing!"

"There's a couple areas I'd like to improve.... for one, the den. Maybe you'll help me while you're here."

"Sure, I'd love to...but it looks good the way it is..."

Ben caught up with them as Lynne was showing Millie the master bedroom.

"Millie, since Dave needs help in the bathroom right now...and he's... ah, kinda embarrassed about it, why don't you both stay here until he can use his hands? It's the least we can do to thank him for saving my life."

"Are you sure? We won't be any trouble?"

"No, you won't be any trouble. We'd love having you. Two of our kids are away at school, and our youngest is at his grandfather's house. He can stay there a few more days. They'll take him to school...." Lynne assured her.

"Sure, it's okay, as long as it won't be any trouble."

"Good! Doc just lives down the road. He can come by every morning and help me with Dave's bath. If not, we'll get a nurse to help him with his personal needs. Somehow, though, I think his personal needs include your being here." Lynne said.

"That's right, Lynne. I DO need to have her around; she's much better than antibiotics." Dave joked as he walked into the bedroom where they were standing.

"Lynne, would you make some coffee?" Ben asked. "I called Doc. He'll be here in a few minutes."

"Boy, I'm getting kinda scraggly-looking. I could use a shave.... maybe he'll help me get cleaned up." Dave said, looking at himself in the mirror. "Maybe I'd better grow a beard and forget about shaving for awhile."

"Why don't you let me shave you, Dave? Do you use an electric shaver or a razor?" Millie asked.

"I have both. Hm-m.... having you shave me might be fun! We'll see how it goes." he smiled.

"Well, let me know if I can do anything..."

While Doc was examining Dave's burns, he shook his head. "Those burns are bad. The wounds are seeping and infected. You should be in a hospital. If the infection gets worse, Dave, it could be life-threatening."

"I don't want to go to the hospital, Doc. Let's try to treat the burns here first, okay?" Dave pleaded. "Hospitals remind me of death. You know I had a battle last year when my Dad died. He was in the hospital for a long time. If the infection gets worse, I promise that I'll go to the hospital; but, for now, let me stay here, please."

"I'll get you started on some powerful antibiotics and pain killers. I can come by every morning and change your bandages. I'm afraid you're going to have to wear these bandages for several weeks. Keep them clean and dry. Under normal circumstances, I'd insist on hospitalization; but, since I just live down the street, and we've known each other so long, I guess I can treat you here. I'll help you get bathed this morning; then, a male nurse will stop by the next few mornings to help you."

"Great! Thanks, Doc. I appreciate it."

"Be careful. Don't make me sorry I'm doing this... You have to rest and take care of yourself. And, stay away from that track! You've got to rest and get better. These pills will make you sleepy. You need to take an afternoon nap. You'll need at least eight hours sleep every night to help fight off the infection."

"Thanks, Doc. Would you do me a favor, too?"

"If I can..."

"Will you ask Father Thomas to stop by as soon as possible to bring me Communion? If he's willing, I'd like him to stop by every day while I'm sick."

While Dave took his nap that afternoon, and Ben was at the garage, Lynne and Millie explored an antique shop. They bought a few things for the cabin in Georgia and went to Mail Boxes, Inc., to have them packed and shipped to the cabin, along with Millie's instructions regarding suggested placement.

On the way home from the shop, Ben stopped by Dave's efficiency apartment to pick up some of his clothes.

That evening, they fixed supper and watched a movie, "*Butch Cassidy and the Sundance Kid.*"

When it came time for bed, Millie decided she would use Angela's room, which had twin beds and contained a bathroom. It was decided Dave would sleep in Ben, Jr.'s room, which was next to the room Millie would be using, since Ben & Lynne's bedroom was situated at the other end of the house.

During the night, Millie heard Dave cry out in pain. She jumped out of bed and ran to his room, finding him in torment.

"The pain is so bad, Millie. Could you please get me a pain pill? Normally, I wouldn't take them.... but this pain is more than I can take. I'm sorry to be so much trouble."

"You're no trouble. I'm just glad I heard you. I'll be right back."

She ran into the bathroom in the hallway and returned with the medication and a glass of water. She helped him take the pills. Once she had him settled, she went back to her room.

About three hours later, she heard Dave cry out for her again. She ran to his bedroom, gave him another pain pill and a sip of water.

He asked her to lie down with him until he went back to sleep. She laid down and ended up falling asleep in his room. Ben woke them the next morning. Millie was embarrassed at being found in Dave's room.

"Man, I don't know what I'd have done last night if it hadn't been for her. The pain was almost unbearable."

"Hey, it's okay. You guys can sleep together if you want to, you're adults," Lynne assured them, "As long as the kids aren't here, I don't have a problem with it."

"It's not like that.... She came to my rescue. She's a care-giver, that's for sure; nothing else happened."

At breakfast that morning, Dave couldn't stop talking about how much Millie had helped him the night before.

"Why don't you both just sleep in Angela's room? After all, there are twin beds. There wouldn't be anything wrong with you sharing a room until you feel better. I'd hate to think about you being in pain and not being able to get her attention." Lynne suggested.

"Oh, I don't know. I heard him okay last night."

"Yes, but how many times did you get up?"

"Two.... and the second time, I ended up falling asleep in his bed."

"What if you hadn't heard him? Doc said it's really important that he gets the antibiotic he prescribed."

Dave smiled. He wasn't getting involved in the discussion between Lynne and Millie; but he hoped she would agree to sleep in the same room with him. He wanted her close to him.

Millie stood firm in her conviction until Dave gave her a special look and said, "Mil', you have been better to me than I deserve; but, it helps me to have you close. Would you allow me to sleep in the other twin bed in Angela's room until my arms are better? It would mean a lot to me. After all, with these bandages, I can't even take a pill without your help."

She stared at him without expression. Then she waved her hands, exasperated. "Okay, I suppose, just until your arms are better." she agreed.

Dave smiled confidently because he was getting what he wanted.

The next three days were repetitious. Doc came, along with the male nurse to give Dave his bath, and change the bandages. Then, Father Thomas would stop by to talk, and give them Communion.

While Dave napped, Millie and Lynne shopped for the Georgia project and returned home early enough to fix supper. Sometimes Millie would bake a pie, mostly Dutch apple, since it was Dave's favorite. One evening, Millie showed Lynne how to make her special potpourri. She wanted to include some of her signature potpourri in the last package shipped to the cabin.

One evening after dinner, Dave and Millie were watching a movie, "*Days of Thunder*," while Lynne went to her parents' house to see Christopher, their youngest son. They were in the house alone. Dave had his arms resting across the back of the sofa, making his chest accessible for her to snuggle.

Millie noticed Dave started to fidget a little. "What's wrong, Dave? Are you in pain?"

"No, Darlin', I need to go to the bathroom. I've been trying to ignore it; but I'm about to burst. Would you call Ben at the garage and ask him to come home?"

"Let me help you."

"I can't ask you to do that. I think it would embarrass us both too much."

"Do you just need to urinate?"

"Yes, that's all."

"Well, for God's sake, Dave, I was married. I've seen a man's naked butt before. Come on, don't be silly. I'll help you." she said, hoping she would, in fact, be able to handle the situation.

They went to the bathroom and Millie pulled his sweatpants down for him from the back, not allowing herself to look at Dave's manhood; but, she couldn't help but notice his firm buttocks from where she stood. As soon as she pulled down his sweatpants, she immediately stepped out of the room and closed the door, keeping her eyes focused elsewhere.

"Let me know when you're finished," she instructed.

After a few seconds of bubbling sounds, Dave told her he was finished.

She politely opened the door and quickly pulled up his sweatpants, diverting her eyes, refusing to allow herself to look at his nakedness.

After they were once again sitting comfortably on the sofa, Dave whispered. "I'm glad you came to North Carolina with me, Millie. I haven't told you that for a while. I appreciate everything you do for me; but, I'll be glad when I get these bandages off so I can do things for myself."

"No problem. I'm glad I came, too."

"We take a lot for granted, don't we? We never appreciate anything until we don't have it anymore. It's nice being together. I'm very glad we're sleeping in the same room."

"Well, after I thought about it, it just made sense. After all, we are adults."

"Your shaves are the most sensual experience I've ever had in the bathroom. Is being together like this hard for you... being close without being intimate?" Dave asked, almost in a whisper.

"Hm-m...being intimate without intimacy. What an expression. We may be writing a new chapter in the book of life. W-h-o-o.... That's a tough question. I'm not used to intimacy ...you know that. It's been a long time. I'm not going to lie and pretend that being in the same room with you isn't hard for me, emotionally. I'm normal in every way."

"I don't doubt it for a minute." he whispered.

"In a lot of ways, we're fortunate to have this time to get to know each other without having a physical involvement. When we make love the first time, we won't have that awful awkwardness, will we? To answer your question, yes, it's hard; but I can handle it. What about you?"

"Yes, Darlin', it IS hard being close without being able to touch you, without being able to show you how much I care. But, think about it. What choice do I have? This desire to get well fast is frustrating me because the healing process is so slow."

"Doc says you're doing well, though. He said you are healing faster than he first expected."

"Millie, this is a special and unique time for us. I don't want to make love until I can use my hands. I want our first time to be something we'll remember for the rest of our lives. I don't want to botch things up. It's probably surprising to hear a man say this.... but, there's a lot to be said about waiting. I can wait. True love waits until the time is right. I think its best when it's as God designed.... kept within the confines of marriage. It's great having you around. I want you beside me every night. It sounds a little weird, doesn't it? However, I promise you, Lady, when I'm able to use my hands again, you'll find out how much I care for you."

"Didn't you say *true love waits*? I share that philosophy. Sex was designed by God to remain within the bounds of marriage. Although I was a teenager during the sixties, I've never been an advocate of free love. Are you saying, in a round about way, that you feel the same way?"

"Yes, I am. We find yet another thing to agree on. Do you think we can remain intimate without intimacy?"

"It's not going to be easy...but it's worth a try. We managed to pull it off a few minutes in the bathroom, didn't we?"

"Yes, we did. Were you embarrassed?"

"A little."

"Can you fathom it; do you have any idea how much I care for you?" Dave asked.

"I have a pretty good idea. I've grown very fond of you, too. You've made a difference in my life. Even if we could, it's too soon to make love. When we make love the first time, I want it to be real love, the kind that lasts forever."

"My feelings exactly. This may sound strange, coming from a man; but, I think sex without love is somewhat animalistic and too soon forgotten. True, passionate love is unforgettable, don't you think?"

"Dave, I haven't made love to anyone since Jacob died. I'm not a carnal Christian. Before I met you, I expected to go to my grave without making love again. I married Jacob for life. Now, everything's changed; and, you give God the credit for our being together. If it's God's will, I look forward to rediscovering love with you."

"I can hardly wait, Millie. It will be unforgettable, I promise. It's hard to imagine how someone so sexy could manage to do without making love for seven years. How were you able to wait so long?"

"I know it sounds a little weird.... a woman with a normal sex drive who can survive without sex for seven years. After the first few months, it wasn't so hard. I got used to it. The hardest adjustment was learning to survive without hugs, kisses, you know, simple human touch."

"And, I can't touch you; I can't make love to you. I can't even hug you. I can, however, with your help, kiss you."

She raised her chin, closed her eyes and enjoyed Dave's loving kisses. She felt herself getting sexually aroused and knew she had to break away. "Watch the movie, Mr. Masden!"

"Yes, Dear! Tonight, I'll watch the movie. Some other night, though, you won't be able to get me to stop!" Dave said as he held his bandaged hands up and growled at them...."U-g-h! I hate these bandages. I want to touch you."

"Some other night, Dave, you won't have to stop," she whispered, "But, right now, we need this time to get to know each other. Now, watch the movie...please. Your kisses are driving me crazy."

They quietly watch the movie for a few minutes; then, became bored and continue to talk.

"How long have you been a Christian, Millie?"

"I was baptized on my thirteenth birthday in a little church in Miamisburg, Ohio. I was a believer; but I wasn't much of a follower. I only prayed when I needed something."

"I see... What happened?"

"My faith didn't grow much during the next few years; but when Jacob was working on the vice squad in Tampa, he was assigned to cover a drug raid. He was seriously wounded. I promised God I'd attend church regularly, convert to his Catholic faith, if he would bring Jacob safely through. A brush with death can certainly cause you to think about eternity. Now, I'm totally committed to Jesus. God's my constant companion. I trust Him with every aspect of my life. I have totally surrendered my life to the Sacred Heart of Jesus, through the Immaculate Heart of His Mother, Mary. What about you?"

"I was always in church when I was a kid—my parents went every Sunday, no matter what. I had a life changing experience when I worked for Lee Petty when my best friend died in a fiery crash. I rededicated my life and began to go to Mass as often as possible. My faith has grown ever since. Pat never shared my love for God. After we were divorced, I was amazed to see how many of my friendships changed. The only true friend I had, the only one I could trust, was Jesus."

"Boy, I know what you mean about relationships changing. When Jacob died, one of my friends told me she didn't want to be friends any longer because she didn't like the way her husband looked at me now that I was single. Can you imagine the heartbreak? She was a good friend, too. I had absolutely no interest in her husband, but I needed her friendship."

"I'll be your friend, Millie, no matter what. You're the kindest person I've ever met. You are truly a gift from God and I thank him every day when I say my prayers. I wake up a lot of times at night. I'll look over at you, sleeping peacefully, and my heart fills with joy. I can't thank God enough for His gift of bringing you into my life."

"I feel a little strange sharing a bedroom with you here....in this house. What if Lynne brings Christopher home with her? Won't you feel funny, too?"

"Yes, I will. We'll see. Christopher stays with Lynne's parents pretty often. She doesn't have to give him an explanation about our being here. Ben and Lynne like you, Millie. They want things to work out. They know nothing's going on in that bedroom right now; but they also know I'm going to get well. Things may change then."

"This is too much to think about. We'd better get interested in this movie, Romeo, before you turn me on with your sweet words!"

"You ain't heard nothin' yet, Darlin! Mark my words, someday, when I'm able to use my hands, I'll show you a mighty love. I predict by the time we make love, it will be love, true love, the forever kind...just like you said."

"Warning noted and challenge taken, Mr. Masden." she said as she snuggled against him. She smiled as she snuggled. She felt safe with Dave. In her heart, she knew it was already love, even though they hadn't said the words. She closed her eyes as she snuggled against him and thanked God for His gift.... Dave Masden!

That night, Millie couldn't sleep. She laid alone in the twin bed next to Dave's bed while he slept. She could see his form in the moonlight and in the dim nightlight that was located on the other side of his bed. She could tell he was dreaming.

She ached to feel his arms around her. Her body tingled with excitement at the thought of making love with him. She longed to touch him.

As Dave dreamed, he got an erection. It was all she could do to keep from climbing into his bed and having her way with him. She wanted to make love to him.

She closed her eyes as tears spilled down her cheek. She kept repeating over and over in her mind..."*true love waits. When we make love, it has to be love.*"

She loved Dave Masden with every cell in her body. She was consumed with desire for him.

Unable to contain her emotion any longer, she got up quietly and went into the bathroom. She turned on the shower and adjusted the water temperature to cool, and stepped into the refreshing spray. The shock of the cool water helped her regain her composure. She adjusted the water temperature to warm and cried out her frustrations under the warm shower.

She toweled her body dry and pulled off the shower cap. She combed her hair and put on her nightgown. When she returned to the bedroom, Dave was awake.

"Come on, Honey, come over here and snuggle with me. I thought I heard you crying."

"I'd better not come to your bed, Dave; a twin bed is too small for both of us. Do you need some more pain medication? It always helps you sleep..."

"No, my hands hurt, but it's not too bad. I can tell they are healing. I'd like to snuggle with you for a few minutes. Were you crying?" he insisted on an answer to his question.

She continued to ignore his question again, but diligently, she laid down on the bed beside him and took a deep breath.

She watched Dave's chest expand as he took a breath. He had a magnificent body. She imagined how wonderful it would feel to have his hairy chest pressed against her bare breast. She tried to think about something else.

She could no longer restrain herself as she slowly moved her hand underneath the sheet and touched Dave sexually, exploring his body with her hand. Dave rose up on one elbow and started to smother her with kisses... her lips ...her cheeks ...her neck. He was moving down her neck towards her breast, which was covered by the nightgown.

Millie's mind was racing. Have they gone too far to stop, she wondered. Do we dare think about doing what we want to do?

She heard a nagging voice....*"True love waits"*. She didn't want to wait. She needed to make love to Dave. Have they gone too far to stop?

Millie thought her head was resting on a pillow. She moved over to better accommodate Dave's ravenous kisses, to wrap her legs around him and she felt wetness on the sheet. She opened her eyes and glanced over to see a dark blot. She gasped when she discovered she'd been lying on Dave's arm rather than a pillow. "Oh, Dave, you're bleeding."

Millie jumped off the bed and turned on the light. She was trembling. Dave's bandage, and one side of his twin bed, was covered in bright red blood. "Oh, Dave, what have I done? I'm so sorry," she sobbed.

"Its okay, Honey. When pressure is put on the veins, they seep blood. Doc said its natural.... its part of the healing process. I'm sorry it scared you."

"Should I change your bandages? Did Doc leave some extra gauze and cotton pads?"

"Yes, they're in the bathroom in the hallway, under the vanity. Would you bring me a pain pill, too?"

She quickly returned, carrying the bandages, his pain pills and a glass of water. She gave him the pill and a sip of the water. Then she carefully removed the blood-soaked bandage on his left arm.

When she saw his arm, she gasped. The burns were much worse than she expected. Even though it had been almost a week, she couldn't see any sign of healing. The flesh was raw, yellow in color, with a tinge of green, oozing pus and blood.

"I'm sorry I hurt you, Dave. If I hadn't been such a hussy...I practically attacked you. I don't know what's happening to me, Dave! There's not a carnal bone in my body. Will you forgive me?"

"Forgive you.... Honey, there's nothing to forgive. We got a taste of what lovemaking will be like. Are you okay? Seeing that blood and now, seeing my hands, must be a shock. Honey, you've got blood in your hair and on your pretty nightgown."

"I know. It's okay. I'm just concerned about your arm. The burns are much worse than I thought. Dave, I think you should be in a hospital."

"I didn't want you to see how bad they were. It's hard to believe; but, Doc keeps telling me my hands are healing. I have to tell you, I'm scared."

"Bless you, Dave. You're such a wonderful man. Can you ever forgive me for hurting you? It's all my fault." She whispered as a tear rolled down her cheek.

"Well, let me ask you this? Do you lust after just anyone else, or is it me you want? You don't have to answer that question out loud," he asked, reluctantly, almost afraid of her answer. After all, she hadn't been with a man in seven years. Maybe she was only interested in having sex with someone.

"You're going to make me answer that question?"

"If you will...it will help us understand what's happening."

"I want YOU, David Masden. I could have had other men. I haven't been with anyone for over seven years. I thought I'd go to my grave without making love again."

"Good! Then, it's nobody's fault. We're simply falling in love."

"Maybe I'd better go back home until you're healed so I won't hurt you again."

"You'd hurt me a lot more by leaving. Come on, Millie, let's ride out this storm, Honey."

"When we were getting dangerously close to making love tonight, this little voice kept repeating.... *True love waits*. Dave, do you think we'll be able to wait? I want you more than I'm willing to admit. I can't believe I'm telling you this... that's why I think I'd better go back to Brandon until you're better. What happened tonight can't happen again. It's like I'm on fire...on fire for you."

"Oh, Lady, that makes my day. I'm so happy I can hardly stand it. What a blessing! Thank you for telling me! You're understandably upset. I don't want you to make a decision you might regret, and I sure don't want you to go home. There are some sedatives on the nightstand. Let's get some sleep and talk about it tomorrow."

"Are you sure you're okay? Boy, talk about a mood changer!"

She joked, wiping her tears.

"I'm fine. You can see the bleeding has stopped. Somehow in the heat of the moment, I wanted to hold you so badly that my hand got under your head. I should have been screaming in pain, but you were giving me quite a distraction. Honey, come on, take one of the sedatives and get some sleep. We'll talk about this tomorrow."

She changed the sheets on his bed and they kissed goodnight. Then, she took one of Dave's sedatives and went to the bathroom to wash his blood out of her hair. She changed her gown and put it in the basin to soak.

When she finally crawled back into her twin bed, Dave was sleeping quietly. She had a heavy heart...she'd hurt him with her passion. In the darkness, she asked for God's forgiveness for her lustful actions, and prayed the Rosary.

Confident that Dave had fallen into a pain-medication-induced sleep, she felt herself getting groggy from the medication. She knew she would drift off soon.

As she listened to the rhythmic sounds of Dave's breathing, she prayed for healing. She asked the Lord to guide them and direct her decision to go home. She felt as if Dave's healing was slower than expected, even though the doctor said he was making great progress. She prayed for complete healing for Dave's hands.

Morally, she didn't know what to think about what was happening to her. It was so unlike her to be wanton. In thinking it over, she realized they had spent practically every hour together since they'd met—day after day—with passion building between them, and in a domestic setting. This, and the accident, had caused their relationship to accelerate at an astronomical rate.

Their relationship was exactly opposite to her old-fashioned morality; but, somehow, she felt she was exactly where she was supposed to be. Dave wanted her there. She wanted to be there. She wanted to spend the rest of her life in his arms.

Millie whispered a prayer, "Lord, you created us, including our sexual desires. Help us, Lord, to wait. If it's meant to be, Lord, let it be. Your will be done in our relationship. Thank you God for creating such a truly good man named Dave Masden. Thank you for changing my life. Amen."

Chapter Eleven

The next morning, Millie decided not to say anything about returning to Brandon. When Father Thomas came that morning, Millie asked him if she could speak to him, in private, to make a Confession. They went into the den where they would be undisturbed.

"Bless me, Father, for I have sinned. It has been two weeks since my last Confession." Millie stammered.

"What are your offenses, my Child?"

"I have developed a lustful passion, Father. I have been celibate ever since my husband was killed, seven years ago. The relationship has grown very quickly between Dave and me, and last night, we almost gave into our lustful passions. I accidentally hurt him, caused his arms to bleed, and we had to change his bandages in the middle of the night."

"But you did not consummate the act?"

"No, Father. For this, and all the sins that I have committed, I am truly sorry. I will try to be stronger in the future."

"For your penance, my Child, pray a full Rosary. Try to attend daily Mass. It will help you through these tempting times. I realize it is more difficult being an adult, and having to abstain from intimacy. You know God's teachings in these matters."

"Yes, Father."

"Then say a sincere Act of Contrition, and try not to commit further sins."

"O, my God, I am heartily sorry for all my sins because of them I deserve the eternal pains of hell, but most of all because I have offended Thee, my God, who art all good and deserving of all my love. I firmly resolve, with the help of Your Grace, to confess my sins, to do my penance, to avoid the proximate occasion of sin, and never to sin any more. Amen."

"I absolve you in the Name of the Father, the Son, and the Holy Spirit. Bless you my Child. Go in peace, My Child, but do not be so hard on yourself. You and Dave care for each other and these are natural feelings."

"That evening, after dinner, Millie suggested that she and Dave take a walk. Ben's farm had a large fence-lined meadow. The air was much warmer than usual that evening...a perfect night for a walk. They put on sleeveless parkas and stepped into the crisp dusky evening air.

Several times as they walked, Dave suggested they stop for a kiss break. Millie would snuggle against him and hug his waist. Although his arms were extremely sensitive, Dave had gotten to the point where he could almost return her hug.

The kisses became intense...hungry. They needed more, to progress to that natural next step. They weren't innocent children. Their passion was becoming voracious, smoldering deep within, and insatiable.

"Millie, the English language fails me when I try to find the words to tell you how much I want you. You've been wonderful all these long days...and, bless your heart, nights; but it must be harder for you. My pain pills help me sleep."

"Its okay, Dave. I feel really bad about what happened last night. All I have to do is remember my shock when I saw that blood."

"I told Doc you had to change my bandages. He checked me real well and said he didn't think I'd done any damage."

"You told him what happened?"

"No…Well, not exactly. I told him I hurt my hand during the night—it wasn't really a lie. He said everything looks okay."

"Does he have any idea how much longer you'll have those bandages?""

"He only said *'be patient!'* I can hear him saying it right now…. it echoes in my head."

"Oh, so your message is *'be patient'* and my message is *'true love waits.'* Isn't that something?"

"Well, true love *does* wait. We *do* have to be patient. Oh, by the way, for the record, I asked Doc to do an Aids test…just to make sure. I know Patricia screwed around on me. She thought I didn't know about it; but I knew there were several others before Butch Smith. They deserve each other. I just want to be sure she didn't give me something that I might pass along."

"Good, I appreciate you taking the initiative to make sure you're okay. I've not had to deal with any of those issues. Do you think I need a test, too?"

"Doc said he'd give you a test, too; but, I'm not concerned about you having any kind of sexually-transmitted disease. As far as you know, Jacob never messed around, right? You said he's the only man you've made love with. I'm glad you've waited all these years, Honey. One day, our wait will be over."

"So, do you think we will make love someday?" she asked, very seriously.

"I certainly hope so. I don't know about you; but, I can't wait to show you how much you mean to me. You've been so wonderful to me."

"Well, I think I showed you last night that I can hardly wait. Do you really think this sexual frustration won't end up splitting us apart? I'm not sure I can wait much longer because it's been so long for me. Whenever we are able to make love, if we're able to make love, I may not let you get out of bed for another two weeks!" she teased.

"Thank you, Love, you're my dream come true. Sometimes I get so excited when I think God may very well have created you for me. You're exactly the kind of woman I need."

"What about Jacob and Patricia? Where do they fit into this scenario?"

"Well, from what you told me, Jacob was a good man. You had a great marriage, right?"

"Super! We should have written a marriage manual....I was devastated when I lost him. I never wanted anyone else, that is, until you."

"Millie, I prayed long and hard before I met you, telling Jesus exactly what I needed in a woman. I begged him to allow me to love again. I prayed for someone like you to come into my life."

"But what about Patricia?"

"Patricia messed up. I'd have never left her if she hadn't insisted on a divorce. I didn't like what she was doing; but I was hoping to somehow work out our problems. She insisted on the divorce. She broke our marriage vows, Millie. God doesn't look lightly upon sin. She never understood when I had to spend time working on the cars. Last year was a really bad year for us. We couldn't get the cars set up right. Our sponsors were threatening to withdraw their support. It's very expensive to maintain our cars. I was coming apart at the seams."

"I understand, really I do."

"I know you understand. You understand because you need to spend time with your business sometimes, too. Patricia never had that outlet. She had no other interests except for our marriage. It wasn't enough. It may have been different if we'd had children; but, there too, God chose not to allow it to happen."

"God?"

"I honestly believe that our lives are destined by a divine plan. Once we surrender our lives to Jesus, from that point on, God predestines everything that happens. He has given us a free will; but, I think he has every area of our lives covered based on our decisions made using our free will. He gives us blessings or disciplines as needed."

"I go along with that, I guess. It was hard, though, when Jacob was killed to understand."

"Who knows, maybe that happened to discipline the drunk driver? God knew you had the guts to face the next day, to raise a fine son by yourself. God's been right there with you, every step of the way. It's like the poem, "*Footprints*."

"'*Footprints*' has always been very special to me, as well as the Serenity Prayer, which helps me to trust Jesus. I guess I'm like a little child when it comes to my trust in Him."

"When I was a little boy, Mil', everything in life was fun. I had carefree dreams and made big plans for the future. It's not so different now. I'm making plans for us. I'm going to find a special way to surprise you, to let you know you are my dream come true."

"There's a risk in being close to anyone. I've worked past the risk and acknowledge I need you. The risk has diminished. Intimacy will come at the right time. It's inevitable when two lonely people find themselves in a situation like this...."

"Isn't it amazing to think about how we met? How much we felt in those few seconds? Ben was rushing to get me out of that store. I stalled. If it hadn't been for that, we'd have missed each other."

"I'm glad I took a chance with you. No matter what happens between us, Dave, I'll never regret it."

"Life's an adventure, Millie. If we fear life and close ourselves up, we'll miss the opportunity of love. Love actually sets us free from our own selfish thoughts. You think more often of the one you love than you think about yourself. I think it's the way God meant it to be. When a man is alone, all he can think about is himself...and how lonely he feels. I had become very withdrawn, feeling so lonely I didn't want to be around people who had a good relationship; and, because I was on a real downer, they didn't want to be around me either. But, God, in his infinite plan for men and women, allowed love. When a man is in love, all he can think about is how to please his sweetheart. Hopefully, she thinks the same about him. In the process, they are both pleased. Our time together has been very pleasurable, with the promise of more pleasures to come. Being with you, pleasing you, is all I can think about. I can hardly wait. I'm not afraid to tell you, I'm seriously thinking about a '*forever*' for us."

At first Millie was unable to speak. Then she cleared her throat and cleared her mind. "Don't you think when two people meet, independent within themselves, with their own histories, dreams, hopes, fears and perceptions; they recognize each other's strengths and appreciate them for who they are...for what they can be. They accept each other's weaknesses. When things are right, everything falls into place. They complete each other, so to speak."

"Millie, you're so smart. I don't know about you; but, I'm starting to feel mighty complete."

"Do we know each other well enough to be this serious so soon?" she asked. She stopped walking, and stepped in front of Dave, facing him pensively. She put her arms around his waist, hugging him.

"What else do we need to know about each other? We're good people. I care deeply for you and I think you feel the same for me, although you're not ready to admit it. We seem to appreciate each another. We've probably spent more time together than most courtships last. Think about it, Mil', we're together almost twenty-four hours a day. We care about each other. We certainly want each other, that's obvious. We each have our own lives, independent of each other, lives that could easily become intermingled. We have a good shot at happiness, God willing."

"Well, I'm sure you've heard what the experts say in those books. They say when something starts with fireworks, soon it fizzles and dies. Neither of us has dated since our marriages ended. Are we really that sure of each other?"

"I know I'm sure. Life's a gamble, Millie; a very fragile gamble. We have the potential for happiness. We're both lonely. We're both Catholic, and have a strong faith in Jesus Christ. I thank God every day for bringing us together. Are you willing to take a chance on happiness?"

"I've done nothing but take chances since I met you, Dave Masden", she said, trembling both from the words he was saying and the chilly night air.

"Just for the record, Dave, what about your marriage? I know I am free to marry again if I choose; but, since the Catholic Church believes in forever marriages, are you really free to get married again?"

"Well, unfortunately, we were not married in the Church. She never shared my faith. Father Thomas filed papers some time ago, because if I marry again, I want the full Sacrament of Holy Matrimony. He led me to believe this is not a problem because she admitted to him that she started to run around on me within a month after we got married. If we had married in the Church, I probably would not be able to receive the full Sacrament if I were to marry again."

"But, right now, we'd better get back inside. It's freezing out here."

"Right."

The movie they chose to watch that evening was "*Always*" as they snuggled together in front of the fireplace, totally at peace with God and each other.

The next afternoon while Dave napped, Millie helped Lynne mail Newsletters to the members of their fan club.

"This is long overdue. I haven't had time to get it together. If you'll help me stuff these envelopes and run them through the postage meter, it will keep me from having to answer the phone so much. Everyone wants to know how Dave's doing."

Millie and Lynne mailed over eight thousand letters that afternoon. "It's a good thing you have this automatic equipment—this would normally take us days to do this little project." Millie said, as she helped Lynne put the newsletters in a mailbag.

"We used to have over twenty-five thousand members in our club. Look at this; I've received over five hundred requests for information on how to join our fan club just this week. If you can help me, we'll send out those packages tomorrow afternoon. We send the new members autographed pictures and biographical information, as well as a few souvenirs. We may need to update Dave's information soon..." she joked. "We may have to add you to his bio!"

"Not yet, okay? It might jinx us."

"No way, you guys have what it takes, and you know it!" Lynne said confidently. "You know what? This is fun, working together like this, isn't it?"

"Well, Dave has kept me pretty busy so far; but, now that we have my Georgia project completed, I love having something to do. It's my pleasure to help you."

In the next couple days, Dave became more impatient because he thought his hands weren't healing as quickly as he wanted. He was frustrated and tense. Millie would calm him down with a facial massage, a back rub, or a few kind words.

One afternoon, after an especially frustrating day, Millie suggested a back rub. "I understand your frustration, Dave... to be incapacitated. But, you *ARE* healing. Doc's happy with your progress. You said you're a patient guy. Well, here's your chance to prove it to me." Millie said as she poured oil into her palms to massage into his tense back muscles.

"You're incredible! Is there anything you can't do? You're the greatest..." Dave purred, lavishing in the expertly maneuvered back rub. "It's going to be so great when I can make love to you ." he whispered.

"I'm sure there are some things I can't do. I like a challenge, though. There's very little you can't learn from reading a book. I read a book about massage and you're experiencing the results. I took a course on interior design; you saw my work. I've been able to build a career on it. I even read a book about basic auto mechanics. I can change a tire if I have to; and, I could change the oil in my car, in a pinch."

"Well, in that case, my truck needs to have the oil changed! Go ahead. I use a good grade of synthetic oil, 20-W-40!" he joked. "In all seriousness, when my hands are fully healed, you'll never have to worry about having to change your oil. I love to tinker with cars.... all cars, well, as least as long as it's a Ford!"

Soon Dave was relaxed by the back rub and fell asleep. Millie quietly walked out of the bedroom, closing the door behind her. She went into the kitchen where Lynne was having a cup of coffee. She poured herself some and sat down at the table.

"How's everything between you guys? He's pretty tense, isn't he? Has anything happened between you two yet?" Lynne asked.

"Boy, Lynne, that's a pretty personal question but I will answer it," she replied, taking a deep breath. "No, not yet. He wants me to snuggle up with him all the time. He says he sleeps better if I snuggle with him until he falls asleep. Sometimes he wakes up several times a night in pain. Doc says the pain is caused by the damaged nerves trying to heal. Curling up with him without doing anything else is certainly causing me to become pretty frustrated, if you know what I mean."

"I realize that, Millie. I think about you guys a lot. It's a tough situation."

"In a lot of ways, though, this is a good time for us. We're getting to know each other. By the time those bandages come off, we'll either hate each other or love each other!"

"Oh, I predict you'll love each other." Lynne remarked. "I've seen the way you look at each other. Having you guys around is good for our marriage, too. It's like we're having a second honeymoon...." Lynne remarked, with a snicker, covering her mouth with her fingers.

"Thanks, Lynne, that has really helped me with OUR problem. We can't touch each other...."

"Hey, I've got a suggestion! Why don't we go to the cabin, and see how our decorating project worked out? It'll be a good change of pace. It'd take several hours to drive there; but, if Ben can get away, he can fly us. Since I helped you, I'd love to see the completed project."

"That's a terrific idea, Lynne. I'd like to see it, too. Lisa always gives me photos; but she takes all the credit for the work. She pays me very well so I can't complain. I'm certainly not looking for fame. But, hum-m, I like your suggestion. As soon as Dave wakes up, I'll ask him what he thinks."

"Why don't I call Ben at the garage? I'll see if he can clear his schedule; get away tomorrow." Lynne suggested.

"I've got a better idea. Dave's been cooped up too much. Since it's a beautiful day, when he wakes up, why don't we all drive down to the garage? It'll do wonders for

Dave's morale.... to see the guys. Then tonight, we'll take another walk. Those walks give us a chance to catch our breath, talk, and who knows, steal a kiss!"

When Dave awoke from his nap, Millie made the suggestion that they go to the garage. The idea excited him. When they got there, everyone was scurrying around, perfecting the car for the up-coming practice laps and time trials. They were glad to see Dave; and he was ecstatic, being at the garage again.

"This was a good idea, Millie. So, tell me, what do you think about our garage?"

"It's so clean and well-organized. Isn't a garage supposed to be dirty? These floors are spotless. Even the tools and tool boxes are immaculate."

"Would you like to see where we started?"

"Sure."

They walked around to the back of their large garage to a small one-bay concrete building. "This is where Ben and I started, many years ago."

"You have certainly come a long way. How many bays do you have in the garage?"

"Twelve, plus the office and lounge, which doubles as a conference room. We have ten cars; five for Coca-Cola and two if we want to run in BUSCH. The others are spares—cars that we have retired from actual racing. They are taken around for special sponsor promotions. We also have two 'funny cars' in case we want to just have some fun and enter one of their races."

"Funny cars?"

"Yes, it's a race using special cars that are virtually impossible to turn over. You'll see them sitting over in the corner. If we enter a funny car race, Ben and I compete against each other. It's a safe race, more or less. Rarely does anyone get hurt in a 'funny' car because of the way they're designed."

"Amazing! I'm impressed."

"We've set up our own practice lap over there." He said, pointing towards the west. "It's a mile long track with different banked turns. We'll pace the cars there to get an idea of how they'll run at the individual tracks."

Ben came running over to where they were standing, and said, "Since you're here, will you pace the car, Dave? I think we'll get a good position if you'll pace me. Hell, who knows, maybe we'll even get the pole position. This is our home track, for God's sake—*let's win this race.*"

Ben put a headset on Dave's head. Charlie maneuvered the stopwatch. They watched as Ben and Dave paced the car. Millie and Lynne decided to get a soft drink from the machine inside, leaving Dave alone at the track.

Dave and Ben communicated over the headset. "Ben, how'd you feel the first time you got back into the car? Do you feel secure? Are any Daytona ghosts spookin' you?"

"Man, the first lap was horrible. I don't think I got the speed over sixty-five miles an' hour. My hands were shakin' and I had spots in front of my eyes. Charlie was screamin' in my ear to go faster. I've missed you being on the other end of this headset, Dave."

"Do you think you'll be okay for this race? You know, we could get a substitute driver. You've had a bad shake-up."

"If I don't get into this race, I'll NEVER be able to race again! You know how it is...when you fall off your bike, you have to get up and get right back on. Same scenario, different vehicle. *I've absolutely GOT to race....* but, I'll admit, I'm scared. I'd never admit it to anyone but you. Don't say a word to Lynne. I don't want her to know I'm a chicken."

"You're not a chicken, Ben. I know what you're goin' through. I'm itchin' to get into one of our cars and hear that engine roar. I can't help it; I wantta drive again, Ben. I've got to get back into that car and overcome my fears...fears I've been harboring since my wreck two years ago."

"I understand completely, Pard."

Millie and Lynne returned, carrying a cup of coffee for Dave. Millie held the cup so he could take a sip.

"So what was that I heard? Something about fear?" she asked.

"I'm not afraid to tell you, Millie, 'cause I don't want any secrets between us. Ben's wreck at Daytona has reinforced a fear I've harbored for two years. When you told me about Jacob's wreck, it also reinforced my fear. I've got to face my fear, head-on, before I'll feel like a man again."

"And, what if I told you I'd stop seeing you...go back to Brandon, if you get back into a race car? I don't think I can handle watching you race. I lost one man I loved in an accident; I don't want to lose another one. Dave, you've got what you wanted. I came to North Carolina to help you get well. Don't ask me to watch you die! Maybe coming to the track was a bad idea..."

"Come on, Millie. If I don't overcome my fear, I won't be worth knowing. Remember when you said, 'When you love something, set it free'? Don't keep me locked in this prison I've built for myself. I have to overcome my fear so I can be a whole man again.... YOUR man, if you'll have me. I can't ask you to settle for a fragment of a man. Life's full of chances ... take a chance with me. You took a chance when we met. It was a good choice. Hang in there a little longer. I can't wait to get these bandages off so I can show you how much I care." he pleaded, touching her face with the tips of his recently-exposed fingers. "But, I've got to tell you, I also want these bandages off so I can enter a competitive race."

"Well, chances are, it'll be a while before you get the bandages off! Doc hasn't said anything about removing them, has he?"

"No, I know I won't be able to race at Rockingham. NASCAR would never allow it because I wouldn't have enough time to get qualified. But, maybe I will be able to race in Richmond...next week."

Goose bumps prickled her skin as he touched her tenderly. He was so excited...so intensely serious about racing. "Okay, Dave. I'll stay until that race; but then I've got to go home. I've already been gone over two weeks."

It was decided they would postpone the trip to the cabin until after the race. Although Dave still had his bandages, he was permitted to be Ben's crew chief at Rockingham.

It was race day.

After the good-luck kisses from Lynne and Millie, Ben and Dave took their respective places for the race. Dave was thrilled to be at the track. The crowd cheered loudly when Randy Pemberton interviewed

Dave. "Dave, we're glad to see your team in full force. How much longer will you be out of commission? I recall some pretty dynamic races when you were struggling for that first place position." Randy said.

"I hope it won't be much longer, Randy. Maybe next week's race, as soon as my doctor releases me."

"Good luck in today's race, Guy. We'll look forward to seeing you race again."

The engines were started, and the pace car slowly led them around the track. Dave and Ben talked to ease the tension. "How do you feel, Ben? Are you okay?"

"I'm fine.... a little shaky. But, we're gonna do well in today's race. This is a great position...third row inside. I'm gonna give it my best shot 'cause it's time the Colson-Masden team made their mark for this season. And, don't forget, as far as your buddy goes...ole Butch Smith is so far back there, all he can do is eat my dust!"

The race began and Rusty Wallace took the lead as Ben Colson and Dale Earnhardt challenged each other for second place.

"Watch that next turn, Ben. A caution flag's out...debris on the track...inside lane."

"I see it...and I missed it, Dave. Thanks."

"Here comes the yellow flag...can you get around Rusty before you get back to the line?"

"Well, he's got a pretty good lead. Do you believe it! I'm in second place. Man, this is great! Move over, Rusty, I'm comin' around." Ben said to himself as he managed to speed around the lead car, followed closely by Dale Earnhardt.

Dale increased his speed and drafted the #19 as their cars circled the track back to the line.

"How's the car handling, Ben?" Dave asked.

"Fine, real fine ... the guys in the crew did a great job! It's a little light in the corners, but handling well."

"Keep the car together and maintain your position. Kyle's movin' up behind you, watch him! Dale's trying to make a move on the outside...."

"Got 'em covered. I'm gonna lead the pack into the pits."

The lead cars pulled into the pit and refueled, changed all four tires and got their windshields wiped. Rusty's crew changed the tires and refueled in record time, enabling him to regain the lead. The other positions were maintained.... Rusty Wallace, Ben Colson, Dale Earnhardt and Kyle Petty in that order.

After a few caution laps, the green flag was waved and racing resumed, and the lead changed several times during the next fifty laps.

On the 100th lap, Dave yelled into the microphone. "Ben, slow your speed! There's a bad wreck at the wall in turn two. The caution flag's out again. Looks like this wreck was caused by our old buddy, Butch Smith."

"Got it...or in other words, I missed it. I cleared the wreck. Davey Allison almost tapped me. Yeah, you're right, Smith's out."

"Come on in for some fuel and tires, Man. Earnhardt's comin' in."

The pit crew was able to change the tires and refuel the #19 race car in less time than Earnhardt's or Petty's crew. Again, Rusty Wallace's crew performed in record time, allowing him to take the lead, followed closely by Ben Colson. The crowd roared, everyone was on their feet.

The lead position changed many more times that afternoon as first one car, then another, passed and charged into first place, awarding them the valuable five Winston Cup points for leading a lap. The crowd stood to its feet as lap-by-lap the leader changed.

Finally, there were only three laps remaining. Dave and Ben were in constant communication as their stress continued. They wanted this win so badly they could taste it.

Final lap.

Ben was so excited he could hardly contain his excitement as he raced towards the finish line in first place. Suddenly the car lunged; smoke poured from the engine and it crawled to a stop, barely missing an altercation with several cars. Ben was able to pull the Coca-Cola-sponsored cherry red race car into the grass. As Rusty Wallace crossed the finish line, Ben waited with his car to be towed to the garage.

Ben crawled out and threw his helmet into the car. The crew gathered around him and congratulated him on running a good race. They felt sad that Ben wasn't able to finish. It would have been a perfect race.

They watched as Rusty Wallace pulled into the Winner's Circle. "Man, I had this race in the bag..." Ben said sadly. "We should be in that circle."

"Shake it off, Man, you ran a good race. There'll be other races... more chances to win. Don't take it so hard. You were pushin' too hard. We could taste the win. Shake it off, Partner. You'll have another chance at Richmond!"

"Yeah, you're right. Rusty gave me a good fight...he had a car that wouldn't quit today. He's good....real good."

Millie and Lynne joined them in the pit. They were somber. "It's okay, Ben. It was a good race." Lynne said, trying to comfort him.

"We didn't need another D-N-F!" Ben said angrily. That's two in a row for us. Richmond's never been our track. What makes you think we'll do any better next week?"

"Well, Ben, if Doc says its okay, I want to drive next week," Dave said, with a firm tone.

"You are a most exasperating man!" Millie yelled, surprising Dave. She was normally so soft-spoken. The anger was evident on her beautiful face. "Don't make me watch you die, please. Don't take any chances. What if your hands start to bleed during the race?! What makes you think NASCAR will even allow you to race?"

"I've seen my hands...they're much better. The bleeding has completely stopped. If I get released, I'm going to run at Richmond. Can't you get it through your head? *I've GOT to do this!!?*"

"Why?"

"To once and for all get rid of the ghosts that haunt me. Ben understands my urgency. I've got to be whole before I can walk away

Take a Chance: True Love Waits

from racing. Then, I'll be free to love you. You deserve the love of a whole man!"

"I accept you the way your are, Dave, without change. You don't have to prove anything. You're more than enough man for me. I can't stand the thought of your being hurt again, or losing you."

"You need to understand, Honey, I'm hurtin' now. I've got to face this challenge. Then, *maybe I CAN walk away*. Time will tell on that one. You said you accept me just the way I am.... Well this is the way I am. Racing made me the man you see. Just trust me; I need you beside me through this, Millie ... today, tomorrow, and, God willing, at next week's race."

"Well, that's a week away. We'll see what Doc says."

"Okay. We'll see."

Millie wanted to change the subject before she let her anger get out of control. "Are we going to Clayton tomorrow to see the cabin? It must be finished by now. Ben said he'd fly us."

"Sure, we'll go as soon as Doc's finished with me in the morning. There's a small airport in Franklin, North Carolina. That's just across the border from Clayton, Georgia. I heard about a restaurant in a small town near there...the 'Trolley' or something. We'll make a day of it!" he suggested.

That evening, Millie and Dave took a walk in the crisp night air. There was a coolness between them. The issue of his racing could be a major obstacle because Dave was determined to race. However, their walk that evening was different than the other times. Dave felt as if a chasm, two miles wide, was now wedged between them.

He lay awake a long time that night, watching Millie peacefully sleeping in her twin bed. He prayed for safety, and *complete* healing so he could claim his new conquest—Millie's love. He wanted to marry her. In his heart, he knew that once they worked out this conflict, things would be better between them. Millie was independent; a survivor. She had gotten along fine without a man for over seven years. Did she really need him? Would she agree to stand beside him as he faced his challenges? He knew they both needed to get past their fears, in order to deal with their insecurities.

What can I offer her if I don't feel like a man, he thought. Once he had challenged his fears, Millie would be his next conquest. If she would have him, he would ask her to be his precious life mate. He prayed to God that he'd be able to pull off the special surprise he was planning. "Oh, Lord, thank You so much for allowing this beautiful woman to love me so much, for putting so much love in her heart for me. I am truly a blessed man."

Chapter Twelve

Doc arrived early the next morning. "Well, I'll be able to remove these bandages in a few more days, Dave. In the meantime, I'll leave your fingers completely free so you'll be able to use them. Your arms are almost completely healed. Your hands, though, are still mending. You'll still experience some pain as the nerve endings continue to mend. This new skin is tough like leather. It doesn't have much elasticity at this point. I can't caution you enough. You'll still have to be extremely careful with your hands and forearms."

"I wish you could take the bandages off today, Doc. We're going to Georgia to see a cabin that Millie decorated. I'd be great to feed myself... and a few other things I'd like to do with my hands." Dave joked.

"Let's leave them on until.... um...maybe Thursday morning. If I like what I see then, the bandages will come off. By the way, you know that test you asked me to run? Your blood is free of any kind of disease."

"Thanks, that's good to know."

"Now, remember, Dave, some areas on your hands are still pretty raw. If you're careful, a few more days should do it. You damaged all three layers of skin. It takes time for your body to heal. It could have been worse. You could have had skin graphs...or we may have had to amputate. No, I'm sorry, Dave, the bandages must stay on!"

"Oh, okay, Doc. What can I say?"

The flight to Franklin only took a few minutes. They rented a car at the airport and Ben followed Millie's map to the cabin that was situated at the very top of a mountain in the southern part of Clayton, Georgia. They found the beautiful wooded gravel road leading them to the cabin, which was entirely secluded from the road.

At first Millie just sat in the car and stared at the outside of the cabin. She didn't say anything.

"Hopefully, everything has arrived, and the work crew had been there to arrange the furniture and hang the drapes. I can't wait to see how it turned out." Lynne said.

"Well, come on. Let's see what a good job you did!" Dave insisted as he managed to open his car door by himself. "There are curtains in the windows so they've probably been here."

Millie knocked at the door. There was no answer. Ben tried the doorknob. The cabin was unlocked, so they cautiously stepped inside.

Dave glanced around the room proudly. "It looks like yours, Mil'. Whoever owns this place wanted you to duplicate your place. Well, you've done it! I can't believe you were able put the cabin together in only two weeks. This is amazing! You sketched each room and the sketches came to life."

"Do you know who owns this cabin?" Ben asked.

"No, Lisa wouldn't tell me. All she said was it belongs to a celebrity."

"Maybe if we look around, we'll find a clue. Let's see what we can find out without making a mess, okay?" Lynne suggested excitedly, with a menacing gleam in her eye.

They walked around the immaculate cabin. It was fully stocked with food, ready for occupancy; however, there were no visible clues regarding ownership.

As they walked around, Millie moved a few accent pieces until she was happy with the presentation. She also put her special potpourri in little baskets and sat them in crucial areas, which immediately flooded the room with a very pleasant apple-cinnamon fragrance.

"Well, I guess they haven't brought any of their personal belongings in yet." Ben surmised.

They suddenly heard the sound of a car moving on the gravel road. The car stopped in front of the cabin; and, they listened as a car door slammed. Millie was apprehensive because she knew Lisa would be angry if she found them at the cabin. The door opened. It was Lee Henderson!

"What are you guys doing here? How did you find out about this place? No one knows I bought this cabin. It was supposed to be my hideaway." Lee exclaimed.

"You're not gonna believe this, Man. Millie decorated it! The cabin you saw in the video was hers." Dave explained. "She does contract work for Lisa, your decorator. We came down to make sure everything worked out. Look at these sketches. She did the decorating without actually seeing the cabin. Lisa takes the credit; but, my friend, Millie did the work!"

"Well, Millie, our paths have crossed again." Lee said, taking her hand. "It's a small world, isn't it? But, I insist this cabin must remain our secret...you understand."

"No problem, Lee. Lisa didn't tell me who the cabin belongs to.... She kept your secret. You can count on us for secrecy as well."

Lee looked around the cabin and again took Millie's hand. "You know your stuff; you did a fabulous job! This turned out much better than I expected. You shouldn't be riding on someone else's coat-tails. You could do this on your own! Lisa gave me the impression that she did all the decorating. I get it! You have the talent; she takes the credit. She needs you...but you don't need her!"

"If you don't mind our invading your privacy a few more minutes, Lee, I'd like to sketch the outside of the cabin. If you like, you can keep the sketch. It's something I like to do for my clients."

"Sure, have at it. We'll talk while you sketch. They were supposed to get some groceries in, maybe some coffee. I'll make some coffee so you can work." Lee suggested. "Ben, Dave, want a beer or somethin'?"

"No, coffee's fine."

"Tell you what, Lee, I'll make the coffee. You guys sit down at this gorgeous new table and talk. Oh, I love the matching place mats and table runner. It looks like its a thousand years old …" Lynne insisted.

Millie walked outside to work on her sketch while Dave and Lee talked about the accident. "So, Dave, tell me, how're you doing? It's been almost three weeks. I see you still have some mean-looking' bandages." Lee remarked.

"I'm healing, Man, slowly but surely. Doc says I'll get the bandages off in a few days. If he releases me in time, I want to race at Richmond. Millie's against it; but it's something I have to do, Lee. If I don't get back into that car, I'll never be able to race again. I've harbored some fears ever since that wreck I had a couple years ago. Remember? It may have been the actual cause for my marriage hitting the rocks. Millie gets upset with me if I mention racing again; but I don't think she understands why it's so important. What would you do?"

"Man, I'm not gonna tell you to get back in one of those cars. Even if the bandages come off, you may not retain full use of your hands. Remember the sponsors!" Ben injected.

"Ben, cut him some slack and listen to what he's saying!" Lee suggested.

Then, looking at Dave, he said, "Only you can answer that question. A man has to do what a man has to do, regardless of what Ben or Millie think. If you think you've got to do it…. Then you've gotta do it! Maybe I'll come up for the race next Sunday and see what you decide."

"You've been a good friend, Lee. You'll enjoy this cabin. I'm so proud of Millie I could burst for her being able to decorate it in only two weeks. She's incredible."

"How's everything between you two?" Lee asked.

"Fantastic. I think its *L-O-V-E*! You know, Lee, we're still on our first date. She came with us when we came back to North Carolina. We haven't been apart since we left Brandon to go to Daytona. Our first date hasn't ended yet!"

"Wow! This could be a Guinness record—a three-week date. That's a songwriter's dream. If I remember right, Millie's a widow. Her husband was a cop who was killed in the line of duty. This could be a bad scene for her.... to fall in love with a race driver who challenges death every time he crawls into the car."

"It's a challenge I have to meet. Millie needs to put her husband's accident behind her, too; and face her fears. We're trying to help each other through it."

"I understand, Dave. Good luck with the challenge, and with Millie. She seems to be good for you."

"Hopefully, she cares enough to stand by me, to wait while I work through this insecurity problem"

"I tell you the truth, Lee," Ben said, "At first I couldn't see what Dave saw in Millie. I thought he'd lost his marbles. Now that I've gotten to know her, she's a jewel."

"You'd better be talkin' about me, Ben Colson!" Lynne joked as she sat down at the table after overhearing the end of the conversation.

"We were talking about Millie."

"Boy, she's something else. She's been like a nurse to Dave, shaving him, giving him backrubs; and, you know what, she gave me some great ideas for our house, didn't she, Ben? The other day, she found a 17th Century antique double-shaker desk that was in Class A condition. She found it but she knew I wanted it. So, she bought it and asked them to deliver it to our house."

"You're kidding!" Ben said. "Why did you let her do it?"

"Well, to be honest, we had a little bet. I bet her an antique that Dave would be able to win Jake over to his side. You all saw how his attitude changed at the hospital. Well, she paid off her bet....and I let her. It was more of a joke to me; but, Millie, insisted on paying her bet. She said she wanted me to have it because we've been so hospitable. She's not been a problem at all...in fact, she's been a big help. She's been helping me with the fan club, too. We've become good friends in this short period of time

...better than Pat and I could ever have been. She wouldn't help with the fan club. Yes, I have to agree, Dave's found himself a priceless gem."

"I know, I've got to find a way to keep her." Dave remarked. "I can't begin to tell you how much she's done for me since I've been laid up. She was always there for me."

"Boy, Dave, you'd better grab her before she gets away..." Lee suggested.

Millie came back into the cabin and sat down at the table to put the finishing touches on her sketch. Then she autographed it and handed it to Dave. He looked at it, winked at her, and handed the sketch to Lee Henderson. He silently stared at the picture.

"You drew this in just those few minutes; your talent continues to amaze me. Thank you, Millie. I'll have this framed and hang it over the fireplace. I'll treasure it always.

"You're welcome, Lee. Enjoy your cabin. Lynne helped me with the accent pieces. Even though we didn't know we were decorating it for you, it was a pleasure to do it for you. Again, let me assure you, this cabin will remain our secret. We know the value of privacy, don't we?" Everyone agreed.

"Lee, I heard about a great restaurant nearby. Would you join us for lunch? I saw a billboard when we came through Clayton. It's only a few miles away. There's also a German village nearby."

"Thanks, I appreciate the invite; but I'll pass this time. I'm really suffering from burnout, and need to just kick back and relax. I don't want to hear a sound except the crickets chirping outside. Give me a rain check, okay? We'll do it next time ...my treat!"

"You can count on it, Man!" Ben said affirmatively. "If everyone's ready, we'll get out of here and let Lee enjoy his crickets. Hopefully, we'll see you at the race Sunday..."

Lee hugged Millie and Lynne, and shook hands with Ben. He slapped Dave on the back instead of shaking his bandaged hand. "Thanks for everything! I'm very happy with the decorating! The cabin looks better than I expected."

Lunch at the Trolley was refreshing. Several people recognized Dave and asked for his autograph. Since he couldn't write very well because of the thick bandages on the top of his hands and palms, they had to settle for Ben's signature.

The return flight to Southern Pines was smooth and uneventful. The next three days were filled with anxiety and ever-building tension between Millie and Dave as he continued to talk, almost excessively, about racing the car in Richmond. His dream hinged on whether Doc would remove the bandages; and, if NASCAR would allow him to qualify.

The next morning, Dave and Millie went to Church to talk to Father Thomas, who informed Dave that, according to Church doctrine, he would be able to receive the full Sacrament of Holy Matrimony if he decided to get married again. The annulment had been granted.

Thursday morning, as promised, Doc removed Dave's bandages. "You must be extremely careful, Dave." he warned. "If you have another injury, the damage could be permanent. There's some scarring; but the burns are almost completely healed. As the nerves continue their healing process, you'll still experience some pain and tenderness. Your skin is very sensitive; and; if it would be re-injured at this point, you could lose your hands, or arms. It's important that you apply this ointment twice a day." He instructed as he rubbed the lotion on Dave's arms. The swirling motions were hurting Dave; but, he didn't wince, not once.

"I want to race this weekend, Doc. Will you release me?"

"What!?! After everything you've been through? I can't believe you'd think about getting back into a racer. You're hopeless!"

"I have to, Doc. I'm not going to take the time to explain. Trust me on this; I have to get back into that car as soon as possible."

"I can't believe you're serious; but, I have no choice but to sign your release." Doc said reluctantly, shaking his head in disbelief as he signed the papers.

"Thanks, Doc. I can't wait to take a shower by myself. Baths are okay; but I'm a shower man. I appreciate everything you've done for me. But, right now, I've gotta go so I can get qualified for the race, okay?"

"I guess so...but, please, Dave; be careful."

"I will, Doc. I've got everything to live for. I hope you understand my urgency."

"I understand more than you think I do. Just don't make me patch you up again. Tell you what; to be on the safe side, I want you to wear these elastic bandage sleeves and these thick rubber gloves for a few more days. You can take them off when you're relaxing."

Dave excitedly ran into the living room to show Millie and Ben that Doc had removed the bandages. Millie walked over to look at the burn scars. The healing process had been incredible—like a miracle. His arms and hands were almost like new, with only a few deep scars.

Millie quickly kissed him and stroked his arms gently. Dave saw tears start to pool in her blue eyes. He hugged her, and looked away, trying to ignore her pain.

"Thank God I don't have to wipe your furry butt any more, Man. That's taking friendship a little too far!" Ben teased.

"It wasn't a thrill for me, either. Guess what, Doc released me. I'll qualify the car tomorrow." he said, trying to contain his excitement. "Let's go to the track and pace the car, Pard. Come on, Millie; let's go to the practice track."

She paled, visibly shaken. It never occurred to her that he would actually be able to drive in the next race. She never dreamt he'd be so anxious to take the reins again. After all, she reasoned, he'd said he was ready to quit.

Unable to speak, she stuttered, searching for a word. Tears spilled onto her cheeks. She shook her head and walked to the window so Dave wouldn't see the fear in her tear-filled eyes.

When she turned back around, Doc was slipping the elastic sleeves onto Dave's arms, and they were laughing....some private joke. Then she heard Dave say...

"Come on, Ben, I need this race! I know I'm the mechanical genius and you're the driver extraordinaire; but *I need one more race.* One more win! Then, I'll be your crew chief, let you do most of the driving…talk you through every race to victory. *One more win and I'll quit!*"

Millie could no longer be silent. "Yeah, if that *one* race doesn't kill you! You've been toying with my emotions, Dave! You made me care for you; all the time, knowing you were going to get back into that car. I don't think I can watch you race…. and I certainly can't watch you die!"

The emotional outbreak was so unlike Millie. They all stared at her, not believing the venomous tone to her words.

Lynne heard the commotion and came into the living room. "Millie, come on. I'll go to the track with you. You can take a lap or two with Dave. Then, after that, we'll talk. I know exactly how you feel."

They got into the front seat of Dave's truck and he drove them to their practice track, followed closely by Ben and Lynne in their Thunderbird. The ride was quiet, anger evident on Millie's face.

Dave finally said, trying to get her to relax, "Boy, its cold in here!"

Silence.

"Come on, Mill', lighten up…. I could use a smile."

Silence.

When they got to the track, Dave helped Millie get into the race car. Since there was only one seat, she had to sit on the floor on a cushion, between two steel supports.

Remembering their conversation when they first met regarding getting into the race car, and wanting to break the silence between them, Dave remarked, "See, that wasn't so hard, was it, getting into the car."

Silence.

Dave shrugged and hit the starter button. The engine roared. He pulled onto the track and revved the motor, shifting gears rapidly as he paced the car.

Millie watched as Dave cautiously and carefully maneuvered the turns. She couldn't help herself; she became excited by their speed as they rounded the track. She surprised herself because she loved the incredible sound of the motor…the tires on the track.

She noticed the instrument panel; gauges kept Dave informed about the rpm's, oil pressure, gas level, temperature, even the tire pressure. The well-built racing machine impressed her. Without expecting it and not wanting to surrender to it, she found herself caught up in the excitement and the challenge of racing.

Dave pulled into the grass on turn four and said, "I want you to drive the car for a lap or two so you can experience, first-hand, the power. You said you love a challenge. Well, I'm challenging you to do something unforgettable."

Reluctantly, Millie changed places with Dave and positioned herself into the driver's seat. She fastened the safety harness and adjusted the face shield on the helmet so she could see better.

Shifting gears, she pulled onto the track, very slowly at first...then at a faster pace.

"Take it easy on the turns, Millie. They're slick and racing tires don't have tread. We don't need to break any speed records on this lap." Dave teased.

The first turn went well. Millie felt a little more comfortable. She pushed the gas pedal and shifted gears until she had increased the speed to sixty miles per hour. It felt as if she was going much faster as the car rounded the corners.

Dave helped her maneuver the next two turns as she began another lap. The cherry red race car slid on the third turn and spun completely around on the last turn. With Dave's help, she pulled into the grass.

"Wow! You're right, Dave. This is great! I don't ever want to take those turns at the speeds you guys drive; but, I have to tell you, it is thrilling."

"What'd I tell you; and, while I'm racing, I have someone talking to me the whole time, letting me know how I'm doing and what pitfalls are ahead."

"That's what you do when Ben races?"

"Yes, our spotters keep an eye on the track, too, because I can't always see a wreck. When a wreck happens, sometimes the driver can't see for the smoke. The spotters are located around the track and immediately radio to the crew chief where the wrecked vehicles are located. Then, I tell Ben to go high or low, depending on the location of the wrecked cars so he won't crash into them."

"Ben does the same for you when you're racing?"

"Yes, he does. In my entire career, I've only had one wreck that was life-threatening; that is, except for what happened at Daytona."

"But, there's so much action on the track. Bumps and scrapes between drivers … little love taps."

"You need to understand, we hit the fence, or the wall, pretty often. It's what racing's about – like I said, competitive 'love' taps between drivers. We call it 'rubbing'. They're nothing to be concerned about. One driver will get behind another and draft him…follow really close until he causes the car to get loose. If he's not willing to move over so you can go around him, the drafting may cause him to lose control so you can take his position."

"And you call this fun?"

"It's a ball! Slide over," he commanded, "I want to go a few more laps and check out this engine. Do you want to come with me? I'll be careful."

"Well, I'm already here. Let's go!"

"Before we pull out, I want you to see how sturdy this car is built. It's like a protective steel cage. See all the braces, roll bars, support brackets. They put *every safety device known to man* in these cars. The seat will be custom-designed to fit my body. It's as safe as possible. You don't hear about deadly wrecks very often anymore, do you?"

She didn't answer. She looked around the car, just as he'd instructed, noticing all the safety devices. "What's that?" she asked, pointing to a piece of equipment which was wrapped in silver matting.

"That, my Dear, is one of the many built in fire extinguishers. They use heat wraps to protect us from the heat generated by the motors. It gets pretty hot in these things when you're racing continuously at two hundred miles per hour."

Dave put the car through its paces as he listened carefully to the sound of the engine and transmission. After three laps, he pulled into the garage.

"Well, what did you think?" Lynne asked Millie.

"It was neat! I'm glad he kept the speed under ninety, though!"

"Let's go to lunch...then I'll take a couple more practice laps before we pack up the car to go to Richmond." Dave suggested.

Millie couldn't help but notice Dave's sudden confidence. She was scared for him; but she knew, deep in her heart, that he needed to race again. She was trying to understand why it was so important.

Although the other three members of their luncheon foursome were cheerful, Millie was somber. Her lunch was delicious; but she couldn't seem to eat. The food was lodged by the "lump" in her throat.

After lunch, they went back to the track; and, after a few practice laps, Dave signaled to Ben to clock him. As he spun the track at incredible speeds, Millie's head was swimming. She was apprehensive. Could she hold her own with such a dynamic personality as Dave Masden? Was she only fooling herself, she wondered.

Ben told them Dave clocked in at 163.8 in their practice run. Dave felt he could do better; but, instead of taking another run, he pulled the #19 into their garage.

"Charlie, I don't like the way this motor sounds. Let's change it out before we pack up to go to Richmond."

Looking at Millie, he said, "We may be here all day. Can you entertain yourself for awhile so we can get our work done?"

"Sure, you know I can. I don't need a baby sitter!" she replied. Then, whispering, she asked Dave, "I didn't do anything to the car, did I?"

"Of course not, Silly, but, before you leave, I want a hug. It's been a long time since I've been able to put my arms around you without those bandages. "I want to touch you."

He pulled her against him and kissed her passionately in full view of Charlie and the crew. They cheered as the kiss broke. Millie was embarrassed and pulled back.

Then she smiled and whispered, "I have you tell you, Dave. You're different since you got out of that car. You're more confident, more sure of yourself."

"You ain't seen nothin' yet, Darlin'! But, this is one of those times we talked about. I need to work on this car; concentrate on what I'm doing so I'll do better in qualifying tomorrow at Richmond. We've got a busy couple of days ahead of us before the race," he said as he patted her on the bottom in a loving gesture. "It'll be a while.... I'll see you later." He was all business.

As Millie drove them back to the house in Dave's pick-up truck, Lynne explained that she spends every race praying for Ben, and that was mainly why she tries to never miss a race.

"Even though things were bad between us at Daytona, I had to be there. It was a good thing I was.... Can you imagine seeing that accident on television and not being able to be with Ben?"

"I understand that philosophy. Because of my past, though, I'm not sure I'm ready to commit my future to someone who takes risks for his profession. I've already done that once and it didn't work out so well...."

"Their choice to live life to the fullest is one of the reasons we love them so much. When you love a driver, it's a love so deep you'll become spoiled. They live hard and love hard. I guarantee you'll walk around with a smile on your face all the time. All the time, that is, except during the race. That's when you'll be praying for their safety. I want to show you some of their racing videos when we get back to the house. Ben and Dave are a great team of professionals who work very hard perfecting their vocation."

That afternoon, Millie and Lynne went to Mass and prayed for the safety of all the drivers. Then, they went home and watched videos of previous races. She watched the video of Dave's accident two years prior. It was difficult to watch.

Finally, Lynne held up another video, explaining, "This one just came. I've not seen it yet. It's Daytona. Are you up for it?"

"I've got to see it. Put it in..." Millie said, taking a deep breath. She watched Lynne put the tape into the V-C-R.

"Look, the car was doing great until Butch Smith hit Ben. He lost control and flipped. Oh, God, there's Dave rushing to pull him from that car. Look at that, they tackled him to the ground to keep him from going to the car. He pulled away and charged right into the flames. Oh, God, look at that! All that fire! By all rights, Ben should have died in that wreck! Dave saved his life, there's no doubt about it." Lynne exclaimed.

"It's the most heroic thing I've ever seen...." Millie said, her voice breaking.

"Don't you see? Dave has to prove to himself, and to you, that he's not afraid to get back into the car. He's got to face his fear, or he'll never get past it. He needs your support, Millie. I'll be with you, talking you through it.... praying with you for his protection."

Millie couldn't say anything. Tears spilled onto her cheek and rolled down her chin. Then unable to contain herself, Lynne got tears in her eyes, too. They hugged each other; afraid for the men they loved.

"I don't want to lose him. I'm in love with him, Lynne."

"I know you are. Does he know it?"

"No, not really, we've talked around it but never really said the words. Things have been a little cool between us for the last few days."

"Why don't you tell him before the race?"

"I will...at least I plan.... ah, I'll try to...."

"Come on, Millie, let's fry some chicken, make some potato salad and take one of your apple pies to the garage. They won't stop and eat unless we make them. If I know them, they'll be there most of the night."

When they arrived with the food, everyone was happy to see them. Ben, Dave, Charlie and the crew washed their hands and ate every crumb of food in record time.

Millie was clearing up the mess when Dave came up behind her and slipped his arms around her waist. "Oh, you feel so good. I'm so glad I can hold you again. Is everything okay? You're so quiet."

"I'm fine." Millie whispered as she leaned her head against his chest. "I'm scared to death that I'll lose you. I lost the first man I loved in an accident; I don't want to lose you...I care too much for you."

"You could never care *TOO* much for me, Millie. I need you to care.... You're my woman. I need every ounce of love you can spare. I.... ah, I guess I....*love*...I mean, I *KNOW* I love you," he whispered.

She turned around and looked at him intently. She wanted to tell him she loved him, too; but the words stuck in her throat. He took her hands and placed them on his face. He closed his eyes, savoring the gentleness of her touch. He kissed her palms and smiled. He needed to hear the words she couldn't say; but, he understood that she wasn't able to say them right then.

She buried her face in his chest, welcoming his embrace. The T-shirt he was wearing absorbed the tears falling from her eyes. He kissed her gently. "Come on, Lady, dry up those tears. I'll be okay, I promise."

"I'm trying to understand, Dave; I really am. Lynne and I had a talk this afternoon. I saw the footage of your first accident; and, we watched the video from Daytona, it was the most incredible thing I ever saw."

"I'd do the same thing for you, Millie. Try not to think about the negative aspects of racing. Build on the positive ... how great it is to win. It's fun going to the different tracks. You'll love piddling around in the antique shops with Lynne while we're getting ready for a race. Can't you see God at work here? He won't fail us now."

"I know, I'm working on my attitude."

"Good, well, I've got to get back to work. I'll see you later. Let's see, what are the words to that song you like so well.... Oh, yes, *'you've got a good love comin' from me tonight'*.... remember that. It may not be tonight, but it will be soon, I hope. Think about that, I dare you!"

She gave him an exasperated look. Then she noticed her make-up had soiled his shirt. "Oh, you! Look what I've done to your shirt. It's your fault; you made me cry with your sweet words. What a mess."

Dave hugged her and kissed her again. "If you didn't care about me, you wouldn't cry. Your tears show me you care more than you're willing to admit. I'm right, aren't I?"

She smiled and didn't say anything. In the back of her mind she knew she loved him. She *wanted* to tell him. She knew he needed to hear the words, and hoped she would be able to tell him before the race ...but first, she had to make sure she could commit her future to such a dynamic man.

"Don't wait up for us, Honey. I'll see you when I get there, okay?" Dave said as he walked back into the garage.

"Can I do anything to help you?" Millie asked.

"No, Darlin' but I appreciate you asking. If you're here, I'll never get my work done. You're too much of a distraction!" he teased. "I'll be home as soon as we get finished. Remember that night in your office? I told you they'd be times when I'd need you to understand. This is one of those times."

"How are your hands and arms doing? Are you having any pain?" she asked.

"Oh, a little...but it's not too bad. These elastic sleeves and gloves help a lot. I'm tough!" he said, joyfully making a fist and gritting his teeth with a throaty growl.

She smiled and watched him walk away. She trembled with delight at the thought that soon they could express their desire for each other. They could extinguish the flames of desire that had been building between them for the past three weeks. A little voice in the back of her mind kept repeating.... *"True love waits."* Could they wait, she wondered. She wanted him so badly she ached.

Lynne and Millie went back to the house and watched the movie, *"Pure Country."*

After the movie ended, Lynne called the garage. "Well, we'd better go to bed; they're not finished. Ben said they'd be home later. I know what that means.... We might see them before dawn. But, don't worry, they're fine."

Millie went to the bedroom she'd been sharing with Dave and took a shower. She put on a cute ruffled nightgown she'd bought earlier that week. After a half-hour of restless tossing, she fell asleep. The little voice in her head kept repeating.... *True love waits.... true love waits...true love waits."*

It was almost three o'clock in the morning when she heard Dave get into the other twin bed. She longed for him to come to her but he didn't.

In only a short few minutes, he was breathing deeply, obviously asleep. Millie turned over in her bed and faced the wall. Soon she was able to go back to sleep. She was exhausted, troubled, frustrated.

Daybreak awoke her the next morning. She wondered what the day had in store.

"Good mornin', Princess. How are you?"

"Sleepy, I guess." she replied nonchalantly.

"I'm pretty tired, too. It was after three when I came to bed this morning. But, I'm excited, too, because I've got a big day ahead of me. The car's on its way to Richmond in the semi, along with Charlie and the crew. We've got to get movin' and fly to Richmond so I can get qualified today. Millie, I haven't been this excited over a race in a long time. If everything works out the way I hope, I'll have a big surprise for you after the race."

"What kind of surprise?" she queried.

"No hints.... something I started planning a few days ago, and when we were working on the car. It's a surprise."

"Well, Dave, I'll stay for this race; but, then, I've got to go home. Before we left Brandon, I called Roberta, my neighbor. She's been keeping an eye on everything for

me, and bringing in my mail. I'll need to go home and pay some bills. Utility companies in Florida aren't very patient. If a bill isn't paid, they'll disconnect the service. Since I don't have the bills with me, I can't send them a check."

"You could call and find out how much your bill is.... Then send a check." he suggested. "Or, you could call Roberta and have her send them to you. I remember you saying you asked her to get your mail every day because you didn't have time to stop it at the post office. I'll give you the address."

"Yeah, I could; but, I need to go home. Lisa may have some work for me. She probably wants to pay me for Lee's job. And, I need to call Jake. He doesn't know how to get in touch with me." She reasoned, adding every possible excuse for leaving.

"Well, those things can all be handled by phone calls. You can call Lisa, Jake, and Roberta. Lisa can send your check here. If it's a question of money, I'll be happy to give you some."

"No, that's not the problem. *I need to go home.*"

"Oh, I get it. You have an excuse for every suggestion I make.... You'll go home even though I want you to stay?"

"I've got to, Dave. I said I'd stay until this race; but, then it's time to go home."

"But, our date's not over until you leave, right?"

"I suppose so, Dave."

"Good, I'll do everything I can to keep you here...to persuade you not to leave," he challenged.

Dave went into the bathroom. Within minutes, Millie heard him whistling in the shower. She wanted to go into the bathroom and join him as he showered...to have her way with him.

"*True love waits.... true love waits...true love waits.*" The words kept repeating themselves in her head as she dared herself to go into the bathroom.... to try to regain what they had lost. She'd have her way with Dave.

The words kept repeating... "*true love waits...*" She grabbed a pillow and put it over her head, frustrated by her conscience, her desire to make love with Dave. Finally, she heard the shower stop. She no longer had to wrestle with her idea. It was too late. The window of opportunity had closed.

When Dave came out of the bathroom a few minutes later, he'd shaved and dressed. He smelled musky...had a very masculine demeanor. "It's more fun when you shave me, Honey. I'm gonna miss that...but now that my hands are healed, it's time I take care of myself again."

"You look nice. That's the outfit you were wearing when we met, isn't it?"

"Yeah, come to think of it, I was wearing this shirt then. We'll probably leave in an hour or so. You'd better pack an overnight bag, because we'll be there a couple nights."

"I'm going to pack all my things. I'll get a flight from Richmond back to Tampa."

Dave was stunned by her stinging words. He didn't say anything. In his mind, he could feel Millie was slipping away from him. But he knew he had until after the race to change her mind...to make things right between them...to claim his gift... his precious Millie. But, first, he had to feel worthy to grab the golden ring...and place it on her finger.

"Well, Mil', if that's how you feel, that's that." He said. "Don't close your mind to the idea of putting our lives together. It's possible, isn't it?"

"I don't know, Dave. We'll see."

"Yes, YOU WILL SEE," he challenged. "Don't give up on me yet."

At first she didn't say anything. She was sitting on the side of her twin bed, looking at the floor. "I'll get dressed and pack my things. I'll see you downstairs in a few minutes."

"Great! I'll have some coffee and juice waiting for you. It's time I wait on you for a change."

She didn't say anything. She watched him leave, closing the door behind him.

She felt as if she had water in her veins that morning. It was a struggle to get up...to get dressed and pack. She styled her hair and applied her make-up.

She was glad they hadn't been intimate. At this point, she could still walk away.... escape to her 'safe haven'...the emotional shell where she's been hiding for the past seven years. One way or the other, she was scared to death of losing Dave. She'd rather lose him by choice, by walking away, rather than see him die in a wreck. She'd tried to pull him inside her safe haven; but he refused. He was determined to challenge life.

The merry-go-round ride with Dave had been fun; but it was time to get off. She opted not to make a grab for the golden ring.

Ben, Lynne and Dave were sitting around the table when she came downstairs. They watched as Millie put her bags near the front door. Dave had already told them Millie had said she would be going home after the race. They were somber when she walked over and sat down.

Millie sipped her juice. It tasted very sweet. She continued to drink it until she'd finished the glass. No one said a word.

"What time are we leaving for Richmond, Ben?"

"In a few minutes, Millie. The plane's gassed up and ready. Richmond isn't very far away. Dave's set to qualify at two o'clock. We'll need to check the car before qualifying." he replied.

"Will we be staying at a hotel?" she asked.

"Yes, we got reservations for two rooms."

"Do you think they'll have another room?" she asked.

"I doubt it. Our motel is the closest one to the track. It fills up first." Lynne said, surprised by Millie's question. She stared at Millie. She wondered what had happened since the previous night. "Millie, what's wrong?"

"Oh, nothing, I just need to go home. I've got bills to pay and things to do. I'll stay until after the race; then I've got to go home. I'll take a commercial flight from Richmond."

Everyone was shocked by Millie's sudden decision. Lynne decided not to push the issue because she'd get a chance to talk to her later, away from Dave. She didn't want Millie to just waltz out of their lives either.

"Don't worry, Millie." Dave said. "You can have my room. If you don't want me around, I'll sleep in the trailer.... But I have to tell you, I don't understand what's wrong. Everything was fine yesterday."

"I can't explain it myself. I feel the need to go home. Forgive me for bringing everyone down. Come on; let's cheer up. You've both got to qualify the car today, right? I want you to do well. Let's shelve this conversation until after the race, okay?"

"Okay." Dave agreed. "I promise you, though, I'm not going to let you just walk out of my life. I love you, Millie. I'm not afraid to say it in front of Lynne and Ben."

"*We all love you*, Millie." Lynne said. "*Please don't leave.* If you have to go home, fine, we'll fly you. You can take care of your business and come back with us."

"I'm not making any promises right now."

"Well, at least you didn't say 'no'...." Dave said. "I'll *'have the pedal to the metal'* trying to change your mind."

She didn't say anything, but his play on words made her smile. She looked down at her coffee cup. The topic of conversation was changed and the mood lightened as they prepared to leave for their Richmond adventure.

While Millie and Lynne rinsed the dishes and put them in the dishwasher, Dave came over and hugged her. "Don't leave me...." he whispered.

"I can't very well stay with you forever!" she remarked.

"Why not?" he injected and walked away. She stood quietly. Tears welled in her eyes. She looked at Lynne as tears spilled onto her cheek. Lynne handed her a paper towel.

"Are you okay?"

"God, Lynne, what am I going to do? I'm crazy about that man; but, I'm scared to death of him, too."

"There's nothing to be afraid of. You'll see."

The flight to Richmond was uneventful and quiet. Ben and Dave sat in the cockpit while Lynne and Millie sat in the back.

Once they'd landed, Ben told Lynne. "I'm going to get qualified for tomorrow's BUSCH race since Dave's going to drive for Winston Cup on Sunday. I've got to qualify before noon."

"Okay, Ben. Why don't you get the rental car? We'll drop you guys off at the track, and we'll check into the hotel. Maybe Millie will talk to me.... Tell me what's wrong."

Their rental car was a Navy Blue Thunderbird. They climbed inside and Ben drove to the track. Charlie and the crew were unpacked and had everything ready to go.

Both cars were shined, glistening in the sun, ready to be qualified.

"We'll be back in time for your qualifying runs, Honey." Lynne said. "I'll bring Millie with me, if she'll come."

"Okay." Ben said as he waved her away. Dave overheard the conversation and ran after them.

"Millie, Honey, wait a minute." he insisted.

She stopped walking and turned around.

"Will you come back for the qualification runs? I'd like you to be here."

"Sure ...okay, I guess I can do that."

"I need a kiss to hold me until then." He said, pulling her into his arms. Dave knew she belonged in his arms. He couldn't comprehend the thought of losing her.

At first she felt cold and rigid in his arms, not at all the warm, passionate woman he'd fallen in love with. He continued to kiss her until she surrendered and threw her arms around him, returning his passionate kisses. They were breathless when the kiss ended.

"That's much better. I'll see you in a little while, Sweetheart." he whispered and walked away.

As he walked past her, Lynne patted him on the back. She wanted things to work out, too.

"Oh, Lord, Lynne, what am I going to do?" Millie said. "I love him so much I ache. I don't think I can stand by his side, week-after-week, while he challenges death. I can't do it again. I'm not strong enough."

"Come on, Millie, lighten up. Dave's crazy about you. You're stronger than you think. I don't know if I could have had the strength to do what you've done … the way you've helped Dave and cheered him up, taking care of him when he was in pain. He loves you."

"I know, Lynne. He told me last night at the garage."

"Love is a priceless gift. You and Dave can have a happy life together. He won't be racing for the rest of his life. They'll be lots of time for the two of you to be together. It takes a special person to be a race car driver's wife. But, it's a good life...well worth the risks, I assure you."

"It's hard being a policeman's wife, too, because of all the stress they face every day. But, I've changed. I'm not that kind of person. I'm not like you, Lynne."

"You're exactly that kind of person. You're exactly what Dave needs. You'll keep him focused. You need to remove the burden from his shoulders about your leaving after the race. He doesn't need to be thinking about that this afternoon.... or during the race. He *loves* you. I know you love him. You've just got cold feet."

"Heck, my feet are *frozen!*" she joked to lighten the mood.

"Let Dave thaw them out, then. He wants to...."

They checked into their motel down the street from the track. The rooms were large, each containing two beds. After they'd put their bags inside and freshened up, they drove back to the track.

Chapter Thirteen

"The BUSCH time trials will be first... then the WINSTON CUP guys. Ben's gonna get qualified for BUSCH... probably in a few minutes." Lynne explained to Millie.

When they got to the track, Ben was ready to take his run. He got a good-luck kiss from Lynne and positioned himself inside the car. As he pulled away, he waved and gave a "thumbs-up" signal.

After a couple practice laps, he signaled to NASCAR that he was ready to take his qualifying lap. He was the last one to qualify for Busch—barely got in under the line. The green flag was waved.

Ben raced the car around the track at an unbelievable speed, clocking in at 183.9. He was ecstatic when he returned to the pit. The crew congratulated him.

Since none of the other drivers had managed to beat his speed, he was awarded the pole position for Saturday's race. Everyone cheered. Their earned victory had been a long time in coming; Ben couldn't remember the last time he'd had a pole position.

"That's great, Ben! You've broken the record for this track." Dave congratulated him.

"Let's see you do the same, Partner.

"I'm gonna give it my best shot!"

"Boy, I have to tell you, this feels good. You've got that championship gleam in your eye."

"So do you. Isn't it great?"

"I've missed it, Masden...seeing that look in your eye. If you do as well on your run, we've got this track locked up."

"Boy, Partner, I was ready to walk away. Sell you my assets. Kiss racing goodbye forever."

"So was I. I'm glad you didn't walk away."

"Me, too! This is going to be our track...a big victory is waiting for us both!"

"Right, Dave!"

After lunch, it was time for Dave to take his qualification run. He hugged Millie and said, "Wish me well, Lady. I hope to do as well as Ben. It'd be great to rule both shows this weekend."

"Good Luck, Dave, I wish you well." She whispered, kissing him soundly. He hugged her so hard she couldn't breathe.

She watched as he climbed into their other race car, and strapped his safety harness. He positioned his face mask and checked the microphone to be sure Ben could hear him.

Word had gotten around the track that Ben had broken the track record on his qualification run. The small crowd of people standing around waiting for Dave to take his run included Michael Waltrip, Bobby Hamilton and Ricky Rudd.

Excitement was in the air and Millie found herself caught up in it. Just before Dave was ready to drive away, she walked over to the car. He lifted his face mask and looked at her.

"Dave, I need to apologize for bringing everyone down this morning. I just.... love you so much, I can't help it. I want you to win, Dave. I know you need this race for whatever reason to work out some problems from your past. I'll be waiting for you when you get back. Kick some butt!"

"Wait, what did you say? What was that first thing you said?" he asked.

"I'm sorry?"

"No, after that?"

"I'll be waiting for you?"

"No, that's important, but, that wasn't it!"

"Kick some butt?"

"No, that's unlike you.... but I like it! What was that other thing you said?"

"I.... love you?"

"That's it! That's what I need to hear. I love you, too, Millie. I'll give you a hug in a few minutes, when I get back." He gave her a thumbs-up signal and pulled onto the track to take a couple practice laps.

Since his practice laps were a little slow, Ben radioed to him...."Only 143.8. If you're gonna do well Sunday, you've got to get up the speed. How are you doing mentally? Everything okay?"

"I'm chasing away some cobwebs, Ben. Let's see how this lap goes." Dave explained.

The cherry-red, Coca-Cola sponsored race car soared around the track.

"That's better, Dave. You clocked in at 159.2. I think the top speed for the Winston Cup guys is 172.5 so far. Are you ready to qualify?"

"Let's do it!" Dave said as he signaled to the NASCAR official. The green flag was waved and Dave pushed the gas pedal to the maximum. The race car met the challenge. When he'd finished his qualifying lap, Dave knew he'd done well."

"Couldn't stand it, could you?" Ben said. "You had to show me up!"

"Why, how'd I come out?"

"185.2"

"Better than your run! Well, what do you know about that!"

"Yeah, you were showing off for your girl. She's jumpin' up and down she's so happy."

"Good, I don't want to lose her, Man."

"I know, good luck in this race and good luck with the Lady. You know I'm pullin' for you. Let's rule the show this weekend. Get Colson-Masden back up front...where we belong."

Dave pulled the #19 back into their pit area and calmly pushed the button to break-away the steering wheel. He slowly unfastened the safety harness and looked up to see Millie's reaction to his run. She was almost glowing with happiness.

Dave pulled off his helmet and smiled at Millie. Before he could get out of the car, Ned Jarrett came over to interview him. "Dave, that was a great qualifying run. Congratulations."

"Thanks, Ned. It feels good to be back behind the wheel. The crew's been working really hard to get our cars in shape so we could both run this weekend. Ben's got the pole position for tomorrow.... and maybe I'll have it for Sunday."

"Good luck to both of you. It's good to have you back. Are you completely recovered from your injuries at Daytona?"

"Not quite 100%.... but close. My friends helped me get better ... especially the new Lady in my life. She's over there..." he pointed out Millie to Ned..."by the fence. I'd never have made it if it hadn't been for her. We've got a winning crew and terrific sponsors. We're primed for a victory this week."

"Good luck to you both." Ned finalized his interview.

Millie was beside Dave's car when he finally climbed out. She hugged him with such force it almost knocked him down. He grabbed her so they both wouldn't fall and swung her around.

"Dave, that was great! I'm so proud of you."

"Tell me again...."

"I'm proud of you!"

"No, the other thing, you know...."

"I love you, Dave Masden. I can't help myself. I love you."

"I love you, too, Millie Greene with an 'e'. Welcome back. I don't know where you went this morning.... but welcome back."

"I'll explain it later. I think I've figured it out."

The foursome went to dinner that evening, then stopped by a party at Davey Allison's suites.

Everyone congratulated Ben and Dave on their qualification speeds. Dale Earnhardt and Rusty Wallace teased Dave about eating their dust.

Butch Smith came over with Patricia snuggled against him. She congratulated her ex-husband. Later, she pulled Dave aside and whispered, "That was great, Dave. Is there a chance we can get back together? I'm not so sure I'm in love with Butch."

"Pat, I would have stood by you, no matter what; but, now, I've got someone else in my life ... someone who *really* cares for me .... someone who'll never screw around on me. You made your decision so live with it. Things haven't been right between us for a long time. It takes two people to make a relationship work. Ours was a one-sided relationship and, unfortunately, our marriage is over. We both have someone new so let's just move on. We have another chance to make a relationship work. Somehow, we failed each other. Maybe things will be different this time. I wish you the very best in your upcoming marriage."

"You look great, Dave. She's good for you."

"She is. I hope I can keep her with me always."

It was late when they got back to the motel. Dave asked Millie if she wanted him to sleep at the trailer.

"No, Dave, there's two beds in our room; we need to talk about some things."

"You're right about that. We need to talk."

They told Ben and Lynne good night and walked to their room down the hall. Millie went into the bathroom and freshened up. When she came out, Dave had plumped up the pillows on one of the beds and was sitting, propped up against them. He patted the bed beside him, motioning for her to join him.

Millie pulled off her boots and pulled up her socks, which had become slouched. She climbed across the bed and sat down next to Dave, putting her head on his shoulder in a hug.

"This feels great, doesn't it?" he whispered.

"Uh-huh..." she purred.

"Millie, there's something I want to talk to you about."

"Okay, then I have something to tell you, too."

"First of all, I'm head-over-heels in love with you. This little voice I hear in my head tells me to be patient. We should be patient with each other while we defeat the fears that are haunting us. Fears from our past.... We both have them. Your fear of falling in love with someone who takes chances is an understandable fear. Jacob's death was tragic."

"Yes, it was."

"I can't promise you I'm not going to die. I can promise you that I'm not going to take unnecessary chances; but, you've got to understand, racing is my life. I don't plan to race forever. The time is fast approaching when we'll step down...retire Colson-Masden, sell our assets. Ben and I agree on that point."

"Really. You discussed it with Ben?"

"Just briefly."

"In the meantime, I'd like to give racing another chance. I get that chance by having the pole position Sunday. My hands and arms have almost completely healed. You played a big part in my recovery."

"It was my pleasure. I can't always say it was easy; but, I'm glad I came."

"I don't want to lose you, Millie. Let me help you get over Jacob's death so you can love again.... love me. I need you to help me get past my fears, too."

"By racing?"

"Exactly!"

"Then what?" she asked.

"Well, we need to do something about US! I ache for wanting you. Since I hear '*be patient*' from my conscience.... and you hear, '*true love waits*', the best thing we can do is see what happens Sunday. If everything works out, I have a big surprise for you."

"Here you go again with this mysterious surprise!"

"Until we sort through these things, let's agree not to have a physical relationship until we resolve these conflicts. Let's do it God's way.... and wait. It's not going to be easy. We want to be close. We have all this sensual energy; but think how wonderful it will be when we finally make love. Do you think we can wait?"

"You continue to amaze me! The reason I was so depressed last night was because you *didn't* reach for me when you came to bed. You made that little remark about my favorite song at the garage. I assumed you had decided not to wait. I was mentally ready for you to make love to me."

"Oh, Millie, I'm so sorry."

"I was awake when you came to bed. It hurt that you didn't come to me. I know this little naggin' voice keeps saying... *'True love waits...true love waits.'* I told it to shut up!"

"Millie, I'm so sorry. I can understand why you were so upset with me this morning."

"Well, the truth is, I believe exactly like you do. I've had to take too many cold showers lately. I thought you gave me the cold shoulder last night. Yes, as long as we both agree and understand that we want God's will for our relationship, I can wait. My body aches for you, too."

"I love you, Millie. I always will."

"I love you, too, Dave.

"Oh, thank you, God, for what you're doing in our lives." Dave whispered.

"Yes, God, thank you." she replied, snuggling closer.

"Millie, will you sleep with me tonight?"

"What? After our conversation, you ask me a question like that?"

"You misunderstand. Will you curl up with me, fully clothed, and sleep in my arms all night. Let's just snuggle, hold each other close. There's nothing in the Bible that says we can't sleep together. We just can't make love—not yet. Do you think you handle it?"

"If you can, I can."

"Goodnight, Darlin', I love you." Dave whispered. "I'm exhausted. You'll be in my dreams. You are my dream!"

"Goodnight, Dave. I love you, too."

Within fifteen minutes, they were both asleep. They held each other all night and an unending embrace, fully clothed.

The next morning, Millie awoke first. She looked at Dave, who was still sleeping. She smiled when he smiled in his sleep. Her body tingled with excitement.

"Oh, God, thank you for allowing me to have another adventure in life...thank you for giving me the love of this wonderful Godly man." she whispered.

Dave woke up. He smiled at her and kissed her sweetly. "Today's race day." he whispered. "We'd better get movin' and make sure Ben's out of the sack. He'll want to take a practice lap or two before the race starts. There's a lot to do." he said, as he sat up. "Good mornin', Darlin'!"

"Good mornin' yourself."

"How did you sleep?"

"Like a baby."

"It's incredible, isn't it? So did I. Words fail me in trying to say what I feel about you. *I love you* doesn't seem to cover it. It's wonderful what's happened between us, isn't it, Mil'?"

"Yes, words fail me, too. I'm filled with joy. I was just thanking God for you!"

"I thanked Him last night, just before I fell asleep, while I held you in my arms."

"I thought you fell asleep before I did."

"I pray a lot, Millie."

"Me, too, I talk to God just like I talk to you."

"Ah, you're my Lady, Millie, tailor made to my specifications. Thank You, Lord … Someday, we'll be able to make love. I'm normal in every way. I could ravage your body right now...tear your clothes off you and make sweet love to you; but, I know we're supposed to wait. I even thank God for our passion...that's a gift from God, too. The rewards of waiting far outweigh the momentary joy we'd get if we gave in right now. That's the reason I want to wait. I think we're supposed to wait!"

"Yes, we are."

Millie allowed Dave to have the bathroom first so he could shower and shave. While she waited, she turned on the television to catch the news highlights. The sportscaster was talking about the Colson-Masden team. "Folks, I think they've broken several records. Not only do they both have a pole position this weekend; but they both set new track records. Do you think they're using rocket fuel in those cars?"

"Dave, did you hear what they said on television?"

"Yeah, I heard it; wonder if Ben did?"

Before he got the words out of his mouth, the phone rang. It was Ben. He was ecstatic.

"We'll meet you guys in the coffee shop in fifteen minutes, okay?" Ben said after boasting for several minutes about the sportscaster's remarks.

"Sure, Ben, that works for me...." Dave said, as he rolled his eyes.

Breakfast was memorable. Dave and Millie couldn't keep their eyes off each other and were continually looking at each other, constantly smiling. It was obvious to everyone they were in love.

Ben and Lynne held hands under the table. People who came into the coffee shop came over to congratulate them. All was right with the world.

They went to the track so Ben and Dave could get situated for the race. Then Lynne asked Millie if she wanted to go back to the room.

"Yes, I didn't get to take a shower this morning. Dave was hoggin' the bathroom." she teased.

"Me, either. We need to put on our jumpsuits. Do you have yours?"

"Oh, sure. I wasn't sure we were supposed to wear them today, since this is a BUSCH race."

"Yet bet your boots we are. We're part of the Colson-Masden team. We wear our colors proudly, right?"

"Right!"

While Lynne drove them back to the hotel, she couldn't restrain herself any longer. "You are certainly smiling this morning. So tell me, Millie, how's everything?" she remarked, knowingly.

"Wonderful...."

"See, I told you. Race car drivers know how to make love."

"Oh, we didn't make love."

"You didn't?"

"No. True love waits. We're being patient."

"Remarkable. You're glowing this morning. When you two finally get together, you may start a nuclear reaction." Lynne teased.

"Maybe.... I'm so much in love with that man. I'm afraid I'm hooked for life."

"That's great news! You'll never have to worry about Dave."

"I know."

"Can we go to Church and pray?" They did.

When they go back to the motel, Lynne and Millie went to their respective motel rooms, showered and changed into their jumpsuits and racing jackets.

They went back to the track. "Let's stay in the infield, Lynne. I want to be close to Dave while he's doing his job."

"Okay."

Lynne gave Ben a good-luck kiss, while Millie and Dave embraced. Ben climbed into the shiny race car where it was parked in the lead spot in the line-up.

Only a few of the Winston Cup guys were scheduled to start in this race. Dale Earnhardt, Ken Schrader, Mark Martin, Ernie Irvin and Bobby Hamilton were further back in the pack.

Ben knew this was his race. If he managed to win, there would be a bonus for having the pole position, and winning the race.

After giving a 'thumbs-up' sign to his crew, he started the engine when the order was given. The beautiful cars circled the track behind the pace car and roared into action when the green flag waved.

Ben maintained the lead until the twenty-fifth lap when Kenny Wallace managed to get around him. They challenged each other and the positions changed several times.

Brett Bodine tried to draft, to get Ben loose.... but he managed to pull ahead of him on the track, to put enough space between them so he couldn't gain from his draft. Dale Earnhardt came speeding around Bodine and was riding Ben's bumper.

A caution flag waved.... a tire blew on the other side of the track. Kenny, Ben and Dale raced to the line; then, made a pit stop during the caution to take on four new tires, fuel, and get their windshields cleaned. Dave decided to leave the set-up as it was on Ben's car. After all, it was decided, why mess with perfection?

Their crew worked at a remarkable speed...enabling Ben to beat the other drivers out of the pits. Mark Martin ended up in fourth position because of his crew's performance.

On lap ninety-nine, a rookie caused a major smash-up; but luckily Ben escaped by going down into the grass. As soon as he was able, he pitted for new tires.

When he returned to the track, Ben was in second place, with Ken Schrader taking the lead. Ben regained first position within eight laps of the restart of the race, and maintained that position until the last lap.

Dale Earnhardt, who'd been experiencing some engine problems, was drafting him, trying to get his car to veer away. Ben held tight, and maintained his position.

Instead of Ben getting loose, Dale's car started to swerve and he had to straighten it up. When he did, Ken Schrader, Brett Bodine and Lake Speed sailed past Dale. Ben had a straight shot to the finish line.... unchallenged.

"Hey, Man, you did it! You won!" Dave said frantically into the microphone. "Congratulations! You ran a good race—the victory was yours from the start."

"Thanks, Dave; it was a piece of cake. It feels great! Well, I've done my job. Now, you have to do yours tomorrow. It'd be great if we both win, right?"

"I'm going to do my best. See you in the Winner's Circle in a minute."

When Ben pulled into Victory Lane, Dave was waiting for him with a container of Gatorade. At first he started to pour it over his head; but changed his mind. He hugged him and handed him the bottle so he could refresh himself.

Charlie sat a big bottle of Coca-Cola on the hood of the car to proudly show the world who their sponsors were....

Randy Pemberton and Jerry Punch interviewed Ben. "The crew deserves all the credit. They've worked really hard to get ready for this race. I knew we had the fastest car on the track today. It's great to have Dave back at the helm, too. Charlie.... and everyone did a great job! Coca-Cola's been incredible throughout the past few weeks. This victory's been a long time comin', Randy. It feels great—WE WON! Where's my wife, Lynne? Honey, come on up here." Ben said, hugging his wife.

After the interviews were finished and the photographs were taken, they went to dinner. Then, they stopped by the victory celebration that was hosted by Coca-Cola and made their "command performance."

The sponsors were elated. "Dave, we expect no less from you tomorrow," they challenged. "There will be a big bonus in it if you can ... and I mean B-I-G!"

After the required appearance was fulfilled, they decided to get to bed early because they faced a much bigger challenge the next day, because the Winston Cup race was a "horse of a different color"—much, much tougher.

When they got back to their room, Dave and Millie curled up in each other arms. They talked for a few minutes.

"I knew Ben was going to win today, Mil'. He makes racing look easy doesn't he? I hope I can do as well tomorrow."

"No matter who wins the race, Dave, you're a winner in my eyes. Don't take any unnecessary chances. Even though we've only known each other for three weeks, you've turned my life around. My head's spinning. Life's worth living again.... as long as it's with you, Dave."

"The first time I looked in your eyes I knew; the first time we danced, I knew ...I knew you weren't a one-night-stand type of woman. *You're the best kind ... a know-forever type.* I hope you'll give me the chance to know you forever.... to fulfill what I saw in your eyes that first day at the store." Dave said.

"What DID you see in my eyes?"

"My destiny.... our destiny. At first, it scared me; but, now, it doesn't scare me a bit!"

"I'm one lucky woman."

"No, I'm the lucky one, Sweetheart. I can't wait to surprise you tomorrow."

"Can't you give me a clue?"

"No."

"Does anyone else know?"

"No ... only God. I've talked it over with Him."

"I'll be praying for you during the race, Honey. You can count on it. Please, be careful.... come back to me."

"I appreciate your prayers. I need them. I have every intention of coming back to you."

"I love you, Dave."

"I love you, Millie. Goodnight."

"Goodnight."

As she watched Dave fall asleep, she said a prayer of thanksgiving. What an incredible challenge God had given her. Would she prove worthy of such a prize, she wondered.

Very soon, Millie was asleep, safe and secure, held tightly by Dave's loving arms. Everything was so right with the world.

Chapter Fourteen

They were jubilant at breakfast that morning. Ben was ecstatic about his victory; and, Dave was anxious to get the race started so he could sail into victory lane.

"I have a good feeling about today's race. If it works out like I plan, I'll have a big surprise for Millie later." Dave said.

"What's that?" Ben asked.

"You'll see, you'll <u>all</u> see." Dave replied mysteriously. "I can hardly wait to spring it on you, Millie. I haven't felt this good in years. My heart is about to burst with joy. I can't miss!"

His romantic remarks surprised everyone because it wasn't in Dave's nature to be so demonstrative with his feelings.

"Were your hands okay when you qualified yesterday?" Ben changed the subject.

"Good as gold. These elastic support sleeves keep the skin from stretching; and these gloves work great." He said, flexing his fingers. "I feel like I could walk into a lion's den and survive. Millie's my good luck charm."

"What a responsibility! You mean, if things don't go well today, you'll blame me?" she kidded. "Don't put me on a pedestal; keep me in your arms, close to your heart."

"That's where you belong; but, you're also on a pedestal."

Take a Chance: True Love Waits

"It's gettin' too mushy in here for me, Lynne. Maybe we should leave these two lovebirds alone." Ben said sarcastically.

"I think its sweet, Ben. You could take some lessons from Dave. We have a good marriage; but, the words are nice, too. We all need to hear the words once in awhile."

Ben got up and went to the cash register to pay the check. The others met him at the door; and, since they were already dressed for the race, they all drove to the track so Dave could check out the car, and they could attend Mass.

After taking the car for a few laps, Dave returned to the garage and said joyfully; "It's ready. I'm ready."

While Lynne fussed around with Ben, Dave and Charlie made final preparations for the race; Millie got her sketchbook to draw some of the scenes that were occurring in front of her. She sketched Ben and Lynne beside the race car. She sketched Dave leaning against the car. She sketched the crew with Charlie pointing his finger at them, planning their final strategies. Then, she sketched Ben and Lynne's house from memory, and drew a picture of Dave standing beside his black truck.

Dave came over and sat down on the concrete slab next to her. He watched as she put the finishing touches on one of the sketches. After looking intently at each picture she had drawn, he smiled. "These are great, Mil'. You know, there could be a market for your sketches through NASCAR."

"Thanks! I just do it for my own pleasure, so I can recapture these moments any time I want by looking at the drawings …"

Very nonchalantly, he whispered, "This feels like a relationship that started a long time ago. I don't believe in reincarnation; but, I feel like we're married, don't you, Millie? I've been searching for you since I was a little kid."

"Well, you found me.... We found each other. Or was it God? Did he bring us together?"

"It was God! He answered my prayers and I'm counting on Him to answer another one today. Then, if everything goes as planned ... well, you know ...my surprise!"

"You're really mysterious about this surprise. Give me a clue!!?"

"Nope, you'll have to wait." he teased.

Charlie called Dave's name. "It's time for the drivers' meeting."

Millie put her pencil down and watched as Dave walked away. Tingles went through her body. How magnificent he looked in the jumpsuit. It fit as if it had been custom-made. He was built the way a man is supposed to be built.... broad shoulders and slim waist and hips. Magnificent, she thought to herself as waves of emotion swept through her body.

She started another sketch depicting Dave and herself. His arm was around her shoulder and her arm was around his waist. They were looking at each other intently.

Normally, she didn't draw pictures of herself; but they seemed to belong together in the sketch. She was no longer alone. Somehow, she'd let her guard down long enough to allow Dave to crash through her 'brick wall'. Instead of staying inside her 'safe haven,' he had torn it down.

She noticed Dave and the other Winston Cup drivers were gathering in front of his shiny red car. After talking for a few minutes, they bowed their heads and prayed. Millie got tears in her eyes as she watched the touching scene and said a silent prayer for protection for the drivers.

After the prayer ended, she immediately sketched that heart-warming scene. It was something not normally seen on television. She wondered if everyone knew how religious most of the drivers were. Several of the drivers made the sign of the cross in the traditional Catholic manner when their prayer ended.

Lynne came over to see what she was doing. After looking at the pictures, she begged, "Oh, Millie, can I have some of these? I love them."

"They're for you.... That is, all except this one. It's special." She handed Lynne the picture she'd just completed.

"Can you draw me one? I'd like to have one of you two."

"How long before the race starts?"

"About twenty minutes."

"I'll draw one now."

"We need to get to our seats, though. If we don't leave now, we'll have to stay in the infield."

"Let's stay here. Just like yesterday, we should be here, close to the guys."

"Okay then, get that pencil flying. I'll watch, okay."

"Sure, but let me know when Dave starts to get in the car. I want to give him a good-luck kiss."

"Okay."

Millie skillfully sketched another picture of her and Dave. This time, she drew them looking towards the front rather than looking at each other. She decided she'd keep her original sketch just for Dave.

"Millie, Dave's about to get into the car...." Lynne interrupted. "Let's go."

Lynne walked over to where Dave was standing and hugged him. "Good luck, Dave. I'm pullin' for you."

"Thanks, Lynne."

"Good luck, Darlin'." Millie said as she put her arms around Dave's waist. She gave him a firm hug and silently prayed for his safety as she held him close. "I'll be waitin' at the Winner's Circle. I'm praying for you; and, remember, no matter what happens today, you're a winner in my eyes."

"Thanks, Honey. If you're in my corner, I can't lose!"

"Just come back to me...."

"I will, I promise." He said as he kissed her.

Millie returned his kiss, then handed him the special picture she'd drawn.

"You've captured us perfectly in this sketch, Millie. I want it with me during the race, okay?"

"It's yours.... to do with as you please."

"I'll give it back to you after the race so you can have it framed. There's no way I'll let anything happen to this picture," he reassured her.

Millie reached into the pocket of her jumpsuit and pulled out a small golden angel, and a St. Benedict metal. She placed the angel on the collar strap of Dave's jumpsuit, and slipped the metal inside his uniform pocket. "This is for protection.... a reminder that I'm praying for you."

"I love it! I've got something for you, too." he said, as he climbed inside the shiny red car. He handed her a long-stemmed red rose. "For you!"

"Oh, how sweet, Dave, I'm touched...with everything you had to do to get ready for the race, and you took the time to get ME a rose. God bless you, Dave!" she said as she leaned down to kiss him again.

"He already has...." he said, winking at her.

She watched as he strapped down the safety harness and adjusted the face shield of his helmet.

Suddenly, Millie heard Jake's voice. "Mom, Mom...."

She turned around. Jake was running towards them, wearing the Colson-Masden jumpsuit.

"Jake, what are you doing here?"

"I almost didn't come, Mom; but, for some unknown reason, I felt that I had to be here for this race. I charged my airline ticket to your MasterCard; but I'll pay you back. Is everything okay?"

"Everything's fine, Jake. I'm glad you came. Don't worry about paying me back. Look, who's racing today.... He has the pole position." Millie said proudly, pointing to Dave as he sat in the car.

"Dave! You're racing today?"

"Yes, Son, I am. Wish me luck."

"You bet I do. I'm glad you're better." Jake replied excitedly.

"Why don't you see if you can help Ben? Keep his head on straight for me, Jake."

"Okay, Dave. Good luck in the race."

Millie noticed that when Dave called Jake 'son,' he hadn't bothered to correct him. She smiled at the thought and then smiled again. Dave seemed to read her mind and gave her a "thumbs-up" signal that everything was a-okay.

"It's great to see Dave doing so well, Mom. I'm surprised he's racing instead of Ben."

"Dave's full of surprises these days. I have a lot to tell you; but it'll have to wait until after the race. Right now, you'd better see if Ben needs anything before the race starts." she suggested.

The announcer said, "GENTLEMEN, START YOUR ENGINES!" The drivers hit the starter buttons and the forty well-tuned engines roared into super-charged action. They followed the shiny green pace car for several laps around the track before the green flag was waved.

Dave shifted into high gear; maintaining his first-place lead, putting several car-lengths between his Lucky #19, and Morgan Shepherd's #21 Citgo Ford. He maneuvered each turn with ease...as if he had wings.

Occasionally, Dave would touch the gold angel Millie had placed on his collar and quickly said a prayer.

Dave dominated the first quarter of the race as several other cars challenged him for the lead. So far, it had been a cautionless race with Dave maintaining the lead. It was hard to believe it had been a cautionless race so far. He might have to make a pit stop under green.

Ben was frantic. "Hey, Man," he said into his headset, "I'm afraid you're gonna blow a tire...check the pressure on the right front. You've got to pit. You've got too many laps on those tires. We don't need another D-N-F!"

Almost on call, Dick Trickle's car scraped the wall and the caution flag was waved. As soon as NASCAR opened the pit area, Dave pulled in for fresh tires and fuel, thanking God for the perfect timing of the wreck.

The next quarter was almost a repetition of the first... Dave found himself in the same position.... tire pressure was declining. He had dominated first place for the majority of the race. If he had to pit under green, he could lose his position.

Ben became impatient and demanded that he come in for new tires. "Hey, Masden, this is no joke. We don't need a wreck!"

"Let's wait just a few more minutes to see if there's another caution flag. If the power starts to decline, I'll pull in. The first caution came at the right time; although, it's a shame that Dick Trickle's out of the race. He was giving me a good run. I'll come in soon, Boss, I promise!"

"I'm half owner of that car. I insist you come in NOW...." Ben demanded, totally frustrated with his dare-devilish behavior. Dave refused.

About five minutes later, a minor skirmish caused a caution flag. Dave pulled in for fuel and fresh tires. Jake handed him a fresh container of Gatorade, and handed him a wet cloth so he could wipe his face shield.

Millie and Lynne were standing by the fence, watching the expertise of the crew as they maneuvered the tire changes and fuel fill-up in record time.

Rusty Wallace's team was three-tenths of a second faster in the pits than Colson-Masden's team, and he took the lead. Dave knew, however, that the number 19 was the fastest car on the track.

When the green flag was waved, Dave shifted into high gear and the engine quickly responded.

The race continued somewhat routinely with Dave struggling to regain the lead from Rusty Wallace. He drafted, a very close second, looking for a chance to get around.

Another caution flag waved. Kyle Petty was out because of engine problems. Rusty and Dave pulled into the pit with only twenty-five laps remaining. Lucky #19 was operating at peak performance. Dave maintained his position behind Rusty, matching his pit stop time.

Ten laps to go. Dave looked into the rear view mirror and saw Butch Smith tapping his bumper. Dave was able to speed away, and put three car-lengths between him and Butch.

"I'll show you, Smith!" Dave said under his breath. Smith continued to challenge him, drafting dangerously close, trying to cause him to lose control of his car. He tapped Dave's bumper again, even harder.

Dave remembered his promise not to take unnecessary chances. Deciding he'd had enough of Smith's reckless driving, he allowed Butch to pass.

Smith isn't going to take MY life...I have too much to live for, Dave thought, as Butch Smith sailed past him. Smith laughed and made an obscene gesture when he passed.

"You'll get yours, Smith." Dave said as Smith charged ahead to draft the leader, Rusty Wallace. Dave held his third-place position a safe distance behind them. He watched as the two battled for first place.

Without warning, Smith tapped Rusty's rear bumper, causing the #2 Genuine Draft Pontiac to swerve and scrape the outside wall. In the process, Rusty's car caught Smith's purple car on the rear quarter-panel, causing him to fly into the grassy area at the end of turn four.

Rusty managed to regain control of his car as the #19 sailed past him. Dave gave him a 'high sign' as they passed as a gesture of 'thanks.'

During the caution and subsequent pit stop, Dave said, "Hey, Ben, patch me through to Rusty Wallace."

Ben radioed to Rusty's Crew Chief that Dave wanted to talk to him. They patched him through.

"Rusty, this is Dave Masden. Smith is going to kill someone if we're not careful. I'm sorry you got caught in the melee. Are you going to be able to finish?"

"I'm gonna try. I bet NASCAR's going to have a lot to say about Smith's tapping procedures. He's too rough. Dale Earnhardt wasn't that bad when he earned the nickname of the Intimidator, was he?"

"That's right; can you give me a run for the finish line? I'm willing if you're up for it."

Miraculously, when they pulled back onto the race track, Rusty managed to maintain his second-place position. Dave was leading the race. They continued their conversation.

"Let's go...race you to the finish!" Dave challenged.

"Well, if Dale or Mark don't beat you there. D-W's moving up on you. Watch your back...you've got a bunch of them chasing you. I'm running... but having a tough time in the corners. I'll be able to finish; but I don't think I'll be able to keep up with you. Smith caused some major damage." Rusty said.

Three laps to go. Dale Earnhardt sailed around Dave like he was standing still. Dave pushed the car to its maximum to stay behind him. There was only a half-second distance between them.... last lap; turn four...the finish line lay ahead.

Dave floored the gas pedal and managed to speed around Earnhardt just as the checkered flag was waved. It was a photo finish! Dave could hardly believe it...he'd pulled it off! God had answered his prayers. He'd won!

"God, this feels great. Thank You, Lord," he prayed, "for seeing the drivers safely through this race; and, thank You for this victory. You continue to bless me. Now, for my surprise, let me say the right things, Lord. We need each other. If it's your will, let it be." Dave prayed as he took the victory lap and waved to the cheering crowd.

As he pulled into the winner's circle, he visually searched the crowd, looking for Millie. He couldn't pick her out among the crowd of congratulatory people who quickly gathered at Victory Lane.

The television crews and photographers were waiting for an interview when he stopped the car. Ben and Charlie were jumping up and down, hugging everyone they saw. The crew dumped the ice bucket on Ben's head as a celebration sign and handed him a bottle of Coca-Cola to give to Dave.

Dave meticulously went through the motions of pushing the button to break-away the steering wheel. He unfastened his safety harness and took off his helmet, trying to straighten his hair.

Ben handed him a wet towel so he could wipe his face and Charlie handed him a Coca-Cola hat. Dave put on the hat and climbed out. He held up his arms in victory as he stepped on top of the car. The cheers were deafening.

He searched the crowd, looking for Millie. He saw Jake. He saw Lynne. He saw members of their crew...but he didn't see Millie.

A microphone was shoved in front of his face when he jumped off the car.

"How does it feel, Dave?" Randy Pemberton asked. "It's been a *long* time since you stood in the Winner's Circle. No one can forget what happened just three weeks ago in Daytona!"

"I'd never been able to get through it without the help of my lady friend, and Ben and Lynne. I wonder where Millie is.... She should be here with me...." Dave said, looking around the crowd.

"Well, congratulations! Your recovery is incredible."

"Randy, I have a philosophy which I've tried to apply to my life. Basically, when life hands me lemons, add some sweetener and make cool, refreshing lemonade instead of accepting the bitterness. Give the glory to God."

"That sounds like a good idea to me. With Ben's win yesterday, you guys have broken records galore at Richmond this weekend. This one will go down in the history books. Ben had the pole position and ended up winning, right? You had the pole position today and won! We hear you're in line for a big bonus! You guys have earned your money...."

"Man, it feels great!! The car was at peak performance and the crew did an excellent job. Coca-Cola pulled out all the stops; and, I have a lot of people to thank today. But, my victory won't be complete, Randy, until I get my Lady up here to share my happiness. She's been my inspiration.... my constant companion since Daytona. I could never have recovered so fast if it hadn't been for her. Millie, where are you?" he said into the microphone.

"Let's get her up here, too," Randy said, turning to look at the crowd of people standing around.

Those who knew Millie started to search for her. Lynne saw Millie and grabbed her hand to pull her through the crowd. "Go, Girl. He wants you up there with him. You're gonna be on television." Lynne insisted.

As soon as Dave saw Millie, he grabbed her hand and pulled her into his arms. "This is Millie, everyone. Tonight, if she'll have me, I want to make her my wife. She's the best thing that ever happened to me!"

Tears welled in Millie's eyes and she buried her face in Dave's chest, unable to say anything, embarrassed by his public display of affection.

"Well, Millie, what's it gonna be?" Randy asked. "Is there going to be a wedding tonight?"

She shook her head affirmatively and wiped a tear from her cheek. "He's a winner...could I refuse him anything after that race? There's no stopping him now..." she exclaimed, hugging Dave, who was smiling like a cat who got the canary.

"Oh, Randy, what a day! Thank you, God!" Dave shouted, waving to the crowd with one hand and hugging Millie with the other. The crowd cheered. The other drivers, including Butch Smith, gathered to congratulate them.

"Hey, Millie .... where's the wedding going to be?" Randy Pemberton asked.

"I don't have the vaguest idea!" Millie replied. "We'll have to make some plans...."

While the sportscasters interviewed Ben and Charlie, Dave pulled Millie aside and whispered in her ear. "I feel like we're already married in God's eyes; we might as well make it legal. Millie Greene...with an 'e'...will you marry me?"

"Yes, Dave, I'll marry you. Maybe we're foolish allowing this to happen after only three weeks; but, you've made me very happy."

"*Then you WILL marry me?*"

"I'm willing to take a chance if you are." she whispered.

"I'm not taking a chance...I'm betting on a sure thing. I see my destiny in your eyes. Everything's going to work out for us, I know it!"

Jake come over and hugged them. "Congratulations, Dave, and welcome to the family."

Dave smiled.

Randy came over to make a final remark. "This day is going down in history for a lot of reasons. For one thing, '*Romeo*', you'll be remembered for this day. Millie, did you know he was going to propose on national TV?"

"Of course not. It was a total surprise."

"Do you think you'll be married today?"

"If we can work things out, we will." Dave said. "We have to find someone who'll marry us on such short notice.... and a church. We want to be married in a church. Maybe we can have a reception during the victory celebration tonight...to celebrate Colson-Masden's wins this weekend, and to celebrate my victory with Millie. Everyone's invited!"

Chapter Fifteen

The entire Colson-Masden race team, including Jake, was pulled into service to help make the plans for the up-coming wedding.

Coca-Cola agreed to handle the plans for the celebration party, including the reception.

Jake and Charlie called their fellow Winston Cup friends to let them know the wedding was going to be held in a little chapel near the track, followed by a victory celebration. Father Thomas agreed to officiate at the ceremony; and a judge agreed to issue a marriage license.

"Lynne, will you be my Matron of Honor?" Millie asked.

"Sure."

"What are we going to wear?"

"Millie, I know the perfect place to get our dresses. Come on, let's go shopping. Ben, give me the keys to the rental car."

They got into the Thunderbird and drove to the shop. They found an antique lace suit with seed pearls and tiny blue ribbon accents. It was cocktail length with a satin ruffled flounce.

"Millie, this is perfect!"

"I know; but, it's a size fourteen."

"Would you like to try it on?" The clerk asked.

"I'm telling you; I can't wear a size fourteen. I normally wear an eighteen or sometimes a twenty." Millie said wistfully, "But, it's exactly what I'm looking for...."

"This style runs a little large. Why don't you try it?" the clerk insisted.

"You look like you've lost weight. My God, Millie, you eat like a bird. Based on how you've eaten since you've lived in our house, you should be 'skin 'n' bones'! Go on, try it on." Lynne urged. "It's perfect."

"Unfortunately, my weight problem is caused by genetics and a thyroid problem. I'd be much larger except I'm very careful what I eat; and, I try to get some exercise every day. Watson Clinic feels part of my problem stems from the fact I don't eat enough! Amazing isn't it?"

"I'll say. Well, go ahead, try the dress. We may get lucky. This is perfect..."

Millie was thrilled because the dress fit as though it had been tailor made for her.

She walked out of the dressing room to show Lynne the dress.

"This is God's gift to me...." Millie exclaimed as she looked at her mirror image. "Course, the best gift is Dave!"

They found a blue silk dress, similar in style to Millie's dress, for Lynne to wear and a gorgeous white negligee for Millie. They also bought the undergarments they'd need for their dresses, a garter, and matching shoes before the left the store.

Then, they picked up some flowers, including baby's breath and small daisies for Millie's hair. Stopping by a bakery, they bought a four-tiered wedding cake. Then, they took everything to the auditorium where the victory celebration—and the wedding reception—would be held.

While they were gone, Ben, Jake and Dave bought some gold wedding bands, and worked on a special surprise for their honeymoon. They were so busy; Millie and Dave barely had time to speak to each other before the wedding. Before long, they were getting dressed for the wedding.

Millie had layers of goose bumps as she stood beside Jake waiting for the wedding march to begin. Ben and Lynne were standing with Father

Thomas. Dave walked out of the side door and stood at the altar. He was so handsome in his dark suit and tie; Millie's knees started to tremble.

"Mom, you're breath-taking. I've never seen you look so beautiful." Jake told his Mom as he hugged her.

"Oh, Jake, am I doing the right thing? We've only known each other three weeks."

"Mom, you're perfect for each other. From what you told me, you've spent enough time together to know it's God's will. You're glowing. Dave brings out the best in you, Mom. I want you to be happy."

"I want us to be happy, too," she stammered. "I want him so bad I can hardly stand it!"

"You two haven't really...how can I say this to my Mother.... Done it, yet?" He asked, somewhat surprised. "I assumed...you two had already slept together."

"You assumed wrong. We made the decision to wait until our wedding night. Tonight will be the first time we'll make love."

"Mom, I'm proud of you. I don't know if I'll be able to wait. I've been seeing Paula regularly. Things are getting pretty hot between us."

"It's worth the wait, Son. Tonight's a dream come true for Dave and me. It was hard; but I'm glad we waited. We know God is going to bless this marriage."

"I hope so, Mom."

"Me, too! Jake, are you going to stay in Richmond tonight?"

"Yes, Ben and Lynne said I could use your room after you guys leave for your honeymoon. Then tomorrow, Ben wants me to fly back with them to help them with a special project. He said he'd pay for my flight back to school if I'd help him tomorrow."

"That's nice. Well, have fun. I'll call you in a couple weeks. I'm so happy, Jake."

"I know...and it shows. Ready to face your future?"

"Ready!"

The wedding march began. Jake proudly walked his Mother down the aisle and placed her hand in Dave's at the altar. The traditional vows were spoken as the couple was surrounded by many of NASCAR's superstars and their wives: Ken Schrader. Alan Kulwicki, Kyle Petty, Davey Allison, Morgan Shepherd, Rusty Wallace, Dale Earnhardt, Neil Bonnett, Ned Jarrett and his sons, Glenn and Dale, Darrell Waltrip, Bill Elliott, Harry Gant ...everyone who was anyone in Winston Cup racing attended.

The wide gold wedding bands were exchanged. Before Father Thomas pronounced them 'man and wife,' he asked if they'd like to say anything to each other. Dave nodded and immediately began to speak.... as if he had it planned.

"Millie Greene, with an 'e', you've made me the happiest man in the world. God, in His Infinite Glory, saw a need deep inside me and gave me a priceless gift. He gave me you. When we met, I knew how it would turn out. At first I had an ego problem because I thought the reason you spoke to me at the store was because you knew who I was. When I found out that you liked me *for me* and *not because my name's in the newspaper*, I was ecstatic. You were concerned because everything's happened so fast; but, in reality, I've been searching for you all my life. Praise be to God, I found you! Why wait to put our lives together? I love you. I cherish you. I'll do my best to never hurt you. I give you my pledge that no problem that we encounter in the future will overcome us. We'll work things out, no matter what. I'm glad we decided to refrain from having a physical relationship ... tonight will truly be a celebration.... a celebration of life and love! Foremost, I pledge to you my undying love.... forever. I can't thank God enough for blessing me with this wonderful gift, your love."

Millie stood quietly, unable to speak. Dave gently wiped a tear from her cheek in a touching gesture. Several members of the audience sniffled, realizing the emotional magnitude that was occurring at the altar.

Millie cleared her throat and took a deep breath. "Dave, I was so lonely until you picked me out of the crowd and asked me to fly to Daytona with you. I had built a brick wall ten feet thick around my emotions. You came crashing through that wall at two-hundred miles per hour. The miraculous way you *unselfishly* saved Ben's life was the bravest thing I'd ever seen. We had a very special time as you healed from your wounds. Because we spent so much time together, we became friends. I knew when your bandages came off, we'd either hate each other or love each other. I'm glad love prevailed. I'll stand by you, no matter what, because I love a challenge. You're my greatest challenge. How many times in the last few weeks have you asked me to take a chance? More times than I can count on my fingers. Yes, I'll proudly stand beside you, pray for you, love you, and respect you as we intermingle our lives. You're MY hero! You saved my life, too. If I can quote from one of my favorite Biblical stories, Ruth said, *'Entreat me not to leave thee, or to return from following after thee; for whither thou goest, I will go; and where thou lodgest, I will lodge; thy people shall be my people, and thy God, my God. Where thou diest, will I die; and there will I be buried; the Lord do so to me, and more also, if aught but death part thee and me.'* In other words, from this day forward, Dave Masden, I'll follow you to any race track in the world.....!"

Father Thomas smiled, and several of the prestigious guests chuckled at her remark.

"Ladies and Gentlemen, may I introduce Mr. and Mrs. David Lee Masden, man and wife. Dave, you can kiss your bride."

Dave made a growling sound in his throat and whispered, "With pleasure."

After the ceremony, photos were taken, and congratulatory wishes were given and received, everyone drove down the street, horns constantly sounding in celebration, for the victory party.

As soon as they got there, Lee Henderson came over to them. "Since we're friends, I've been chosen to provide entertainment for this party. Congratulations and best wishes to you both!"

Lee went to the make-shift stage, picked up the microphone and started to talk...."The day this couple met, Dave Masden asked me to sing this special song. This song is appropriate tonight as they share their first dance as husband and wife. *'You've got a good love comin' from me tonight....'*" Lee sang as he smiled joyfully.

The audience cheered as Dave pulled Millie into his arms to dance to what would forever be "their" song. As they swayed to the music, Dave pulled a handkerchief from his pocket and gently wiped away Millie's tears.

"You're so beautiful, Millie Masden! Thank you for making me so happy. Thank you for being my friend, my confidante, and my wife.... And soon, Honey, my lover. I'll always love you!"

"Right back at you, Dave Masden. Who would have thought that morning when I took my neighbor to the store that my life would change forever. I face each new day with excitement...and my nights will be filled with love. Thank you for noticing me, thank you for pulling me out of that crowd of lonely people and helping me to escape from that emotional prison I'd built for myself inside that brick wall. I tried to pull you inside my safe haven; but you knew we had to break free and rejoin the living. That brick wall's in a shambles. I'll try to never rebuild it! Thank you, most of all, for loving me and saving my life, too!"

Dave hugged and kissed her as the dance ended. The crowd applauded.

Lee sang several more songs for their wedding celebration that night, including: *Two-Heart Serenade; I.O.U.; Wind Beneath my Wings; Lean, Mean, Lovin' Machine; the theme from Robin Hood;* and finally, *God Bless the USA.*

Before he left the stage, he said. "I wish you guys the very best! What do you say, People? I think Randy Pemberton hit the nail on the head today when he called Dave '*Romeo*'. The nickname fits!" He gave them a thumbs-up sign and walked off the stage.

A little later, Lee managed to corner the newlyweds for a few minutes. "I'd like to write a song about you guys," he said, "Everyone in this room is touched by your love story."

They gave Lee the details about how they met, the loneliness that became affection because of their chance meeting. As they talked, Lee noticed they were touching each other lovingly, or hugging each other. It was obvious they were deeply in love.

"You guys managed to grab that golden ring on the merry-go-round of life. Good luck! You have a good chance to make it work...you seem to be crazy about each other. No one knows it yet, but I've found a wonderful lady, too. I'm happy for the first time in my life. I'm going to ask her to marry me."

"Congratulations. We want an invitation to the wedding, Lee!" Millie exclaimed. "We're happy for you."

A few minutes later, Lee went back to the stage. "I hadn't planned to sing these two songs tonight; but, I'm so touched by the love I feel in this room, if you'll bear with me, I'll sing them for you. I've not rehearsed them..." He sang, "*Thank you for Changing my Life.*"

When the song ended, he said, "Let's get the bride and groom on the dance floor for another dance solo while I sing this last song.... a special dedication to them." He sang, "*Love Don't Get no Better Than this...*"

In the middle of the song, he said, "Everyone dance with the love of your life. Tell them you love 'em. Every word of this song describes Dave and Millie's love for each other. Best wishes! You two will make it work. May you always be as happy, or happier, than you are tonight."

The wedding festivities were enjoyable for everyone in attendance. They had a twenty-dollar dance wherein Millie and Dave has to dance with anyone who handed them a twenty-dollar bill. When the long dance ended, they had their hands full of money.

Dave accidentally spilled a little champagne on Millie's dress when they had the wedding toast. Cutting the wedding cake was fun. Dave very nicely put a morsel of cake in Millie's mouth. She took a large piece and pushed it into Dave's mouth, smearing some icing on his face. Lynne handed Dave a wet towel so he could wipe the icing off his face.

"Boy, thanks, Millie. I was afraid I wasn't going to get any cake. You gave me a whole piece in one bite!"

"Hey, I told you'd I'd take care of you...." she laughed, kissing him, icing and all.

Millie threw the bouquet that was caught by Jeff Gordon's girlfriend, Brooke Shealy. Jake caught the garter.

The party continued for two more hours before Dave and Millie quietly slipped away to begin their honeymoon at the Hyatt Regency in

Richmond. The room had a beautiful view; but they didn't spend much time looking at it. Dave freshened up first and waited while Millie changed clothes. When she came out of the bathroom wearing her new negligee, she looked like an angel.

"Well, Mrs. Masden, the time has finally come. Can I make love to you now? You look so beautiful. I have to keep pinching myself to see if I'm awake. Is this a dream?"

"If it's a dream, we're both having it."

"Do you realize, we're still on our first date? Think about it. Since you got on the plane to go to Daytona, we've not spent a night apart. Our first date was go great; we got married before it ended. Now, it never has to end!"

"What a romantic man you are. Am I lucky or what?"

"I'm the lucky one...." he whispered, as they snuggled.

"Do you think your newly-acquired nickname will stick?" she asked.

"What's that? *Romeo?*" He answered.

He reached behind her and turned on the stereo in the luxurious honeymoon suite. George Strait was singing, "*I Cross My Heart*" from the movie, "Pure Country."

"Hum.... this song seems appropriate. Since I met you, this has been MY favorite song, Millie. It says what I'd like to say to you."

"Yes, Romeo," she said as she listened, "That's a beautiful song. I hope we'll always love each other as much as we do right now."

"We can make it happen, can't we?"

"Why don't you come here, Romeo." she whispered, pulling him closer. "The sweet words to your favorite song are turning me on... Why don't you just shut up and kiss me?"

She touched his lips with her finger. The breath caught in her throat as his mouth came down hard, passionately on her willing, yearning mouth.

Their passion continued to grow as Dave kissed and caressed Millie. As the passion grew, her knees got weaker. She could hardly breathe for wanting him.

"I'm trying to take it slow, Honey, so we'll never forget this first time together." he whispered as he untied a pink ribbon on her gown, freeing her breasts.

After their next kiss, they found themselves on the bed...their hands discovering each other's secrets.

Finally, unable to wait any longer, Dave pushed his rock-hard manhood into her willing body. He expertly and successfully brought them to mutual satisfaction, bringing tears of joy to their eyes. Millie smiled and hugged Dave with such force; she almost knocked the breath out of him.

As they basked in the afterglow, Dave whispered. "Wow! I'm glad we waited. I feel God's special blessing in our marriage. Because of having to go to so many tracks, we may not be able to actually go to church very often; but, I want God to be the center of our lives, Millie."

"He already is.... Can't you feel His blessings?"

"Yes, I've felt it for a long time.'

"Me, too."

"Guess what? I have another surprise for you tomorrow. We're going to another honeymoon spot where we'll have two weeks before we have to return to civilization. We'll have a real honeymoon! We had to make a few phone calls; but I think you'll be surprised. Or, if you don't like my surprise, Lee offered us his cabin at the party tonight.... Would you rather go there?"

"You're full of surprises, Dave. I can't imagine what you've got up your sleeve now."

"You'll see! Ben and Lynne flew back to Southern Pines with Dale Earnhardt so we'll have the plane at our disposal. My truck'll be at the airport where we left it. We'll fly back tomorrow so Ben can have the plane next week. The next race is in Atlanta. I told Ben we'd be there the day before the race. I also told him we needed to use the plane to fly to Brandon after the race in Atlanta. He said they'd get a ride back with someone so we can go pick up your things and take care of your business."

"Sounds fine to me. Right now, I can't think of anything I'd rather do than snuggle in your arms. I'm so happy, Dave. You're more than I ever hoped for..."

"You've not seen nothin' yet, Mrs. Masden." he challenged as he began to kiss her again. Their passion returned and they made love again.... leaving them breathless and satisfied. Neither felt their brief courtship had been a mistake. Finally, exhausted, they fell asleep.

Millie smiled and stretched. She could tell it was daybreak by the amount of light coming through the window. Dave snuggled against her and whispered, "Good mornin', Sweetheart. Boy, did I have a dream last night! It was incredible; the best dream I've ever had!"

"I had the same dream, Dave. And this morning, I can't seem to quit smiling. You're terrific. I feel wonderful...."

"H-um. It wasn't a dream! We're really married? We made love? Good, let's wake each other up by doing it again.... I'd like to get in the habit of snuggling with you in the morning. It feels natural to wake up with you lying next to me."

"Yes, it does. You've won me over, Mr. Masden.... You dropped your hook in the water and I jumped for it!"

"It's about time," he whispered as he stroked her breast gently and kissed her passionately, awakening their insatiable desire for each other. He slowly, expertly made love to her again.

In the afterglow, Millie whispered, "I saw fireworks! I could lie here in your arms forever. I didn't think I'd ever feel this way again."

"A feeling you'll never have to do without. You came into my life, Millie, took a chance and look what happened. We can tackle any problem that comes our way. We've had enough heartache, pain, anxiety and depression. You are my heart mate, my helpmate, and my lover-friend. Nothing's impossible. We'll have our struggles; but, together, we can succeed, don't you think?"

"Absolutely, I can't believe how my life has changed. I think back to that Saturday we met. I'm a different person. I didn't realize how much I lost in Jacob's wreck. You helped me pick up the pieces of my life. I was wishing for a valentine when you walked over and sat down on that bench. I got my wish. You went out of your way to make me feel special. Thanks for everything you did for me on this.... our first date!"

"What a date. It never has to end. My life was in shambles. You fit the pieces of my life together, too. I struggled with those pieces long before the divorce. You're my completer. Something was always missing before.... You complete that part of me that was missing. Does this sound crazy? Do you know what I'm talking about?"

"Yes, when Jacob and I were together, we were complete. When he died, I was empty. I've been empty ever since; that is, until you took me out of the crowd of lonely people three weeks ago and put me on a pedestal. I don't want to be on a pedestal. I want to be in your arms until the day I die. I don't know what's ahead of us, Dave; but I want to be there, no matter what. If you continue to race, I'll stand proudly beside you, praying for you, loving you every minute."

"God bless you, Millie. I appreciate your prayers and your love. I've been given a gift from God, namely you. Just like the words to Lee's song last night.... *'thank you for changing my life'*."

After a leisurely breakfast in bed, they packed and Dave piloted the plane back to Southern Pines, with Millie adoring him from the co-pilot's seat. As he drove his truck to their secret honeymoon spot, Millie curled up beside him and rested her head on his shoulder. She paid little attention to where they were going. She felt so safe in his arms; and she knew they were in the mountains. It was chilly, and it was beginning to rain.

Finally, Dave pulled the truck over to the side of the road. "See in that direction as far as you can see, Millie? This is the property I told you about. There was a farmhouse; but it burnt down. Ben and I have done a lot of huntin' and fishin' up here. The only shelter is the barn, which was converted into temporary living quarters after the house burnt."

"Oh, Dave, it's lovely."

"If you can handle the rustic living conditions, I'd like to spend our honeymoon here. There's a bathroom and kitchen. Jake got in touch with Lisa, and she air-expressed a bed. If it's not here yet, we'll have to sleep on the floor!"

"I'll gladly sleep on the floor as long as you're there, Dave!"

"I know you will. As a wedding gift, Lynne stocked the refrigerator with everything we'll need for the next two weeks. While we're here, we'll decide where we want to build our house. Is this okay? Lynne said she'd make sure you'll be comfortable."

"This is wonderful, Dave! What a beautiful piece of property. The mountains are on one side, and a beautiful stream on the other. There's so much you could do with this property, Dave. Is that the farmhouse?"

"No, that's the barn." he explained.

"From here, it looks pretty sturdy. I've always wanted to restore a barn ... convert it into a home. Can we do that first?"

"Hey, it won't bother me to live in a barn as long as you're there, too!"

"Let's go.... I can't wait to see it!" she said excitedly.

"Do I see another challenge in your eyes? You're already making plans. I can see it!" he kidded her, relieved that she was as excited as he was by the prospect of spending their honeymoon in their secluded location.

"Come on, Dave...take a chance! Are you willing to take a chance with me," she teased.

"Delighted!" he said as he put the truck in gear to drive to the barn. She jumped out of the truck before he could open her door. They walked to the door and Dave quickly swept her into his arms and carried her over the threshold.

"Dave, you can't carry me like this...I'm not a small woman!" she remarked.

"You're my woman. If I didn't carry you over the threshold, we'd have had bad luck! I don't have a problem with your weight, so quit worrying about it! You're a beautiful woman. I plan to make love to you for the rest of my life, no matter what size you are...."

"God bless you, Dave. I got lucky when I met you! You're so much better than winning the lottery! I don't even have to pay taxes for you!" She joked.

"Take a chance, Millie, you'll never know!" he teased. "Let's see, what's that other song you like so well...the one Lee sang that first night....'*She turns into a lean, mean, lovin' machine; better than a centerfold in any magazine.*' That's how I see you."

"You've got me, Dave. See this band of gold on my finger? It matches the one on YOUR finger. That means we're married. So, act like it! It's cold in here, Husband. Why don't you start a fire in that fireplace?"

"Boy, pretty bossy, Wife!" he teased. "Get mean with me, I'll divorce you!"

"Hey, the word divorce isn't in my vocabulary! Now, you promised to love, honor and obey... Well, act like it!" she kidded.

"Yes Ma'm, I'll start a fire in the fireplace; then, I'll start a fire in you.... in that beautiful bed over there." he promised. "Guess what, the bed arrived! We don't have to sleep on the floor."

"I'd sleep with you anywhere, Dave."

"I know you would; but, I'm glad we don't have to sleep on the floor, Honey. That's not exactly what I had planned for our honeymoon. What do you think about the barn?"

"I'm not going to give too much thought to this barn for the next few days 'cause we're on our honeymoon. Then, I'll get my sketchbook out. After our honeymoon, I'll get Lynne to help me find a contractor and get some more furniture. At this point, I see beamed ceilings, big ceiling fans, wainscot and wallpaper in the kitchen. You get the idea!"

"Sounds like a Millie Masden original!"

"This place is big enough, we can have a second floor, leave the center area open all the way to the roof. We'll put a skylight there. We already have the basics...a good foundation and a fireplace. We'll have a two-story great room in the center of the barn, surrounded by secondary rooms on both floors."

"Fix it anyway you want.... Give it your signature trademark, Millie. You'll have it beautiful in no time. Right now, it has everything we need for a honeymoon.... You and me." he whispered.

Millie walked around the large barn. It was structurally sound with a large circular fireplace in the center that used to be used by a blacksmith. Besides the beautiful bed, there was a love seat and a table with two chairs. The table was set with a beautiful flower arrangement in the middle. Candles adorned the cabin. In the corner was a small television, V-C-R and stereo.

"Ben and Lynne did a great job getting these things together. It'll be fun turning this into our home."

"Oh, look, Mil', they left us a note." Dave read the note to Millie ....

> *"Congratulations, Guys. We hope only the best for you two forever. It was fun getting this place in shape. There's plenty of firewood and food. Television reception is terrible out here without an antenna so we brought a stereo and some tapes. Enjoy.... We'll see you at Atlanta. Love you guys, Ben and Lynne."*

They walked over to the television and looked at the tapes.... They were some of their favorites. Next to the stereo was a package of twenty-five brand-new CD's.

"Do you know how much these CD's cost?" Millie remarked. "Aren't they about twenty dollars a piece?"

"The CD player is from my efficiency apartment; but, my selection of disks was pretty slim. I gave Jake some money and asked him to pick out some of your favorites."

"Is there anything you didn't think of...."

"Well, I've been planning this for a few days. Many nights I'd lay awake, watching you sleep in the other twin bed. I'm basically a fairly-organized man. Jake, Ben and Lynne know how to follow instructions. I could never have done it without their help."

"Dave, you're such a blessing."

"So are you."

"Dave, you're talking too much. Shut up and kiss me!"

"Yes, Dear, with pleasure..."

Their secluded location was perfect for a honeymoon getaway. They took long walks in the woods. The stream was natural and beautiful... one sunny afternoon, Millie packed a picnic lunch and they made love under the trees beside the rippling brook. A young doe stumbled out of the thicket and stared at them precariously before bounding across the meadow. "This is God's country." Dave whispered.

After a few days of marital bliss, Millie pulled her sketchbook from her luggage and drew some basic ideas for their barn home.

After getting Dave's input, she finalized the plans. They included building a detached four-car garage. They would keep their bedroom on the main floor, with four more bedrooms upstairs. There would be an office they could both use. In their bedroom, Dave suggested she allow enough room for a hot tub. She loved the idea. On the main floor, Millie included a trophy room for Dave's awards, trophies, and prized memorabilia.

Saturday Morning, March 12, 1993

"Well, Mil', you'd better pack a few things so we can go to Atlanta. We'll drive to the airport. If we can't get a ride from there, I'll rent a car so we can drive to Atlanta for the race tomorrow. I promised Ben we'd be there. That way, the truck will be parked at the airport when we get back from Brandon. I promised you we'd go to your house."

"Okay, thank you for such a beautiful honeymoon. It's been great to be completely away from civilization and snuggled in your arms; but you're right, it's time to rejoin the human race. I'll never forget this week, though. You're so much more than I ever expected."

"An answered prayer...God is so good. I can't thank Him enough for what He's done in our lives."

Millie quickly packed a few things and got dressed while Dave cleared their breakfast dishes. They drove to the airport. Dale Earnhardt was landing his plane at the airstrip. Dave met him when he disembarked. They shook hands and Dale teased him about being on his honeymoon.

"If we can't hitch a ride with someone, I'm going to rent a car so we can drive to Atlanta. I promised Ben I'd be there for the race."

"Oh, then, you don't know. An unbelievable ice storm came through Atlanta. I almost didn't get clearance to take off from the airport. It's a good thing it happened in Atlanta or I wouldn't have been able to fly out. NASCAR canceled the race until Saturday. Rusty's got the pole position. I think Ben's somewhere in the middle of the pack. You'd better call him."

"Yeah, I guess I'd better. I'm glad I ran into you, Dale."

"Well, listen, I'm flying back on Wednesday morning if you and Millie want to fly down with me."

"That would be great!"

"Be here Wednesday morning at nine o'clock."

"Okay. We'll see you then. Thanks!"

Dave and Millie went inside the small terminal and called the motel where Dave knew Ben and Lynne would be staying. Lynne answered the phone.

"Hi, Lynne. This is Dave. I saw Dale Earnhardt. He told us the race has been canceled. Is everything okay?"

"Everything's fine. We miss you guys. How's everything going for you?"

"Great, Lynne. It couldn't be better."

"Well, Dale told you right. Everything's covered in ice in Atlanta. Ben got trapped at the track last night, almost didn't make it back to the hotel. He's up in the coffee shop right now talking to some of the guys."

"How'd he do in the time trials?"

"He missed you, that's for sure. He ended up in the twelfth row, outside. He's not really happy about that; but what can he do about it? At least he's in the race. I guess Dale didn't tell you he's got the second spot."

"That rascal, he didn't say a word!"

"Well, we'll be down sometime this week. Is there a room for us at the motel where you're staying?"

"Yes. It'll be ready whenever you get here. The race has been re-scheduled for Saturday. You probably should get here by Friday afternoon at the latest so you can pace the car with Ben."

"I think we'll be down before then. Dale said we could catch a ride with him Wednesday morning. Do you want to speak to Millie?"

"I'd love to..."

Dave handed the phone to Millie. "Hi, Lynne. How are you?"

"Freezing to death. Atlanta isn't usually this cold. We have ice everywhere. The race has been re-scheduled for Saturday. Was everything okay at the barn?"

"It was great, Lynne. Thank you for everything you did for us. We've had a really great honeymoon. I noticed you even put some of my potpourri in the barn."

"No problem. It was my pleasure, Millie."

"How are the roads now?"

"They're pretty slick. They have to shut down the Atlanta airport occasionally to de-ice. I've never seen anything so beautiful, while at the same time, so treacherous."

"That's amazing...isn't it?"

"Well...Millie, how's everything?"

"Unbelievable, I'm so blessed. I can't believe how my life's been turned around. I think I owe you another antique!" They laughed.

"Well, Lynne, say hello to Ben for us and let him know we called. We'll see you guys Wednesday. Do you need Dave back?"

"No, that's okay. We'll be glad to see you when you get here."

Dave and Millie went back to the barn and spent the next few days in each other's arms. Wednesday morning, they met Dale at the airport and flew to Atlanta with him. The trip down was fun as Dale joked in his usual manner.

After picking up a rental car, they drove to the motel, dropping Dale off at his hotel on the way.

Ben and Lynne welcomed them and they went out for dinner. Whenever they saw a WINSTON CUP driver, they were teased about their romantic wedding.

Ned Jarrett saw Dave the next day at the track and interviewed him for his television program: "Well, Romeo, congratulations on your wedding. You guys really broke the records at Richmond. How's everything for this week? Ben's pretty far back in the line-up. Do you think he'll be able to move up and win this race?"

"Anything's possible, Ned."

"Can we get Millie over here so we can talk to her, too? I've had so many calls about your romantic proposal. Maybe she'll agree to be interviewed, too? The fans would love it. You know, NASCAR's gaining popularity with the women. Racing is the number-one spectator sport and fifty percent of the crowd consists of women. In view of that, I think they'd love to have you both on the show."

Dave waved for Millie to join them. At first she was reluctant. Ned explained to her, off the microphone, that the response to Dave's proposal had been overwhelming. He asked if she'd agree to be interviewed for his 'Inside Winston Cup Racing' program. He also indicated that Neil Bonnett had mentioned he might try to get them on his "*Winners*" program. Millie finally agreed to the interview.

"Well, Millie, congratulations on your marriage to *Romeo* Masden. Were you surprised?"

"He's full of surprises, Ned." she said, "We'd only known each other for three weeks; but, we had spent every minute together since the accident in Daytona. I'm not a celebrity. Dave's the one who masterminded the whole thing."

"What about you, Millie? Will it be hard for you to change your lifestyle so you can go to all the tracks in the circuit?"

"I don't think so. I'm a country decorator. Lynne Colson will assist me when I have a project. She told me there are antique shops and decorating stores in every town where we'll be racing. I took forward to putting our lives together, even shopping around for some new distributors."

"Do you have a family?"

"I have a twenty-four year old son who's in pre-law. He's fine, practically on his own. Soon he'll pass the bar exam, and have his own life."

Ned noticed she was holding a framed picture. "What's this in your hand, Millie, if you don't mind me asking?"

"It's a picture I sketched of Dave and me. We had it framed."

"Millie, you drew this? This is amazing. You could have a career drawing lithographs. There a big market for it." He said as he put the picture on camera.

Dave interspersed, "She's incredible, Ned; but, I don't want our relationship to sound seedy. I want to clear up any misconceptions before it goes any further. Millie and I made the decision not to have a physical relationship until after we were married. I don't want any of our fans to get the wrong idea. I prayed to God for someone special to come into my life.... for God to give me another chance at love and life. He gave me Millie. God has been so good to us. The word divorce isn't in our vocabulary... we're going to make this work, no matter what. We're totally committed to each other."

"That's terrific, Dave. Best of luck to you and Millie."

After the interview had ended, Ned remarked, "I plan to send you some of the mail I've received. We all wish you and Millie the best things life has to offer in your future. Best of luck in the race this week."

Neil Bonnett caught up with them on Thursday and asked them to appear on his *'Winners'* program, a half-hour show. He asked Millie to bring some of her lithographs. Since she didn't have any but the one of her and Dave, she had to sketch some more for the program.

She sketched Dale Earnhardt with his # 3 Goodyear Chevrolet, and Rusty Wallace with his # 2 Miller Genuine Draft Pontiac. She also made another sketch of Ben and Dave standing beside the #19 Coca-Cola Ford Thunderbird.

Neil gave the highlights of Dave and Ben's career, and then touched on their romantic meeting and Dave's proposal on national television. The program was well received by the fans.

Saturday, March 20, 1993—
Motorcraft 500, Atlanta Georgia

Rusty Wallace maintained his first place position for the first twenty-three laps of the race until Mark Martin overtook him and led for the next ten laps. Rusty regained the lead on lap thirty-four but Mark was able to regain the lead on lap fifty-eight. Ken Schrader grabbed the lead for a few minutes; then Geoff Bodine charged ahead.

There were a couple accidents and several cars were out of the race with mechanical problems. All in all, there were nineteen lead changes and four caution flags.

Morgan Shepherd managed to win the race after capturing the lead from Rusty Wallace on Lap two hundred sixty-five. Ernie Irvan came in second, with Rusty Wallace close behind in the third position. Ben ended up in 12th position, unscathed.

While they were preparing for the next race at Darlington, four bags of mail were delivered to Dave and Millie. The mail was the result of Neil's *'Winners'* program.

After their honeymoon was officially over, they contracted to have their barn home restored to their specifications. Millie and Lynne searched for furniture while they traveled with their men to the different races in the circuit.

Ben did most of the driving; Dave did most of the flying. They were, in essence, the perfect foursome of old fuddy-duddies.

Ben managed to win three more races that season; but he led in nineteen races and finished 10,942 accumulated miles out of the possible 11,490 miles.

It had been a sad year because the racing profession lost two valuable drivers in accidents not related to racing. Alan Kulwicki was killed when his plane crashed; and Davey Allison was killed in a helicopter incident. They were sadly missed by all.

By the end of the season, Ben had racked up enough points to win the coveted Winston Cup award! Their total earnings for the season were over two million dollars, with an additional three-and-a-half million in residuals and promos.

"*Romeo*" Masden and Ben Colson had become legends in their own time. Ben took an Alan Kulwicki lap, turning around and going the other direction on the track. Carrying a #28 flag, in honor of Davey Allison after he'd won the championship. Rusty Wallace, who'd won the final race, carried a Hooters' flag in honor of Alan. The sight of the beautiful race cars circling the tracks in the traditional Alan Kulwicki victory lap, carrying the flags to honor their fallen fellow racers, was so beautiful, most of the audience stood silently with tears in their eyes.

When they returned to Southern Pines after the victory celebration in New York, the renovation had been completed on their barn home.

Word got out about the restoration. Several decorating magazines contacted Millie, requesting permission to feature their home in their publications.

Millie accepted several offers and received enough money in her endeavors to pay for Dave's four-car garage, and a practice track, which doubled as a landing strip for the airplane.

Millie also earned enough money from her racing lithographs to build a gristmill on their stream. Her lithographs increased in value each time she sketched a driver and his car. Her talents were very much in demand.

Dave and Millie spent a beautiful Christmas in their new barn home. On Christmas Eve, Dave gave Millie a little box.

"What have you done?" Millie asked him.

"You'll see... Open it!"

"But, it's not Christmas yet. You already have so many packages for me under the tree."

"I want to give you this one while we're alone. I have to leave in a little while to pick Jake up at the airport. This is a special Christmas moment for us.... Go ahead, open it!"

Millie opened the box and couldn't believe what she saw. The box contained a beautiful diamond forever ring."

"Doesn't a husband usually give his wife one of these for their thirtieth or fiftieth anniversary? We haven't even been married a year!"

"Well, I never got around to getting you an engagement ring. This is just my way of letting you know how much I love you. I expect our marriage to last for the rest of our lives."

"So do I; I'm so happy, Honey. No matter what lies ahead of us, Dave, we'll work it out."

"I know we will. I love you, Millie. Thank you for making my Christmas so special."

"I have a surprise for you, too; but, I've decided to make you wait a while before I give it to you." she said, mysteriously, pensively.

"Oh, come on, give me a clue..." he pleaded.

"Not a chance. You'll see. You're not the only one who can plan a surprise!"

They kissed and made love on the bearskin rug in front of the fire, with only the lights from the Christmas tree, and soft Christmas music playing on the stereo.

Later, Millie rode with Dave to pick up Jake at the airport. Paula was with him. As they drove back home, Jake told them, excitedly, that he'd passed the bar exam with flying colors. He said he was starting to get offers to join prestigious legal firms.

"So far, the one I like the best if for a firm in Chicago." he said.

"Congratulations, Jake. We're proud of you. Plan your future carefully, and then go with it." Dave said. Millie smiled and nodded her head in agreement.

Since it was past midnight by the time they attended Midnight Mass and got back to the barn, Millie quickly got them settled in two of their four bedrooms.

The next morning, they exchanged their Christmas gifts. Since Millie hadn't planned on Paula being with Jake, she had to scurry around and find a few things she could wrap up for her. Luckily, she kept a supply of her favorite accent pieces so it was easy to select a few presents for her. Millie also included two packages of her signature potpourri, which was now being marketed for consumers. Paula was touched by Millie's thoughtfulness.

"Mrs. Masden, I don't have anything for you guys." Paula commented.

"The smile on Jake's face is enough. You're very good for him, Paula."

Jake smiled and agreed.

Millie and Paula prepared Christmas diner while Dave showed Jake around their farm, riding a couple of Dave's Harleys. Working together in the kitchen gave them a chance to get to know each other better. Millie liked Paula very much. She could see a lot of herself reflected through Paula as they talked. She smiled to herself and thought... they say a son chooses a wife exactly like their mother....

By the time the guys rejoined Millie and Paula in the barn home, it was snowing—large, powdery flakes that transformed everything into a wintry splendor. Millie served hot cider with cinnamon sticks as they warmed themselves by the fire.

After they had eaten their Christmas dinner, Jake announced he'd asked Paula to marry him. "We're planning a spring wedding, Mom;

and, for the record, we're waiting until our wedding night to make love, too!"

Paula blushed and Jake hugged her.

"That's great, Jake. You need the love of a good woman to complete your life. Be careful, take your time and work out your problems. No matter how much you love each other, there'll be problems. Never go to bed angry. If you have to, stay up all night and work out your problems."

"The fun part's the makin' up, Son!" Dave said, "I'm happy for you. It's a pleasure to welcome you to the family, Paula."

"Thanks! I look forward to getting to know you both better." Paula responded.

"Congratulations, again on this season's victory, Dave." Jake said proudly.

"You know, Son, I'm so blessed. Not only did I win over your Mom's love; but also, we have so many sponsors who want to support our team, we'll have nothing to worry about next year! And, guess what, your Mom's gettin' decorating offers from all over America; and, her lithographs are selling like hotcakes!"

Jake looked at his mother and realized she was glowing. "Mom, you look so happy! Marriage to Dave is good for you. If he hadn't asked you to go to the race, I'd never have gotten together with Paula. I love her, Mom, more than life itself. So, not only did Dave turn your life around; he turned mine around, too." Jake said.

Then, turning to Dave, he said quietly, having to clear his throat, "Thanks, *Dad!* Is it okay if I call you Dad?"

"Yes, Son, it makes me very proud when you call me 'Dad'."

Millie, who had been smiling to herself all afternoon, said quietly, looking at Jake, "Now don't spoil my surprise, my special Christmas present...." she insisted.

"Mom, what are you talking about?" Jake asked. He and Dave looked at each other quizzically, not having the foggiest idea what she was referring to....

"Well, Jake, '*DAD'S* the right word." she said as she looked at Dave. "You know, I thought I couldn't have any more children after you were born. Well, guess what, I'm pregnant! Doc called this morning to confirm the news..."

Dave's mouth fell open. He was shocked by her announcement. At first, he couldn't say anything. Then, finally, he swallowed hard and said, "You're kidding! I thought it was impossible. Are you sure? Did the doctor say it was okay to have children at our age?"

"He said we'd have to be careful; but, he thinks we'll do fine." she said, patting her tummy. "I've always taken good care of myself, took vitamins and ate healthy foods. Merry Christmas, Honey! What do you think about my special surprise?"

"It's fantastic! Thank you, God! Thank you, Millie! I can't believe it! A baby.... I never expected to have my own child. Here we go again, Millie, taking chances. You've got to be careful. We can't let anything happen to this miracle, this gift from God."

"I'll be careful. Isn't it wonderful?"

Dave didn't reply to her question. He pushed back his chair and walked over so he could hug his wife. Joy was evident on his weathered face. He knelt at her feet, taking her hands in his.

"Jake," he said, while looking at Millie. "If Paula makes you half as happy as your Mom has made me, you're a very lucky man. I thank God every day that she's my wife. I've come to think of you as my son. This new baby will only increase our happiness. I wish you and Paula the best life has to offer...."

"You guys have the best, now. Paula and I will use you guys as role models.... We'll strive to be as happy. Thank you, *DAD*, for everything."

Dave and Millie whispered to each other.... "Thank you, God, for everything."

Epilogue

A New Beginning

The first trimester of the pregnancy went well with only a few minor problems.... A little morning sickness. However, when Neil Bonnett was killed during the time trials at Daytona, Millie took it so hard she had to be hospitalized in Daytona, almost losing the baby. They had become good friends.

Dave and Millie had their first argument when Dave told her he planned to race more than usual that season. Ben and Dave both qualified for the Busch Clash, and the Daytona 500.

"Honey, remember what you said when we were married? You said you'd follow me to any race track in the world."

"I know; but, I thought you were going to quit racing. It was easy to say it then. Now, I'm scared ... what with the baby comin' and everything. We both need you to stay with us. If something happened to you, I don't think I could go on..."

"Sure you could; but, remember, only the good die young. I'm too mean to die!" He teased.

"There's not a mean bone in your body!"

"What do you want me to do? Withdraw from the race? If it's going to cause you a physical problem with the little one, I'll quit in a second."

"Do you really want to do this?" she asked.

"Yes, Honey, I do; but, not at the cost of you or the baby."

"I made a promise.... but I can't be there. I have to stay in bed."

"Lynne said she'd stay with you. You can watch the race on television."

"Don't worry. Everything will be okay, I promise. I know you can't be with me because of the baby; but I don't want you to worry. I'll drop out if you say the word. I have to believe God's going to protect you, and our little one here."

"You know I love you, Dave. I keep my promises. I'll trust God to take care of you. Please be careful. You know I'll be praying for you."

"And, I'll be praying for you, too. Everything will be fine, you'll see. Let's take a chance at life, okay?"

"Okay, I guess. I'm willing if you're willing Dale Earnhardt won the Busch clash, and Sterling Marlin won the Daytona 500; but Ben and Dave came through unscathed. They made a good showing in the line-up.

Millie was able to relax, and understand that God was in control. Dave was doing what he was supposed to do. She was doing what she was supposed to do ... pray for God's will in their lives.... a total surrender of their wills to His Divine Will. He had brought them safely so far. They had to trust Him with their futures.... and the future of their unborn baby.

In a couple weeks, Millie was able to check out of the hospital and the remainder of the pregnancy went as scheduled.

Millie was fine by the time Jake and Paula were married in May.... a lovely old-fashioned Victorian wedding.

Since Jake was valedictorian of his class, and graduated with honors, Jake continued to receive offers from ivy-league legal firms. He considered each offer carefully before making his decision where to put his future.

When it came time to deliver, as a precautionary measure because of her age, Millie was again ordered to bed. Dave and Ben had no choice but to go to Pocono, Pennsylvania, without her. She was understandably upset at having to stay behind.

"Don't worry, Honey. I won't be racing. I know you'll be praying from home. I'll call before the race, if I can; and, I'll be home as soon as the race is over. Stay in bed, and take care of yourself and our little one. I'll miss you." Dave said, reassuring her, rubbing her swollen tummy affectionately. The baby stirred in the womb, and kicked his hand.

"I'm sorry I can't be with you. Ever since the night we met, we've never spent a night apart. Take care of yourself for me, okay?" she pleaded. "Somehow, I have an uneasy feeling."

"Don't worry. Everything will be just fine. I'll be home before you know it, I promise."

Everyone, including the pit crew missed Millie's presence. They had all become very fond to her because of her quick wit and charm, and didn't even mind her occasional pregnancy-hormonal bantering.

Just before the start of the race, Ben accidentally tripped over a tire jack and sprained his ankle. He could hardly walk, let alone drive the race car. Dave had no choice but to substitute for him.

Because of this last minute shuffle, and getting approval from NASCAR, Dave did not have time to call home. He knew Millie would worry if she knew he was racing. He would have to smooth things over with her later, he thought, as he hurriedly climbed into the race car.

Because Dave was forced to take a provisional position at the end of the pack, his chances were slim at being able to finish in the top ten. There were a few busted fenders, blown engines, and twisted bumpers. Butch Smith hammered relentlessly at Dave's bumper. Whenever Dave felt frustrated, he touched the little gold angel Millie had given him, which he always wore on his jumpsuit. In spite of everything, Dave managed to finish in eighth place. Smith, however, was unable to finish the race because of a blown head gasket.

As he pulled into the pit, Ben announced to Dave over the headset, "Hey, Man, get your ass in gear and get outta that car. We've gotta get home. Lynne called to let Millie knew you were racing. They told her because we didn't want her to find out on television. Guess what! She's in labor. Jake, Paula, and Lynne are with her."

"Really! Let's get moving!" Dave said as he waved away the reporters and rushed to their rental car.

"I've already called the airport. They'll give us clearance as soon as we get there." Ben said.

"Great! Thanks for taking care of things for me."

"Thanks for taking over for me today. You ran a good race, Partner. Charlie's gonna take care of everything here so we can get home in time for that baby!"

When they got back to Southern Pines, they went directly to the hospital. Jake and Paula were sitting with Millie.

Dave hurried in.... "Honey, are you okay?"

"Yes, we're fine. Congratulations, '*Daddy*!' You have a son!"

Suddenly, Dave became aware of the small blue bundle Millie had cradled in her arms. His eyes filled with tears at the beautiful sight that lay in front of him.

"Oh, God, Millie, he's beautiful. I'm so sorry I missed this. Are you okay? Did you have a rough time?"

"No, I was only in hard labor for two hours. I swear, Dave, an angel laid him in my arms. We have a beautiful son, handed to me by an angel!"

"Oh, thank You, God! First You blessed me with a beautiful wife and stepson; then, You gave us another miracle. I can't believe it! Thank you, too, Millie. You're pretty special, too!" Dave exclaimed. He could no longer contain his joy as tears spilled onto his cheeks.

"Congratulations, Man!" Ben said, slapping him on the back. "I've got another surprise for you. From now on, our racing team will have to be Colson-Masden-Greene-Colson-Colson-Masden!"

"What!?! What do you mean?"

Take a Chance: True Love Waits

"Well, Dave.... Dad, "Jake stepped up to explain."Although the name sounds more like a law firm than a team of car owners, if you'll have me, I'd like you to teach me to race the cars. I'll open my practice here, in Southern Pines ...and become a part of the team on the weekends. When the Little Squirt here gets old enough, you can bring him in, too, if Mom will let you!"

"We'll see, Son!" Dave said proudly, hugging Jake. "You've made me very happy. I'm proud to have you as part of our team."

"*YES, WE'LL SEE, SON!*"Millie loudly protested, jokingly. Everyone laughed.

"Don't worry, Dave, you'll win her over. She can't say '*no*' to you, can she?" Jake teased.

"I don't know about that! But, Ben, I need some more explanation. I understand all the names you said except the third Colson and second Masden. What's the deal?"

"Well, just like we thought, Ben Junior wants to become part of the team, too. I thought we might as well step aside and sponsor the boys for a change. We'll run the BUSCH circuit, and the WINSTON. You and me, we'll just sit back and take it easy—let the younger men take over under our leadership. The third Colson and second Masden are just speculation on my part, my Christopher, and your baby here. Do you think you can handle that?"

"Well, what do you know? This is incredible! Before this Lady came into our lives, we were ready to dissolve Colson-Masden Racing. It was almost a washout ...now; we're stronger than ever ...bigger than ever!"

Dave sat down on the side of Millie's bed, and gently kissed her as if she was a piece of delicate porcelain. Then, she carefully laid the baby in his arms. Dave held him close to his chest, speechless, unable to find adequate words to express his feelings.

"Millie, he's beautiful. He's got your eyes."

Trying to judge his weight by bouncing him in his arms, Dave remarked, "This is what I call a baby. How much does he weigh?"

"Almost ten pounds." Millie answered. "They say he's healthy. Doc's so proud that we all came through it, he's about to burst his buttons, too. He needs to know what we're going to name him."

"Let's see....a special name. He's got a lot of hair; maybe we should call him Samson."

Millie and Dave looked at each other...."Nah, it doesn't fit!"

"Well, he's a big baby; maybe we should name him Goliath!"

"No, that name doesn't fit either." she said.

"You're right....Samson was weak when his hair was cut, and Goliath was slain by David. Of course, it's obvious! DAVID! David defeated Goliath.... And because it's MY name!"

Millie smiled. "Okay, David it will be. Can we give him 'Greene' as a middle name? A final tribute to my late husband. Do you think it would be appropriate?"

"Of course. He'll always be a part of you, too!"

"You know there's a race car driver with the name David Green.... without the 'e'. He's a good driver, predominately in BUSCH at the current time; but, I don't think that will be a problem for Little Davey later on. DAVID GREENE MASDEN—a real winner —there's no way he can miss!"

From the time she came home from the hospital, Millie and Dave never spent another night apart.

When it was time to go to a race track in another part of God's beautiful country, Millie would pack up Little Davey; and off they'd fly to watch the team race.

David Greene Masden literally grew up at the racetrack, trailing after his Daddy, whom he worshipped, and his big brother, Jake, who eventually was hired by NASCAR's legal department.

Little Davey considered Ben and Lynne to be his aunt and uncle. He was a happy go-lucky child, whose eyes twinkled menacingly when he spoke. Rarely was it necessary to discipline him; and when they did, he quickly learned from his mistakes.

Dave and Millie Masden had taken a chance on life ...and won! God is so good...

The End

ACKNOWLEDGMENTS/NOTATION

- THE OFFICIAL NASCAR PREVIEW & PRESS GUIDE 1993
- THE OFFICIAL NASCAR PREVIEW & PRESS GUIDE 1994
- PIT PASS MAGAZINE, April, 1993
- ON TRACK MAGAZINE, March 12, 1993
- STOCK CAR RACING MAGAZINE, May, 1993
- STOCK CAR RACING MAGAZINE, March, 1993
- WINSTON CUP ILLUSTRATED MAGAZINE, March through August, 1993
- WINNERS—Television Program on Cable TNN
- INSIDE WINSTON CUP RACING—Television Program on Cable TNN
- RACEDAY—Television Program on Cable TNN
- Various BUSCH and WINSTON CUP races for 1993 and 1994
- Superstar LEE GREENWOOD, and his special songs
- NASCAR Superstars and Commentators

TECHNICAL ADVISERS

- Dan and Jim Steck
- Ruth Kaiser
- Michael David Knight
- Wendell and Juleta Poole
- Mike Reisinger
- Jerry Tompkins
- Fred Tompkins

NOTES

- Dale Earnhardt won the actual 1993 Winston Cup Award.
- Mark Martin won the actual 1993 Richmond Busch Race.
- Davey Allison won the actual 1993 Richmond Winston Cup Race.
- Ken Schrader held the Actual Richmond Winston Cup Pole.
- The actual Richmond Busch Pole was held by (must research).
- The other races mentioned in this novel were won by the driver stated.

www.ingramcontent.com/pod-product-compliance
Lightning Source LLC
Chambersburg PA
CBHW020720130726
47899CB00011B/586